THE MODERN DEITY'S GUIDE TO SURVIVING HUMANITY

Other Anthologies Edited by:

Patricia Bray & Joshua Palmatier

After Hours: Tales from the Ur-bar
The Modern Fae's Guide to Surviving Humanity
Temporally Out of Order * Alien Artifacts * Were-
All Hail Our Robot Conquerors!
Second Round: A Return to the Ur-bar
The Modern Deity's Guide to Surviving Humanity

S.C. Butler & Joshua Palmatier

Submerged * Guilds & Glaives * Apocalyptic
When Worlds Collide

Laura Anne Gilman & Kat Richardson

The Death of All Things

Troy Carrol Bucher & Joshua Palmatier

The Razor's Edge

Patricia Bray & S.C. Butler

Portals

David B. Coe & Joshua Palmatier

Temporally Deactivated * Galactic Stew
Derelict

Steven H Silver & Joshua Palmatier

Alternate Peace

Crystal Sarakas & Joshua Palmatier

My Battery Is Low and It Is Getting Dark

THE MODERN DEITY'S GUIDE TO SURVIVING HUMANITY

Edited by

Patricia Bray
&
Joshua Palmatier

Zombies Need Brains LLC
www.zombiesneedbrains.com

Interior Design (ebook): ZNB Design
Interior Design (print): ZNB Design
Cover Design by ZNB Design
Cover Art "The Modern Deity's Guide to Surviving Humanity"
by Justin Adams of Varia Studios

ZNB Book Collectors #20

Kickstarter Edition Printing, June 2021
First Printing, July 2021

Print ISBN-13: 978-1940709383

Ebook ISBN-13: 978-1940709390

Printed in the U.S.A.

COPYRIGHTS

Table of Contents

SIGNATURE PAGE

Patricia Bray, editor:

____

Joshua Palmatier, editor:

____

Crystal Sarakas:

____

Juliet E. McKenna:

____

Tanya Huff:

____

Edward Willett:

____

Daniel Roman:

____

Jennifer Dunne:

____

Jean Marie Ward:

____

Mike Marcus:

____

A.L. Tompkins:

____

Daryl Marcus:

____

Alma Alexander:

____

Kari Sperring:

____

A.J. Cunder:

____

Irene Radford:

____

N.R. Lambert:

____

Justin Adams, artist:

____

The Weight of a Feather

Crystal Sarakas

It used to be that when I pulled a heart out of someone's chest, there was a reverence to it, a ritual that honored both supplicant and god.

Today, it's just another stage show in that wannabe Vegas known as Branson.

I stood off to the side, in the shadows, while my assistants helped the old woman up on stage and into the ornate golden chair between two towering statues of jackal-headed men—arms crossed, each hand holding a flail. One assistant stayed with the old woman, kneeling next to her. The other faced the audience as she began to speak in a hushed voice that reached every part of the theater thanks to the sound system.

"What you will see now is not a trick of mirrors or glamour. The Great Lord Anubis, Lord of the Dead, Savior of Lost Souls, will pull our brave volunteer's heart out and lay it upon the Scales of Judgement." Darla was good. You could hear the capital letters as she recited her lines. "Please do not move or applaud. We don't want any distractions during this very dangerous moment."

I frowned at the lack of reaction from the crowd and watched as Heather, the other assistant, tried to pry the old woman's smartphone from her hands. "You can't record this," I heard her whisper, a smile plastered to her face. "But you can buy a DVD recording of tonight's performance at the gift shop after the show."

The music swelled to a crescendo of wailing, wordless vocals spiraling with the beat of a tabla. That was my cue.

I swept across the stage, expecting at least a few gasps when the audience saw me in my true visage. My head was that of a jackal's, complete with sharply-pointed ears and even sharper teeth. Gold paint swirled around my eyes and down my neck to my still human torso. Half-jackal, half-man, and entirely bored with everything.

I stood in front of the old woman, just enough to the side so that the audience could see what I was doing. Darla paced gracefully across the stage, holding a large set of gold scales in her hands. I pointed at the altar table next to the golden chair. She sat the scales down, then knelt on the other side of the woman, just in case our volunteer decided to run for it or passed out.

The frantic drumbeat suddenly stopped. I plunged my hand into the woman's chest, my fingers gently closing around her beating heart.

"Oh oh!" she giggled. "That tickles!" Heather rolled her eyes at me.

I held the heart high overhead, making sure the audience got a good look at it. Then I knelt in one smooth motion, setting the heart on the left side of the scales. I pulled the feather from where it had been tucked into my belt and showed it to the audience before placing it on the other scale.

The scales teetered back and forth. I looked down at the old woman. Tears filled her eyes, but she was smiling broadly, one hand reaching out as if to touch someone. This would be a good balancing, I thought. I watched carefully, though, ready to grab the heart back the moment the scales found their balance but before the soul moved on to whatever came next. It wouldn't be good publicity to have volunteers actually dropping dead on stage.

"Behold! The heart is as light as the feather!" Darla's voice was a triumphant shout. I plucked the heart from the scale and passed my hand over the old woman's chest. All good, back in place. A soft but uplifting melody echoed through the room as we faced the audience, hands held high, anticipating the roar of applause.

The audience—all thirteen of them—gave a few perfunctory claps and then lurched to their feet, anxious to get out of the theater and on to the early-bird dinner. For them, that was the best part of the Dinner and a Show(!) savings package. Meatloaf, mashed potatoes, green peas, sweet tea, and pecan pie. That was the main attraction here—not Anubis, Lord of the Dead, Savior of Lost Souls, He Who Wields the Scales of Judgment and Opens the Gate to the Darkness Beyond.

I'm just the opening act these days—and not even a good one.

"Oh, is it time for the dinner now?" the old woman asked Darla as she was escorted from the stage. Heather was already heading to the lobby, no doubt to try to direct at least a few people toward the gift shop before they departed for the all-important dinner.

I exited stage left, nodding to the bored stagehands who were waiting to reset the stage for the next show. They barely looked at me as I walked past, ducking so that my ears didn't scrape against the entry to the backstage hall.

When I got to my dressing room, I shifted. The black muzzle and sharp, pointed ears melted away, letting my human form take shape. I studied myself in the mirror, making sure that everything was as it should be. One time, I'd left the theater without checking and spent the walk home getting stopped over and over to take pictures with the tourists. It turned out that my ears were still jackal-shaped, and my teeth sharper than they should be. I'd been pretty annoyed that no one was scared—they were just looking for another freak-show photo op to post on their social media accounts.

I scrubbed the gold paint off my face, the swirls and hieroglyphics that were just another kind of smoke and mirrors. They certainly had nothing to do with the ritual bullshit that Darla whispered to the audience as I assumed the mantle of the Dark Lord before their old and cataract-clouded eyes.

I'm so exhausted all the time.

I'd just buttoned up my shirt when there was a sharp rap at the door before it opened and a woman breezed in. She was a little shorter than my six-foot height, with pale skin dotted with freckles and long, black hair. Morgan—known to some as the Morrigan, goddess of death, a member of the council that ruled Branson and an all-around pain in my ass.

"Jack! How ya doing? Great show. Too bad about the audience, but hey, we've got at least a dozen tour buses scheduled for the weekend. Most of the other shows are already sold out. I'm sure you'll pick up some of the overflow crowd here."

I rolled my eyes as my unwelcome guest landed with a thud on the leather couch. "Morgan. So not good to see you. Please leave."

Morgan rolled her eyes right back at me. "I can't imagine you got much off of that crowd. Most of them have been dead three days, at least." She laughed at her own joke as she leaned back on the couch, crossing her legs just enough to show off an ample amount of skin. "Seriously though, we've got to get you some better numbers or…" Morgan made a cutting motion across her throat. "You know what happens then."

"Morgan, my darling, you assume that I care." I rubbed a hand across my face. "Now, it's late, and I'm tired, and there's nothing I can do about any of this tonight. I'm sure it's going to be fine. Numbers will pick up in the summer. They always do. Are you here just to annoy me, or is there some other reason for you being here?"

Morgan's face grew still. "I was trying to be polite, but fine. I'll be blunt. The Council isn't happy, Jack. You aren't pulling enough to sustain yourself, much less contribute to the tithe. And it's not just a slump. You're in a full-blown rut, and you need to figure out a way out of it before I come back and be a whole lot less friendly."

She stood and smiled. "Frankly, I don't want to have to do all the work to find another act. You know how boring the little gods are, all scattered in their hovels, barely eking out an existence. We've got a good thing here." She stepped close enough to rub her hand over my chest. "Maybe you can spice things up a bit. That old heart-and-feather routine is getting a bit stale, don't you think? Ever consider getting something a little more…sacrificial going onstage? Maybe something with hypnosis? You know, cloud their minds so they're not sure what they actually saw. I bet that would bring them in like crazy! People love that mentalist shit."

I said nothing. Just waited.

"Fine." She flipped her long black hair over her shoulder. "Just think about what I said. I mean it—if you don't get a little more nectar flowing up the hill, then I'll be paying you a totally different kind of visit. One involving a lot of running on your part." She cocked her head as she looked at me. "Then again, it's been a really long time since I've gone on a hunt." She shrugged. "Either way works for me." She patted my cheek and left.

I sank down on the couch, my knees suddenly a little wobbly. For all my bravado, it was never a good thing when the Morrigan came calling. I could pack up, leave town, and hope the Council didn't send the hunt after me, but where would I go? I sighed. And leaving wasn't even that easy, not when we were all bound one way or the other to the tithe.

That's how we survived. A century ago, many of the old gods were starving. A few of the bigger-name gods—the ones who still had enough believers scattered around the world to give them that edge of power over the rest—got together and picked a spot in America to build a… well, not exactly a home. More like a mutually-beneficial co-op.

The earliest settlers had opened up a few of the nearby limestone caves, carved out steps, put in a few handrails, and called it a marvel of the world, charging a nickel to come take a look. We set up shop in the valley, and the tourists came to us for a bite, or even to see a stage show full of juggling and sleight-of-hand. The energy that poured out of the humans was our salvation. Wonder, awe, laughter, joy—it fed us, kept us going. After a few years of everyone doing well for themselves, and as more and more gods—big and little—flocked to the region, the founders created the Council, made up a few rules and began to govern. Rule number one: the tithe.

You contributed a bit of energy from your own reserves to the tithe, which, in turn, was shared equally—everyone getting enough to keep going. No one would ever starve and fade away again. You did your part to bring tourists into Branson and, in return, you had a place of safety, a home, and a regular source of the energy that kept us all going. Occasionally, if a human was annoying enough or someone that wouldn't be missed, there might even be a little blood and bone to go with the energy we pulled.

There's a catch, of course. Once you checked in, you can't check out. Being a part of Branson is a forever kind of deal—unless the Council decided otherwise.

I'd been offered a place on the Council back then, but I'd never wanted to rule anyone. Sometimes, like tonight, I regretted that a little. Especially when it would have meant that I'd be the one telling Morgan what to do, instead of being blamed for ever-declining audience numbers.

That's what pissed off the old ones more than anything. Not the dwindling money or the bad reviews or even the fact that they couldn't snack on the humans as much as they did in the olden days. It was all about the vibe, the chi, the energy that flowed along the streets of Branson like a fine wine. When the flow was high, then everything sparkled. The lights were brighter, the glitz and glamour louder. Those days seemed to be gone, though. Branson was a pale echo of its past glory, and so were we.

* * *

A few weeks went by and the numbers in Branson weren't getting any better. Even the big acts were starting to hurt. The little gods were hiding, mostly because rumors flew that the Council was actively looking for someone to blame. Or eat.

Tonight's show had been a disaster. The volunteer actually fell asleep in the middle of the rite and Darla tripped and accidentally knocked into the scales, sending the heart sliding across the stage. Not that anyone in the audience noticed. Most were either looking at their phones or whispering to each other. I'd shoved the heart back into the old man's chest and stomped off stage, leaving Darla and Heather to wrap things up.

I didn't linger after the show—just changed clothes, locked up, and headed out through the lobby. I waved to Charlie, the night guard who kept watch over the theater.

"Good show, Mr. Anubis?" Charlie was a stickler for manners and never referred to me with my modern name.

"Not our best, Charlie. But I'm sure tomorrow will be better."

"It surely will, Mr. Anubis. Have a good night now."

There wasn't much for Charlie to do most of the time, but he had permission to eat anyone trying to break in, so he considered it a fair exchange. Most of the time, he just read from the stack of books he kept behind the gift shop counter.

I walked out past the two towering jackals that flanked the entrance. The gold gilding around their necks and eyes was flaking again, another sign that things were getting worse.

"I know who you are."

A woman stood a few feet away, hidden in the shadows of the jackals.

I shook my head and kept walking. "I don't think so."

"I didn't at first," she called out. "Not until I saw your show a few times. Then it all clicked. That whole heart-and-feather thing is real, isn't it? Not just some show."

I sighed. I did not need this kind of trouble right now. Rule number two in Branson—no one gets to know what really goes on under all the lights. I turned back toward her. "I don't think you heard me," I said, my voice a low growl. "You don't know anything. Now I suggest you enjoy the rest of your stay. Catch the *Titanic* show or go see the Roundup. And don't repeat what you just said. Ever."

She stepped forward into a circle cast by the parking lot lights, holding a gun in her hands. "I'm not going anywhere. Not until you tell me what you did to my father."

I laughed. I couldn't help it. She didn't mean to use the gun on me, and it wouldn't matter even if she did. This was nothing but bravado, some little pissant of a human thinking she could threaten me, even though her fear was a thick and delicious smell on the breeze. But there was something more there, something under the fear. I inhaled, letting her scent play over my tongue. She smelled of earth, of grain ripening in the fields, of apple blossoms in the spring. She made me hungry in a way I hadn't been in a very long time.

I took a deep breath, stepping away from the edge. "I don't think a gun is necessary. Especially one that isn't even loaded." It was a fair guess.

She lowered the gun, hands shaking. "I just want to find out what happened to him," she whispered. "He was a totally different man after his trip here. Something happened here and I think it killed him. Or worse."

I rubbed my hands across my face. All I wanted to do was go home, eat a steak, and drink a bottle or two of wine. But she'd landed on my doorstep and claimed to know more than was allowed. I knew the rules: You break it, you clean it up. "Come on. But not here." I started walking.

"My name is Katie," she said, falling in beside me. "Katie Mc—"

"No!" I stopped and put a finger over her lips to silence her. "I don't need to know your full name. No one around here needs to hear it. Just Katie will do."

"I don't know, Jack." The voice came from behind us. "I'd like to know more about Katie. A lot more. Like why you haven't snapped her tiny little neck yet."

I glanced up at the heavens, wishing for patience. I looked over to where Morgan stood, flanked by two creatures that were human-shaped one moment, giant crows the next. I took a step forward, pulling Katie just behind me.

"I've got this, Morgan. I don't need your help."

"Oh, I know you don't, darling," she purred. "I'm just hurt that you didn't invite us over for dinner." She pulled a dagger from thin air, its long blade reflecting the lights. "But we're here now, aren't we, boys?"

I whistled sharply, a trill of notes cutting through the dark. Seconds later, I heard the click of nails on pavement. Katie gasped and pushed closer against me. "It's okay. They belong to me."

The jackals stood in a semicircle around us, a dozen pairs of golden eyes fixed on the shadow creatures flanking Morgan. The largest of them leaned up against me, her head as tall as my waist, a purr rumbling in her chest. I called her Kalil, an old word for "friend." They were the closest things I had to friends anymore. They were also my guardians. Their sleek, black bodies seemed to swallow up the night, their coats void-like. Then they would shift, and flecks of gold would catch in the light, like tiny iridescent scales or fireflies.

"Oh, come on, Jack." Morgan crossed her arms across her chest. "Are you out of your mind? She's just some human. You've had more than your share in the past."

She was right. There was no reason for me to stand between the Morrigan and some human woman who didn't matter at all. But I'm just sick and tired of Morgan showing up just to stir the pot, sick of having to bow to the other gods' whims.

Damned if I'd let her know that, though.

And beyond that, there was something intriguing about this human, something that tickled the edges of my mind before dancing out of reach.

Morgan looked at Katie, who had edged out slightly so she could see around me. "What did you mean, human, when you told Jack you who know he is?" She took a step forward, her hands dropping down by her sides, fingers curling. "What do you think you know, Katie? About Jack…or anyone else here?"

"Leave it, Morgan. She's just making shit up."

Morgan narrowed her eyes at me. "You're already drawing too much attention to yourself, Jack. You know they're watching you. Why push it?"

I shrugged, putting my hands in my pockets. "Maybe because I just don't care anymore."

The shadow-shapes lunged. The jackals met them halfway, snarls and growls and ripping sounds filling the air. Morgan leapt forward—not at me, but at Katie. Before she could grab her, though, a sharp crack split the air. Morgan stumbled, then fell to the ground. I whistled again and the jackals backed away from the shadows, still snarling.

"Well, I'll be damned," I said, taking the gun from Katie. "I was sure that thing wasn't loaded."

* * *

Rule number three: No fighting amongst ourselves. The council's laws forbade violence—unless they were the ones ordering the violence—and since I'd acted as Katie's protector, I would be found just as guilty as she was.

Katie got lucky with her shot. If Morgan hadn't been a god, she'd have been dead before she hit the ground. Even still, she'd be healing for at least a day, which might give me the time I needed to get Katie out of town before the Council came after her.

I took her back to my dressing room. We'd be safe there, for now, and I could pack and figure out where we might be able to go that the hunt couldn't find us.

My dressing room was small but still elegantly furnished, with overstuffed leather couches and a deep, thick red carpet. Katie sat on one of the couches, her green eyes wide. Kalil had come into the room with us and sat near the couch, her eyes locked on Katie's face. It was strange. The jackals didn't usually react to humans, much less take a shine to them the way Kalil had.

"Did I…did I kill her?"

I shook my head. "If you really do know who I am, then you can probably guess she's like me, and we don't kill easy."

I messaged Charlie and told him to keep an extra eye on the boundaries, warning him that we might have trouble on the way. Judging by his reply, he seemed perked up at the thought of a possible battle.

I stuffed a few changes of clothes into a bag and tossed it on the floor near the door. "Why don't you tell me exactly why you're here?" I said, turning to look at her.

She blew a dangling strand of hair out of her face. "I just...I wanted to know what happened to my dad. Something happened to him in Branson. He came home a different man. He used to be the guy that everyone came to. He fixed people's cars, had coffee every morning with his friends, bought all the cookies and candy from the kids selling door-to-door." She looked down at her hands. "He came here on one of those senior tour things, and when he got back...well, he just wasn't himself."

"I'm not sure what to say. I—"

"Just tell me you remember him," she interrupted, "and that you can tell me what happened to him."

"Why are you so sure that it has anything to do with me?"

"You were the last show the group saw in Branson. And everyone said he was fine...until he was pulled up on stage for that magic act."

I knelt on the floor in front of her and reached out to touch her hand. It was enough to give me a flash inside her mind. I saw her memory of the man—his face a little smudged around the edges, a little blurry like all memories usually were. But it was enough for me to recognize him, to know exactly who she was talking about.

I've held millions of hearts in my hands. I remember each and every one. I just don't always know their names.

"I remember him. He was joking when they pulled him up on stage. Thought it was big fun. He joked about me giving his heart a good cleaning-out while I was in there. A tune-up, he said. The audience laughed. I think he was a better showman than I am."

Katie looked away from me, tears spilling from her eyes. "What did you show him? What did you do that made him a stranger to everyone who knew him?"

"I...can't tell you." I gently grasped her chin, forcing her to look at me. "And even if I could, you really wouldn't want to know. The secrets of a person's soul, the things we don't tell other people, are usually the stories that will most hurt and destroy the ones we love. We hide those stories fromourselves, until we're forced to look at them when the scales are brought out."

"But why him?"

I shrugged and stood up. "He volunteered. And like everyone else who raises their hands, he thought it was all a show, a bit of smoke and mirrors. They never believe it, sometimes not even after they leave here." I could tell she didn't believe me, either. "It's not about what god you believe in. It's about how you lived. Religion doesn't matter at the end, Katie. It never has."

"So what happens up there? When you…when you do the heart thing…?"

"It's a moment where time stops, and you know who you really are. Beyond that…" I shrugged.

"Your life flashes before your eyes?"

I hesitated. The weighing was such a personal moment. Intimate in a way that you never experienced with anyone else. "It's different for each person. It's not so much about the things you did day to day. Oh, you may see certain events play out again, or see different people or places that were part of your life. But it's more than that. You judge yourself, without filters, without excuses. You are stripped down to nothing, standing in front of your own soul and weighing whether or not you are leaving this world a better place when you are gone."

"And you're saying that my dad didn't think he'd done that?"

"Katie," I said gently, "it's not my place to judge or interpret. But the scales know the weight of a feather and the truth of what a soul is worth."

She was quiet for a long time, tears rolling down her cheeks. I looked away, giving her some privacy.

"Is he…is he in hell?"

I shook my head. "Like I said, this isn't about religion. Everyone has their own idea of what happens after, but no one knows for sure. Not even me, and I'm the Lord of Death. I know something happens—the soul goes on, but in what form? And where? I don't know."

"So what's the point of the scales if it doesn't decide your fate?"

"Because no one gets to move on without facing their own truth."

I picked up a small scale that sat on my desk. It had been a gift from the Council, a small joke back when I built the theater.

"Honestly, once the weighing begins, I'm as much a part of the audience as anyone else. But I can say that the scales don't do anything but weigh. Anything that comes after? That's on the person."

"What do you mean, 'move on'? You just weigh the heart and then put it back."

"I cheat a little. I don't complete the rite with them. It's showbiz, remember?" I eyed her. There was something that kept bugging me. "So how did you take your father's change, and his death, and put two and two together to decide the Lord of the Dead was in Branson?"

She started, a guilty look in her eyes. "Just, you know, rumors, I guess."

"Rumors?" This wasn't good. Katie wasn't exactly connected to powerful people, so if rumors that old gods were alive and well in Branson had trickled down to her, then the Council had much bigger problems. "What rumors?"

She looked away. I crossed the room, leaning over her as she sank back into the couch. "What rumors, Katie?" I asked, my face close to hers.

"Family legends!" I could feel her heart beating faster. "My great-grandmother used to tell me stories that we had some sort of special kin in Branson, that could be traced back all the way to the lineage of the gods." She shrugged. "I used to think she was just making stuff up. She was real old, and her mind wasn't what it used to be. But my great-grandfather lived well past a hundred. He said that we had strong blood, that we came from Branson."

I took a step back, my mind awhirl. "Is that all?"

"My great-grandfather managed to take more than a hundred acres of rocky mountain land up in the Ozarks and turned it into the most beautiful farmland you ever saw. And Granny always could grow anything she wanted. Even managed to have an orchard of oranges and lemons, and so many olive trees. Said that the smell of olives on the tree reminded her of home."

"How old was your granny when she died?"

"Oh, she's still around. 101 years old, but she still gets out and tends to her own garden, does her own shopping. She's real spry."

"What about your mother?"

Katie looked away. "She died when I was young. No one ever told me how, just that asking questions would cause a whole lot of hurt and that if I loved my family, I'd keep quiet."

It's like I heard the click of several little things piecing together. "Katie, can I try something? I have a feeling about this, but I don't want to say what it is—in case I'm wrong."

She looked at me, wary. "What do you want to try?"

"I just want to touch you, like I did to get the glimpse of your father. It won't hurt, but it might make your head feel a bit odd."

"Okay, I guess."

Once more, I knelt in front of her. "Close your eyes," I said, my voice soft and low. "Don't try to do anything. Just sit there and breathe. Feel your body here and now. Breathe. Breathe."

I reached out to her with my magic, gentle tendrils of peaceful darkness. People make more out of death and the dark than they need to. The transition from life to death may be hard, but death itself? The place where my powers are drawn? That's a place of peace, of rest. I pulled on that power, entwining it gently around Katie until she was cocooned in strands of black, glowing at the edges with starlight. I took one of those strands and gently pushed it into her. I watched as her skin paled, the color leeching from her face and hands. I pushed a little further. Just a little more to see if I was right…

She gasped, her eyes flying open. A sudden wave of energy burst out of her. If my power was dark and peaceful, this was golden light, the smell of green and growing earth, of honeysuckle carried on a summer wind. The plants near the window burst from their pots, trailing vines up along the walls, curving around the room while their roots cracked the foundation of the building and shot downward, connecting with the earth below.

Her magic pushed into mine, life and death intertwining. Where death bruised her, her spark of green healed. It was everything that this world should be, light and dark, neither good nor bad. It just was.

I withdrew the tendrils of my power, untangling them from hers. She blinked at me as I sat back on my heels. Her face was flushed, her breath coming in gasps. "What the hell was that?"

I sighed and rubbed a hand over my face. "That, little sister, means things just got complicated."

She opened her mouth to say something else, but she was interrupted by the buzzing of the intercom.

"What is it, Charlie?"

"Sorry to interrupt, Mr. Anubis. But I thought you should know—the Council just crossed the boundary. They'll be here soon."

* * *

I've always found a certain amount of peace on an empty stage. No stage lights, no one in the audience, no noise from the lobby. Moments like that are when the theater is most like a temple—hushed, expectant, full of magic just waiting to be unleashed. Even when there's an audience and a show, it's still serving its purpose, channeling that magic for all to see.

But tonight, my temple was a tribunal.

I stood at the center of the stage, my hands crossed in front of me. The big double doors leading out to the lobby slammed open and Morgan stalked down the aisle. She faltered when she saw me, glancing back over her shoulder. Several of the little gods and sycophants followed her. Everyone in Branson loved a good show.

Katie stood near the side, her face composed as the others stopped in front of the stage. She rested a hand on Kalil's shoulder. The jackal had definitely turned traitor—not that I minded. No one was going to bother Katie as long as Kalil was guarding her.

"Anubis, Lord of Death, greetings." Morgan spoke, but it wasn't just her. She was speaking as one of the Council, allowing the others to use her voice and body as their own.

I nodded my head in reply. "Greetings to those who sit on the Council. What can I do for you?"

Morgan's eyes were dilated, the black of her pupils so wide there was almost no white showing. "You are not the one we summon to stand before us, Anubis. Judgement must be passed on the human who violated our precepts, through claim of forbidden knowledge and by committing violence against one of our own."

"These are serious charges, and if they were found to be true, they would carry a serious penalty."

Morgan's eyes rose. "Do you doubt the veracity of the accusation, Anubis? Were you not present for both violations?"

I bowed slightly. I had to step carefully here. "Forgive me, Council. I see that the Morrigan did not convey the full truth of the events to you."

Morgan blinked at this, her pupils receding a bit. "What the hell are you talking about, Jack? There's no way you can deny what happened."

"I don't deny what happened," I said, my voice silken smooth. "But the facts of who was involved are in error."

"Be careful before you call me a liar, jackal," Morgan hissed, stepping toward me. Behind her, two of her crow-shadows flickered into being. I heard a low growl from Kalil, one that was echoed as the other jackals misted into shape along the aisles of the theater.

A sharp smell filled the air, the smell of ozone just before a lightning strike. Thunder rumbled and Morgan's eyes turned black. "Explain yourself, Anubis, before we grow weary."

I snarled, unleashing some of my own power. A cold wind blew through the theater, swirling around Morgan. She stumbled back, her breath turning to ice in the air. "I remind the Council that I am one of the elders here, too, and you will speak to me with the respect I am owed."

There was a tense silence. Morgan bowed slightly. "Our apologies, Anubis. We await your words."

I beckoned to Katie, putting one hand on her shoulder when she stood next to me.

"Katie is not a human, therefore she did not violate our laws. Her claim of knowledge is one she was born to."

There was a murmur of conversation from the spectators. They hadn't expected that and, judging from Morgan's silence, neither had the Council.

"What do you mean, she's not a human?" Morgan asked.

I beckoned Katie over. "Katie is descended from a little god. Probably an agricultural deity, based on her powers. She's one of our own." I paused. I wanted everyone in the audience to hear me. "She's descended from someone who left Branson and had a life outside of this miserable place."

Silence. Several of the others shifted in place, looking at each other, then at Morgan. I could feel the other gods in the room weighing my words, absorbing them.

I glanced back at Morgan. "And because she's not human, she didn't break any of our laws."

Morgan snarled, rage in her eyes. "She may not be human, but she still broke a law." She walked over to me, leaned in close. "If she really is a little god, then she attacked me when she shot me. And that is a death sentence."

Morgan threw out her hands, sending a blast of power at Katie. Katie went down, even as her own powers flared in response, forming a bright green shield around her. Kalil snarled and lunged at Morgan, who simply backhanded her with another whip of power. Kalil howled as she was thrown through the air, slamming into one of the stone columns with a sickening crack.

"No!" I grabbed Morgan, spinning her around to face me and felt her own death magic sliding over me, like black lightning.

A fury swept through me like the searing desert winds of my homelands. I snarled, my body shifting into my true form. I released power in a wave of energy and broke through her lightning attack, managing to slash her across the chest with my claws. Morgan cried out as she stumbled back, bright-red blood blooming from her wounds. I saw her gathering her powers for another strike, but I didn't have enough to counter her.

"ENOUGH!" The voice thundered through the theater, knocking paintings off the walls and exploding light bulbs in their sconces. The little gods dove to the floor, cowering, while the others knelt, bowing their heads as three figures walked down the aisles and onto the stage. One of them tossed up several balls of energy, which brightened until the room was lit up like a summer's day.

Morgan dropped to her knees, but I remained standing, a not-so-subtle reminder that they didn't outrank me.

"Anubis." The old man spoke, his deep voice reverberating through the room as he peered at me with his one eye. He looked around and sighed. "Well, this is a mess now, isn't it?"

"Not one of my making, Odin," I replied, letting my body meld back into its human form. It was a lot easier to talk without a mouth full of sharp teeth. "But yeah. It's definitely a cluster—"

"Let's remember our manners, Anubis," the woman chided. She wore a long blue gown, her dark skin shimmering in the light. "Elder you may be, but our position still demands respect."

I bowed my head, placing a hand over my heart. "My apologies, Ala. No disrespect intended." I looked to the third of the elders and bowed again. "Coyote. It's been a while."

Coyote grinned back. "It's been too damn boring around here! At least we're not sitting in another damn meeting about branding and increasing tourism numbers. I'm so sick of meetings. Give me a little mayhem anytime." He walked over to where Morgan knelt. Her wounds had already started to heal over, but judging by the amount of blood on the floor, I'd nailed her pretty good.

"You should clean that up, Morrigan," Coyote said. "I'm sure you don't want to leave your blood lying around where any old person can take it. Who knows what they could get up to with such a gift."

Morgan glared up at him but ran a hand over the floorboards, the blood vanishing. Coyote chuckled as he walked back to stand with the others.

I heard a moan and looked over to where Katie slowly pushed herself up off the floor. A wave of relief swept through me. She was alive. She looked around, paling when she saw Kalil lying in a heap near the stone pillar. "Oh no!" she cried out, scrambling over to where the jackal lay. She picked up Kalil's head, cradling it in her lap as tears ran down her face.

"Oh, my child," Ala crooned, walking over to kneel next to her. She placed her hand on the jackal's chest. "Her heart still beats."

Katie looked up at her. "Can you fix her?"

Ala smiled. "Better yet, you fix her. Just reach out with your—"

"I still claim retribution against that bitch," Morgan sneered.

Ala looked at Morgan, her face still. "Your claim is unfounded. This is no mortal."

Morgan sneered. "She shot me. She drew blood."

Ala looked at me, sorrow on her face. "Is this true, Anubis?"

I bowed my head. "There were extenuating circumstances," I replied, looking at all of them. "Katie may have struck the first physical blow, but she believed it to be in self-defense." Even as I said the words, I knew it wouldn't matter.

"Did the Morrigan lay a hand on the not-human first?" Coyote asked.

I hesitated, then shook my head.

Ala looked at Katie, laying one hand against her cheek. "I'm so sorry, child. But we have certain laws that are immutable, even under—as Anubis puts it—extenuating circumstances."

Katie looked around the room, her eyes wild. "Jack, what is she talking about?"

"We are beings of power," Odin said. "Some of minor power, like yourself, and others who wield vast reservoirs. We could do great harm to this world if we were to battle." His eye unfocused for a moment, as if seeing something else entirely. "And when violence among our kind is tolerated, then we step closer to certain prophecies that none of us want to see unfold."

Coyote nodded his head in agreement. "When the other gods came to this land, there were skirmishes. They were fun for a while, but if enough of the humans die, then so do we."

Ala's voice was a lament. "Our existence is threatened every day as the humans turn away from their gods. Only a few still command worship enough to refuse the pact that we made. And that pact must be enforced for the sake of everyone here."

"What…what does that mean for me?" Katie whispered.

"Death." The three spoke in one voice, a ringing tone echoing through the room.

Morgan laughed, ignoring the glares of the elder three as she stood up. "You get to die, and I get to drink down your power."

I coughed slightly, getting their attention. "The law commands death, but it doesn't specify whose."

Ala shook her head. "Anubis, no. Don't do this."

I straightened, ignoring the way my hands were starting to tremble. "I am an elder, Ala, just as you are. It is my right to intercede, not to circumvent the law, but to choose the manner of its fulfillment. I am willing to offer restitution myself."

Morgan cackled. "Oh, this is just brilliant!"

I ignored her, keeping my attention on the elders. "But as is also in keeping with the laws, I get to make a request, and I get to choose the manner of my own death."

"Agreed," said the three.

"My request is this." I took a deep breath. "Katie gets to leave and return home." I looked at Ala, who stood near Katie and Kalil's body. "And I would ask that she be able to take her guardian with her."

Ala smiled and knelt down, placing one hand on Kalil's lifeless body, holding the other out to Katie. "Time to learn how to use those powers, child."

Katie clasped her hand, then gasped as a current of power flowed from Ala, bright gold and blue. Katie's own power responded, the two strands weaving together before pouring into Kalil. The jackal stirred, her head coming up to lick at Katie's face.

Ala stood. "That was well done, little one."

"I have one more request." I spoke carefully. "I understand the importance of the tithe, but Branson is stagnating. And without something to renew not just the city, but each other, ultimately it will fail."

"What are you asking for?" Coyote looked back at me, his head cocked to the side.

"Allow some of us to leave. Maybe not forever, but just to get out and experience the world, to bring back new ideas that could benefit everyone."

The three elders looked at each other.

"We do not promise, but we will think on your words, Anubis," Odin said.

I bowed my head to them. It had to be enough to plant the seed. "Thank you."

"Can we get on with it?" Morgan sneered. "I'm hungry."

I smiled at her. "It's my choice, remember?"

"Agreed." Ala joined the other elder gods as Odin spoke. "For the crime of violence against one of our own, the sentence is death. And by his own choice, Anubis will step into her place. His death is his own."

"No, Jack!" Katie lurched to her feet, running over to grab my arm. "You can't do this."

"It's my choice, Katie. And it's done. There is no turning away from this path." Kalil gently took Katie's arm in her teeth, pulling her away from me. "Don't be afraid. Go home. Tend your olive trees and let Kalil get fat chasing rabbits." Kalil snorted at me, clearly offended. "Well, maybe not fat."

I gestured. The golden scales appeared on the altar table, the blue feather already in its place. Before anyone could move or say anything else, I plunged my hand into my chest, my fingers closing around my heart. I felt it beating, even as I lifted it out and placed in on the empty scale. There would be no last-minute snatching it back. This time, the rite would play out to the end.

I sank to my knees in front of the scales, watching as the heart sank lower and lower. I closed my eyes, listening as millions of voices whispered to me. Millions of hearts, millions of lives judged, millions of souls brought to truth. The heart sank lower still, and I felt a great blackness opening up around me, an immense abyss beneath my feet. I could feel the edges of my soul start to disintegrate, eaten up by the whirling wind that came up from the abyss.

The world paused.

The scales began to balance, the heart rising higher and higher until, finally, it stood evenly with the feather. Light and dark, death and life, everything for one moment in perfect balance. Dimly, as from a great distance, I could hear Morgan scream as she realized there would be no great release of my life energy. You cannot harvest what is already laid upon the altar in offering. My heart beat once, then again, then stilled. The abyss retreated and, instead, a door opened. I glimpsed a sky full of a billion stars, the echoes of laughter and welcome reaching out to gently tug at my soul.

"It's okay, Katie." I opened my eyes and smiled, as I took that last step. "It's all very much okay."

Old Gods, New Tricks

Juliet E. McKenna

The rain hadn't let up all day. Autumn's colors were muted to a dull palette of ochre and brown. The visitor in the yellow raincoat looked cheerful regardless as her bright red boots squelched along the muddy path to the lake. She looked around the woodland, her brown eyes bright with curiosity. Then she focused on the solitary figure tossing handfuls of food to the wild geese at the edge of the water.

"Hello!" The visitor's voice had a lilt that suggested a laugh.

The figure feeding the birds spun around. As she pushed back the hood of her old, weathered coat, her resemblance to the visitor was striking. No one could doubt they were sisters, though an onlooker would be hard-pressed to decide who was the elder. Come to that, it was anyone's guess how old either woman might be. Both had flawless skin that might be taken for youth at first glance, and there was no hint of silver in either woman's long black hair. However, a closer look would see infinite wisdom born of experience in their faces.

"Tyche!" The woman was as pleased as she was surprised to see her sister.

The visitor extended her free hand to offer a one-armed hug beneath her umbrella. "You really have hidden yourself away. It's taken me ages to find you."

The other woman tossed the last of the feed to the waterfowl and walked into her embrace. "It's lovely to see you. How long has it been?"

"Too long." Tyche's arm tightened around her. "And it's long past time you came back to work."

"What?" The woman broke free to stare at her. "Why?"

"Humanity needs you. We need you." The skies were clearing. Tyche lowered her umbrella and shook it to shed the raindrops before she furled it. "I've been to see the others already. I'm getting the band back together."

The woman in the weathered blue coat was bemused. "What band? What are you talking about?"

Tyche waved that away. "Never mind. Let me show you how things have changed. Then you'll see how much people need us. How we can help them."

The woman in blue shook her head. "No mortals remember me. They certainly don't pray for my help. I can't have any influence on their lives these days."

"They may not pray in the ways they used to, but that doesn't matter now. How many mortals call me Tyche, beyond historians and literary scholars? That's never stopped millions of them begging for Lady Luck's favor, even if they're just buying a lottery ticket these days." She smiled with irrepressible charm. "I don't mind what they call me. Why should you?"

"Luck's something mortals always long for." Her sister shook her head. "Justice? Not so much as I recall, even when they dedicated temples and altars to me."

"You need to move with the times," Tyche chided. "People still know your name, even if they don't realize you're a goddess. Nemesis is a concept that everyone understands. More than that, they want to see it—they want to see you—in action. Not nearly enough people are getting their due out in the world these days. You're the only one of us who can make sure that happens. Like I said, we need you, to help keep humanity honest."

Nemesis looked at her, incredulous. "I have no power anymore."

"You'd be surprised." Tyche's grin widened as she hooked her umbrella over one arm. She reached inside her raincoat.

"You won't get a signal out here," Nemesis remarked.

Tyche raised her eyebrows as she produced a smart phone. "So you're not that much of a hermit."

"People come up this way in the summer to camp and go boating on the lake." Nemesis shrugged. "They'll be determined to go off the grid, to get a proper break. That lasts until they get themselves into some sort of trouble. Then they'll come knocking on my door, to see if I've got satellite broadband or another way they can call for help." She nodded at the cabin set back from the water. "It *is* the only house for miles around."

"What do you say?" Tyche was intrigued.

Nemesis shrugged. "That they have to hike out to the highway. A vehicle to give them a lift will come along sooner or later."

She might have said more, but Tyche was busy with her phone, tapping at the screen.

"I've got a couple of bars." She looked up with a grin. "Just lucky, I guess. Come and see."

Nemesis walked over to join her. "See what?"

"Social media," Tyche said with relish. She swiped a beautifully manicured fingernail across the screen. "See how many sorts there are now? Twitter, Facebook, Instagram, Tumblr, Reddit, and that's just the start. See how mortals use these portals to pour out their longings and frustrations, to beg for validation or approval? They're as quick to share their dreams of an unexpected windfall as they are to long for well-deserved misfortune befalling a person who's wronged them."

Nemesis watched the thumbnail pictures and snatches of text fly by. The phone screen flickered far too fast for mortal eyes, but navigating this stream of information was no challenge for a goddess. She had once been accustomed to expanding her consciousness through time and space to encompass and comprehend every detail of prayers and offerings made to her at countless shrines. To her astonishment, she sensed the faint presence of the power she had once known so well. The power she had used to bring down petty tyrants and mighty empires alike. It was like hearing distant music that stirred a memory of some half-remembered tune.

"You can feel it, can't you? Just like the others did when I showed them. They're already seeing what they can do." Tyche's finger halted the dizzying torrent of images. "Here's one for me. A talented comedian who could use some good luck. He'll be at an open-mic night this weekend and an established star will be in the audience. She'll heckle him to see how he copes and he'll do brilliantly without being sexist or rude. A video clip will go viral and he'll get his chance on a TV show. That'll be his big break. Before the end of this year, he'll set up a charity offering drama lessons to underprivileged kids."

She double-tapped the screen. A flash from the phone momentarily lit her face with a reflection of incandescent power.

"Luck, good or bad, is your business, not mine. You don't need my help to punish the people you've blessed if they're not suitably grateful,"

Nemesis protested. "I used to give mortals what they earned through their actions, no more and no less."

"Exactly, and there's plenty for you to do nowadays. You'll see once you get online." Tyche was swiping the screen again. "That comedian? He'd be working in a bank for the rest of his days if I didn't throw an unforeseen blessing his way. However much time he devoted to his jokes, it would make no difference without a lucky break. But this man—" her finger halted.

Despite herself, Nemesis glanced at the phone. She looked onwards through that palm-sized window to take in every detail of the unsuspecting mortal's life, laid out in tweets and posts and pictures on a handful of different platforms.

That sense of the power she had once known grew stronger, like music growing steadily louder until she recognized the elusive tune. Perhaps, if she were to reach out, to hum along as it were…

"See?" Tyche persisted. "He'll never get what he deserves unless he does something to get himself noticed. There's no twist of fate I can throw in his path to change that. Believe me, I've tried. Anyway, this is your job, not mine. I've got more than enough to do."

"Why should I?" Nemesis demanded, obstinate.

Tyche shrugged. "Why not? Why not remind everyone who knows him that there can be justice in this world? That nice guys don't always finish last while the bastards get ahead."

"Mortals don't care—" Nemesis broke off as she contemplated the swirling clouds of posts and pictures that she could see beyond the smartphone's screen. She saw far too many people lamenting unfairnesses great and small.

No, not unfairness. Injustice. Abuses of power, from the petty to the breathtaking. That was the thing about power. Unless you were a god or a goddess, it could be horribly corrupting. As long as there were no consequences, why shouldn't people see what they could get away with? Once upon a time, she had been there to make sure they realized their mistake. Before mortals had turned to other gods and she had drifted away from humanity.

"They still put up statues of you holding a set of scales," Tyche said, merciless. "Seriously, don't you think it's time you helped redress the balance? To make people think more deeply about their actions? Start with something easy. You'll soon get into the swing of things, once you start wielding your power again."

She held out the phone. Challenge was bright in her eyes.

Nemesis took it. As she wryly acknowledged to herself, even goddesses can be tempted.

* * *

"Have you seen the new temp?" Nicholas paused beside Jacob's desk. "Very easy on the eye."

He looked up from his screen. "Shall I tell Emily you said that?"

Nick spread his hands in mock-protest. "Hey, I'm a married man. You're the one who hasn't had a date in three months."

"It hasn't been—" Jacob realized he couldn't actually recall when he'd last gone out to dinner or a movie with someone special, rather than his usual group of friends.

"Here she comes." Nick hurried away, heading for the office plotter as it printed out some large-scale plan of whatever office block renovation he was working on.

Jacob was about to go back to the architectural drawing on his middle screen when all three of his monitors momentarily went black. His heart pounded and his stomach hollowed, but before he had time to wonder if he had just lost half a morning's work, everything reappeared just as it had been. All the same, he hastily saved every file he had open and reached for his phone to call Ellie in IT.

Then he realized the new temp was looking at him as she walked between the well-spaced desks. He hastily checked his email. Ignoring the messages he really didn't need to be copied into, he found the notification from Leo in HR. He was sending up the new temporary assistant Jake had asked for, since the last one sent by their regular agency had been late every day last week.

Nick was right, Jake had to admit, as the woman approached. She was very nice-looking, with her long black hair drawn back into a neat braid. Not impossibly glamorous or model-thin, or anything else intimidating like that, just…nice.

He guessed she was about his own age, so not fresh out of college, and she looked around with the confidence that meant she could pick up a new office routine. She was also clearly here to work not to flirt, wearing comfortable shoes and a business-like skirt and blouse. That was a relief. Jake was too busy for time-wasters like some of the temps he'd been sent since Amanda had gone on maternity leave. All the same, once they got to know each other, if this new girl—woman—was here long enough, maybe they could go for a coffee…

She arrived at his desk and he shoved such thoughts aside. "Hi, I think you're looking for me? I'm Jacob Milton. Everyone calls me Jake."

She smiled. It was a very nice smile. "I'm Remy. I'm supposed to ask you to get me up to date with the Elysian Fields development. I'll be working for you and—" she checked the first page of the notebook in her hand "—Oliver Widford."

"Right. He's out on site this morning. That's his desk when he's in the office, and you'll be over there. Bring your chair over here for a moment though. Let me show you where we are with the project."

As she fetched the seat, Jake closed down the drawing he'd been working on and opened up the brochure showing the concept artist's vision of the houses the company was halfway through building. "Can you see this okay?"

As Remy adjusted her chair and nodded, he went on.

"The site's on the other side of the city. It'll be a mixed development of houses from two-bed town-houses all the way up to these five-bed detacheds with double garages. We're managing the whole project, from the designs through to construction. That's Oliver's side of the job, liaising with the builders and other contractors. We're selling the houses off these plans and with a range of options. I'll be making the modifications the customers choose, and we can discuss other things buyers might ask for. We like to make their new homes exactly what they want."

He scrolled through the brochure's pages, glancing over to be sure that he wasn't going too fast for Remy. She surprised him with a laugh.

"How many people ask you to lose those columns?"

Jake grinned. "Fewer than you might think. They're surprisingly popular."

Personally, he thought the fake Greek-style porticos looked ridiculously out of place.

Remy shook her head, amused. "I suppose they're in keeping with the name. But whose idea was that?"

"Elysian Fields? Oliver came up with that. It means 'paradise,' doesn't it?"

Seeing Remy grimace, Jake suddenly wasn't so sure.

"It's the nicest part of the realms of the dead, but it's still in the Underworld." She broke off, looking self-conscious. "Never mind me. Greek myths are a bit of a hobby, thanks to my family history. That's where my people came from, way back. They called me Rhamnusia, can you believe it?"

"I can see why you go by Remy." That explained her attractive Mediterranean complexion. Jake turned his attention back to the screen.

"Well, the name's not putting our customers off. Calls and email from people interested in buying a house will come through to you. You'll have access to this directory on the server, so you can send them the brochures and layouts. This is where you'll find my calendar, to set up meetings on site or here in the conference room, to discuss whatever tweaks they're interested in. You'll be keeping those records, and making sure Oliver's kept fully updated, so he can brief the contractors."

Remy nodded. "Okay."

"Have you been given your login and password?"

She nodded again. "All part of this morning's induction."

"Okay then." Jake was reassured by her calm confidence. He offered a friendly smile. "Is there anything else I can do for you, or would you like to get settled in at your desk?"

Remy smiled back. "What's the time? We're allowed fifteen minutes for tea or coffee mid-morning, aren't we?"

"We are." Jake glanced at the lower right-hand corner of his central screen and saw that had worked out just right. "Let me show you where to find the break room."

* * *

At the end of the week, Jake was so deep in thought that he didn't even notice when Nick paused by his desk. He looked up, wide-eyed and startled, when his grinning friend snapped his fingers to get his attention.

"So, how are you getting on?"

Jake stared at the drawing on his screen. "They want the integral garage turned into another reception room, and a free-standing garage built somewhere else on the plot. The work on the house is easy enough, but I can't decide on the best place for the garage. There are the trees to consider; not just the ones already there, but the ones we're going to plant. Then there are the lines of sight for the neighbors—"

"Never mind your fussy clients." Nick waved that away. "How are you getting on with Remy?"

Jake was tempted to remind Nick of all the times he'd monopolized their Friday evening conversation over a beer with complaints about the impossible things people expected from repurposed industrial buildings. He answered his question instead. "She's great; well-organized and really good with the customers. I hope she stays until Amanda gets back."

Nick shook his head, exasperated. "I didn't ask how Remy was getting on. Have you found out if you've got any interests in common? What sort of films does she like? How about her favorite music? How does she take her coffee?"

That at least was something Jake could answer. "Like mud. Seriously, she likes it stronger than espresso. She brought in some special sort of coffee pot to make it on the hotplate."

Thankfully she hadn't taken offense when he'd been unable to hide his reaction after tasting the cup she'd offered him the other afternoon.

"And?" demanded Nick.

"And nothing," Jake retorted. "She's a nice person and she's good at her job, and I'm not going to make her uncomfortable by being nosy."

Nick sighed theatrically. "What you need—"

He broke off, looking past Jake. "Well, here she comes. Try to find something to talk to her about besides coffee?"

He walked off and Remy arrived back at her desk. Jake looked at his screen again, then turned towards her. "Could you do me a favor? Take a look at these options and tell me what you think. I've been staring at different possibilities for so long, I can't see the wood for the trees—literally."

"I'll help if I can."

"You remember what the Brewsters wanted?" As she came over, Jake clicked his mouse to open up the three possibilities he'd come up with. "What do you think?"

She took her time looking thoughtfully at the screens. "I think you'd get a better idea of the best option if you went out to the site and took a look there."

"You know, I think you're right." Jake realized that was the obvious answer. As he leaned back in his chair and stretched his shoulders to ease his stiff neck, another thought struck him. "Why don't you come, too? You haven't seen the site yet, and I'm sure it would help when you're talking to the customers. As long as you can spare the time," he added hastily.

Remy smiled and glanced at her desk. "Give me five minutes?"

"Fine. I'll print these off to take with us and I'll see you in the car park."

Remy was as good as her word. He'd just had time to check he had two hard hats and spare hi-vis vests in the trunk of his car when she arrived beside him.

"Is it going to be muddy?" She gestured at his battered boots. "I can bring my walking boots in from home, if we go tomorrow instead."

"No, we'll be fine." Jake closed the trunk lid. "This plot is close to a finished section of the site. We can see what we want from the paving that's already laid."

He wondered about opening the passenger door for Remy, but before he could decide if that would look stupid, or even a bit creepy, she had gotten into the car. He took the driving seat, handed her the folder of printouts, and started the engine.

As he made his way carefully out of the car park and accelerated along the road, he remembered what Nick had said. He could start a conversation now, couldn't he? That wouldn't be weird. The two of them making this journey in silence, that would definitely be weird. So what should he ask her about? Music? Films? What sort of food she liked—or would that seem like a hint that he wanted to ask her out to dinner?

Remy spoke first. "Can I ask you something?"

Jake forced himself to relax. "Of course."

"Oliver said something about you reporting to him, but I thought your line manager was Mr. Compton. I don't want to get something wrong…" She left the query hanging in the air.

Jake discarded the questions he was considering. "We both report to Mr. Compton. Come to that, I've been with the company longer than Oliver. I certainly don't answer to him." His grip tightened on the steering wheel.

They drove the rest of the way in silence. Jake turned down the new side road cutting between the houses that were already finished. He pulled up beside the show home where the sales team's bold flags were fluttering. There were several cars parked close by the fencing around the back garden.

"It's not far, and we won't need to go near any of the construction that's going on, but rules are rules." As they got out, he opened the back of the car and handed Remy a hard hat and hi-vis vest.

"I'm all in favor of people following the rules." Remy looked around as she put on the protective gear. "I can see why these houses are selling so well. This is going to be a lovely place to live."

Jake was about to casually ask whereabouts in the city she lived, when voices surprised him. Someone had opened the sliding glass doors at the back of the show house and come out into the garden. He recognized Oliver's voice and looked again at the parked cars. He hadn't noticed before, but one was Oliver's BMW. That made no sense. The office calendar said he had meetings all afternoon with the estate agents marketing these new homes.

"Honestly, these houses sell themselves." Cigarette smoke floated through the air along with Marcus from the sales team's words. "They're so well designed. Everyone says the same."

"Thank you, I'm glad you think so." Oliver's voice was sunny with satisfaction. "I put in a lot of hours getting everything just right."

"You—?" Marcus clearly rethought what he was going to say. "I didn't realize. Jake showed me the plans originally."

"Oh yes," said Oliver, unbothered. "He did a good job of getting everything drawn up, once I'd walked him through the concepts I'd come up with. I barely had to tell him to make any changes when he showed me the final layouts."

Jake wondered what on earth Oliver was talking about. He hadn't played any part in designing these houses. That wasn't his job at all. He thought he could take credit for it though?

Oliver was still talking. "I told Jake, it's the attention to detail that matters, and understanding what people need as well as what they think they want. He got the idea soon enough, once I showed him how to make best use of the storage space in the first couple of designs. I was happy to give him the nod when he asked if he should put the proposals forward."

"A lot of people like the built-in storage," Marcus agreed.

Jake was ready to vault over the fence and punch Oliver in his lying mouth. He had never sought the bastard's input on any aspect of these designs. He sure as hell hadn't sought his approval before sending the drawings to their boss. Oliver's only contribution had been putting together the costs.

Then he caught Remy gazing steadily at him. There was a knowing look in her warm brown eyes. She didn't believe any of Oliver's bullshit. That was a relief. Jake opened his mouth, but she raised a finger to her lips, unblinking. That meant Jake heard what Oliver said next.

"I was telling Darren Compton, Jake's a hard worker and a quick learner. I said, I'm glad I've been able to mentor him."

Now Jake gaped as he looked at Remy. He was lost for words. When Oliver had joined the company, it had been Jake who'd shown him the ropes. He'd saved the newcomer more than once, when Oliver had been about to screw something up because he hadn't listened to what he'd been told.

"Well, I can't hang around here chatting all day," Oliver said breezily. "I'd better get back to the office and make sure everything's ticking over okay."

His voice retreated back towards the house. Jake heard the sliding doors being drawn closed.

Remy looked at him and waved the folder of papers she held. "So, are we going to look at the best place for this garage?"

"What?" It took Jake a moment to remember why they had come here in the first place. "Right. Come on."

He couldn't help glancing over his shoulder, as he led the way down the newly paved path that would link this first completed phase to the rest of the housing development. As he saw Oliver come out of the show home, he wondered if the lying swine was taking credit for this idea as well, when it was Jake who had devised the network of footpaths and bike routes that would keep walkers and cyclists well away from the cars.

He had no idea about that, but he saw Oliver didn't even glance their way before he got into his car and drove off. Not that he would have recognized them, Jake reckoned. All he'd see would be two people in hard hats and fluorescent vests, half-hidden by one of the site's mature oak trees that Jake had made sure wouldn't need to be felled. That had been a fair bit of extra work. He wondered if Oliver was taking credit for that as well. The bastard.

Remy took the plans out of the folder. "That's the Brewster plot over there, isn't it?"

Jake dragged his thoughts back to the job in hand. "Yes, you're right."

Remy held up the plans one by one. "What do you think?"

"The second one." Jake could see that clearly now. "You were right. We just needed to come out here to see it."

They made their way back to the car and dumped their protective gear in the trunk. Jake drove them back through the city, and thankfully Remy didn't try to start a conversation. He was fully occupied with his irate thoughts.

How dare Oliver tell Marcus that so much of the design work had been his idea? But how could Jake prove he was lying? As he ran through everything they had overheard, he realized how clever the bastard was. The fact that Jake's name was on all the computer files proved nothing, if Oliver was claiming to have been the project's guiding hand. It would be Jake's word against his, and anyway, how could he bring up this subject with anyone back in the office? "I just happened to overhear a conversation when I was lurking on the other side of a fence…"

Saying anything would sound like whining. Even so, it was infuriating to think that Oliver could get away with telling these lies. Then Jake wondered uneasily how long this had been going on. How many of his co-workers thought he was no more than a draftsman, turning Oliver's brilliance into the company's plans?

He hadn't found any answers by the time they got back to the office. He pulled into an empty parking space and they both got out of the car.

As Remy shut the passenger door, she looked around and her forehead creased.

"Didn't Oliver say he was coming back here? I don't see his car anywhere."

"Maybe he got caught in some traffic." Jake hoped so, as they headed for the office, and not just because the bastard deserved as much aggravation as city center gridlock could offer. The longer it took Oliver to get back, the more time Jake would have to cool off. Losing his temper wouldn't solve anything.

But there was no sign of Oliver before Jake realized it was time to call it a day. As he shut down his computer, he saw Remy looking thoughtfully at the empty desk. He wasn't going to say anything, but she glanced his way and her gaze met his for a long moment. Then the printer on her desk churned out a piece of paper.

"I'm starting to wonder how reliable Oliver's work calendar really is," she remarked, as she brought over her time sheet for him to sign.

Jake realized she made a very good point. Before he could find the right way to say so, Remy surprised him with a smile.

"Those boots of yours seem to have had plenty of use. Do you like hiking? Maybe you could show me some of the local trails?"

Jake's day suddenly improved by about a thousand percent. "Are you free sometime this weekend?"

* * *

Remy was a serious walker, there was no doubt about that. Jake was impressed with her stamina and fitness by the time they reached the turn where the trail that flanked the nature reserve skirted around the golf course. She also looked very good in her well-worn outdoor gear.

"If we walk up there, we can take a path that loops around the far side of the lake," he said casually. "That'll get us back to the car in an hour or so. Maybe we could head into town for a coffee after that?"

If they sat and chatted long enough, perhaps he could suggest they went somewhere for an early dinner.

"That would be nice." Remy broke off and raised the binoculars slung around her neck. It turned out she was a serious bird watcher. "Isn't that Oliver? Over there, with those other golfers."

Jake raised his camera and used the zoom to see for himself. "You've got good eyes."

"He's with Jason Lovell, Evan Welch, and Phil Shifford," Remy said slowly. "Well, I suppose that makes sense."

Jake nodded as he watched the foursome making their way along the trimmed turf. He had no idea how far they were through their game.

He'd been hopeless the few times he'd tried playing golf. "They must have set this up when Oliver was getting some quotes for the next block of houses."

"Haven't you seen his social media?" Remy asked, surprised.

Something in her tone made Jake uneasy. "No. Why?"

"They play a lot of golf together, and not just around here." Remy let her binoculars hang from their strap and got out her phone. "Look at this."

"You've got a signal?" Jake was surprised.

"I'm on a really good network." Remy smiled. Before Jake could ask which one, she held out her phone. "See what I mean?"

Jake moved to stand beside her, so he could see the screen without a sheen of reflected light. "Where's that?" he asked, astonished.

"Portugal, it says, last summer. Here's somewhere else in the Algarve. This was a trip to Ireland. They go there a lot." The photos slid across the screen, drawn by Remy's finger. "Oh, here's Scotland, just for a change."

Jake stared at the pictures. The details were different, but the same four men were playing golf every time. That or they were enjoying some meal in a fancy hotel, with or without the women he guessed were their wives. "I had no idea they were such good friends."

"Are you surprised, when he puts such a lot of business their way?"

The edge to Remy's voice made Jake look up, startled.

"What do you mean by that?"

"Lovell Carpets. Welch Kitchens. Shifford Plumbing." She looked at him, her fine black eyebrows arched.

Jake was even more unnerved. "Their quotes are always competitive."

"Are they?" Remy stared at him, unblinking. "Who else does he go to?"

"There's a whole file of contractors and suppliers…" Jake realized he'd heard Oliver on the phone in the office to these golfing pals, but he couldn't actually recall when he'd last heard him speaking to anyone else about their price for some part of a project.

That didn't mean anything though. Oliver would send out his requests for quotations by email, wouldn't he? All the same…

Another thought struck him. "Do you always go looking at their social media, when you meet new people?"

"When I'm starting a new job, yes, of course." Remy seemed surprised that he needed to ask. "Wouldn't you want to know what you were walking into?"

"I suppose so," Jake agreed reluctantly.

He wondered what Remy had made of his own online presence. She must think he was pretty pathetic. He only used Twitter to follow football, and his Facebook friends were the local mates he played online games with, as well as his mum, his sister, and his brothers. Then there were the handful of old friends from school and college, and those three cousins he got on well with…

"Come on," she said briskly as she put her phone away. "Let's get going. I don't know about you, but I'll be ready for a hot drink and maybe a doughnut when we get back to the car."

"That sounds like a plan." Jake tried to throw off the doubts hovering around him.

He managed pretty well. They enjoyed the walk. Remy had a talent for spotting birds, and Jake managed to get some satisfying photos of the autumn trees over the water. The cafe he suggested was bustling without being too crowded, and as they sat and chatted over hot chocolate and blueberry muffins, he learned a whole lot about Remy's favorite books and films. He'd never realized she was such an avid mystery and whodunnit fan.

When she went to join the line at the counter, to get them each another drink, Jake took out his phone to check the news headlines. That was odd. He didn't have a connection. Oh well. He went through the routine to restart his phone and put it down on the table. He'd be back online in a moment.

As he gazed idly through the cafe window, Jake couldn't help thinking about Oliver and that golfing party. Then a sudden cold draft on the back of his neck made him shiver. He turned around to see if someone had left the cafe door open. No one had, but as he looked, an estate agent's sign across the street caught his eye. Leafield Properties.

Before he could talk himself out of it, Jake picked up his phone. He had a full signal again so he scrolled through his contacts to find his friend Matt's number. Matt worked for Leafield, and Jake knew he was working this Saturday. Matt has said so, the last time they'd been setting up a gaming session. Jake drummed his fingers silently on the table as he made the call.

"Hi, yes, I'm fine, thanks. Listen, I know this sounds odd, but can I ask you something without going into why?"

Matt sounded puzzled, but willing to help. "Okay."

"You know Oliver Widford? Who did he come to see at Leafield's yesterday?"

"Yesterday?" Matt was surprised. "No one."

"Really? Are you sure?"

"Certain. I was in the office all day. We haven't seen him for ages." Now Matt was curious. "What's up?"

"Honestly, I'm not sure. Look, forget I asked, will you? I've probably just got some wires crossed."

"Okay," Matt said amiably. "Are you up for a session online tomorrow afternoon?"

Jake looked at Remy, and saw she was about to be served at the counter. "Maybe. Actually, I'm not sure. I'll let you know if I'm free."

"Okay, cheers." Amiable as always, Matt ended the call.

Jake put his phone away, and wondered what to do. He also wondered just how many things Oliver Widford was lying about, and how long that had been going on.

Then he saw Remy walking towards him with their fresh drinks on a tray. He decided problems at work could wait until Monday.

* * *

"So what happened?" Tyche leaned forward to top off her sister's wine glass.

"Jake did a bit more digging, and after wrestling with his conscience for a week, he went to their boss. The truth soon came out. Oliver wasn't doing half the work he claimed when he was out of the office. He was making sales calls for his brother's IT firm on the side. When he was in the office, he certainly wasn't asking a full range of suppliers to quote for fitting out those houses. He'd just send details of whatever the customers wanted to his friends, and say they came back with the best prices once he had taken quality and workmanship into account."

Nemesis took a sip of retsina. "Which was a complete lie. People were paying top prices for bargain basement materials. Fire doors that weren't even fire proof, things like that. Meantime, Oliver was enjoying five-star golf trips without ever reaching for his own wallet. Let's hope those memories help him pass the time in prison."

"That news must be going viral," Tyche said with a sly grin.

Nemesis nodded with satisfaction. "A lot of people who might be tempted to pull a fast one will be thinking better of it, for a good long time. That's not all. Oliver might not have been getting brown envelopes full of cash, but his wife's hair salon has a lot more money in the bank than she can account for. Apparently, he did her bookkeeping. Now she's facing a full audit."

She laughed. "He couldn't understand how everyone had been able to see those photos. He was sure those accounts were locked so only the four of them had access."

Dionysos raised his glass. "Praise be to me, the god of drunken fat fingers and butt dialing. You'd be amazed at the results I can get when someone's had enough booze. When one of my beloved sisters needs my help," he added piously.

"I'm very grateful," Nemesis assured him, "and to you, Tyche, for showing me what I was missing. Anyway, Jake's got a pay raise, a promotion, and a whole lot more self-confidence, so everyone's got what they deserve. Well, nearly."

"I'm on it." Aphrodite put down her wine and reached for her phone. "What dating site did you talk his friend into convincing him to try, in case he was pining after you left?"

"I sent you the link." Nemesis drained her glass.

"The online world offers us endless possibilities. Even the humans who are experts have no idea how it really works." Tyche's eyes gleamed, bright as sunlight. "I knew you'd enjoy getting back to work, once you started with something small. What do you think you'll do next?"

Nemesis reached for the wine bottle. "Have you seen the state of mortal politics these days? I was reading the comments on the local paper's website. We really should do something about the next elections."

Your Three O'Clock Is Here

Tanya Huff

"A marriage counselor, Mother?"

"Why not?" Hera leaned closer to the mirror and adjusted her eyebrow until it arched into the exact curve she desired.

"You're not a therapist."

"So? You're not a doctor and you work as an OBGYN."

Arms folded over her…

What were those ugly things called again? Hera wondered. Oh yes. Scrubs.

...Eileithyaia scowled. "I'm the Goddess of Childbirth!"

"And I'm the Goddess of Marriage. Not to mention that I've been married to your father for millennia."

"He's your brother!"

Hera glanced down at the phone. "Different times."

"He tried to kill you!"

"Forgive and forget."

"You don't forgive. Or forget."

She considered that for a moment. "Fair."

"You turned his lovers into animals. Into trees!"

"So he'd leave them alone. That man is incapable of hearing the word no and impossible to stop." She frowned. "And I'm fairly certain I turned them back once he lost interest."

Eileithyaia exhaled vigorously. "You haven't seen Zeus for three and a half centuries!"

"But we're still married."

"Mother..."

"You can't deny I have experience dealing with the worst a marriage can offer."

"Well, no, but..."

"And, frankly, I'm bored."

"That's not..."

"I've got to go, sweetheart. I have two new clients booked today."

"Mother..."

"Khaîre, darling." Hera tapped a gilded fingernail against the screen and wondered why she'd ever thought settling in the same city as one of her children would be a good idea.

* * *

Mackenzie Whyte sat in the tastefully decorated waiting room and tried not to stare at the clock. Raymond had agreed to meet her at two forty-five for their three o'clock appointment. He knew where. He knew when. It was two fifty-five and he wasn't there. She'd texted. She'd called. She'd even run down to the Tim Horton's on the first floor of the office tower and used their wifi to Facebook message him. Nothing.

She drew in a deep breath and released it with enough force that the lilies in the vase beside her swayed.

If he'd gotten *distracted* again, she was going to...well, evidence suggested she'd go to marriage counseling.

At two fifty-six the inner door opened and a not very tall woman emerged, light brown hair brushing against her shoulders as she threw back her head and laughed with the couple following her. She wore a turquoise suit, gold high-heeled sandals, and moved with the kind of grace that made Mackenzie suspect years of dance lessons. She looked... elegant. The couple, a pair of women in their late thirties or early forties, looked happy. Like Dr. Próta had solved the problem that had driven them to a marriage counselor.

If only...

The clock striking two drew her attention. Mackenzie hadn't realized it was a cuckoo clock. Distracted by the cuckoo's broken neck, she didn't see the couple leave.

"Dr. Whyte, I presume." Dr. Próta smiled down at her. She gestured to the empty space on Mackenzie's right with one long-fingered hand, the glitter of gold nail polish drawing the eye. "And the other Dr. Whyte?"

Mackenzie checked the clock. The cuckoo's head had gotten jammed and stopped the mechanism. It was three-oh-two. It might have been three-oh-two for a while. "He's, uh...late."

"So it appears."

She shrugged. "He's got a heavy course load this semester. He was probably distracted by some...thing.

"I understand." Her smile suggested she did. "Why don't I sit down here with you and we can wait together."

If she lived to be a hundred, Mackenzie knew she'd never be able to sit with even half the grace Dr. Próta exhibited. Actually, if she lived to be a hundred she'd probably feel grateful she could sit at all. Here and now, she felt guilty for taking Dr. Próta's time. She felt guilty about Raymond's absence. She felt guilty about feeling guilty when she was paying for the doctor's time and Raymond was a grown man with a doctorate and full professorship. Finally, when the silence stretched toward uncomfortable, she said, "He's not going to show."

"Did he not want to come? Counseling works best when both partners are at the table."

"He wanted...he was willing to come for me."

"He wanted you to shut up about counseling or he wanted to make you happy?"

"He didn't...I don't..." She took a deep breath. And it all spilled out.

They'd never had a monogamous marriage. They'd both had lovers, people they were more or less serious about, but they'd respected the relationship. Acknowledged boundaries. They'd talked about everything. Everyone.

"But he doesn't talk to me anymore. Over the last six months, he's had a string of one-night-stands. More of a rope than a string actually. Objectively, for a man in his late forties his stamina is impressive. He's not ashamed. He's not lying to me. But he's not talking to me either..."

"And you want the women punished."

"What? No! They haven't done anything wrong!"

"Then you want the children of their union punished."

"Children? There aren't any children. Raymond had a vasectomy."

"Ah, so you want your husband punished."

"I don't want anyone punished. I just want..."

"Yes?"

Mackenzie sighed. "I want him to talk to me. I want him to tell me what's going on in his head. I want him to tell me why. But if that's not in the cards..." She glanced around the waiting room. At the open door to the inner office. At the vase of lilies. At the hotel-tasteful still life of pomegranates. At the woman sitting beside her. And surrendered. And sighed again. "...then I just want him to get tired of tom-catting around."

Dr. Próta's eyes glowed gold. Which was impossible, Mackenzie acknowledged. "I think you'll find the next time you see Dr. Whyte, the *other* Dr. Whyte, he'll be considering his choices."

"You haven't even met him." Mackenzie sighed and stood. "You may have a wonderful reputation, Dr. Próta..." The marriage counselor had come very highly recommended, although Mackenzie couldn't remember by who. "...but you can't possibly know that."

"I think you'll find I can, Dr. Whyte."

"Doctor..."

"Far too many doctors in this conversation." Golden nails drew another gilded arc in the air. "Call me Hera."

* * *

"Raymond?" Mackenzie left the front door open behind her. If he wasn't home, she wasn't staying. She had work to do at the university and, with luck, she'd find him in his office just down the hall.

She heard footsteps on the stairs and turned as Raymond stepped into the hall. He'd showered recently, his hair in damp curls against his neck. She had time enough to acknowledge what a shower in the middle of the afternoon probably meant, then there was a pile of clothing on the hardwood floor and a large tabby cat racing for the open door. She grabbed for it, missed, and reached for the door handle. But the cat was fast, the tip of its tail flicking to safety just as the door closed. By the time Mackenzie got it open again, the cat was halfway across the lawn. She stepped out onto the porch in time to see it dive under the scruffy hedge of bridal-wreath spirea on the other side of the driveway.

"That was weird."

Then she realized how weird.

Heart pounding, she pivoted on one heel and stared into the house.

At the pile of clothing.

* * *

The world looked unsaturated. And bluer than Raymond remembered. He could see every vein on the leaf in front of his face, but when he looked back at the house, the woman standing on the porch was distinctly fuzzy.

Where were his glasses?

He raised a hand...paw...he had a paw. He had a paw because...hey, he had four paws!

If he didn't stop to think about it, he could walk. And run. And...

And swish his tail!

He had a tail!

If this was a dream he was all for it. If this was some kind of an acid flashback, cool. Also, unlikely, but he was a cat and that had shifted his base line for unli....

He could lick his own balls!

That was...

A bird shifted on its perch with a rustle and a scrape. He caught the flicker of movement from the corner of his eye. Far around the corner...

His leap was instinctive. He twisted in midair, bending his back in ways he hadn't managed even back when he'd been studying iyengar yoga at the ashram.

He hooked his claws around the branch, but the bird flew free.

Oh well, he wasn't sure what he'd do with a bird anyway.

He opened his mouth and sucked air past his teeth, tongue curling.

What was that incredible smell?

Tail lashing, he stalked off to find it.

* * *

Mackenzie pounded on Dr. Próta's door with both fists.

"I doubt she'll be in much before ten." The elderly man unlocking the office down the hall shrugged when Mackenzie whirled around to face him. "She never is."

"Ten?" It was eight twenty-seven. "I'll wait."

He shrugged again. "There's a public bathroom at the end of the hall if you want to clean up."

She had spirea branches caught in her hair, mud on both hands and knees, and a scrape on her forehead where she'd slammed into the side of the neighbor's garage, her eyes locked on the fleeing tabby cat. The calico he'd been with had shot her a look that should've been fatal, leapt over a garden gnome, and disappeared.

Branches removed, hands washed, water splashed on her face and swished around her mouth, helped. A little. Enough that when she tucked herself up against Dr. Próta's door, she drifted off to sleep.

"Dr. Whyte?"

Her eyes snapped open. "You!"

Dr. Próta cocked her head. "Yes. It's my office."

Lurching up onto her feet, Mackenzie followed the other woman inside. "My husband is a cat!"

"So you said."

"No. An actual cat. Four paws and a tail. And you..." She pointed a trembling finger. "...you're responsible."

"Me?" One hand over her heart, Dr. Próta raised an elegant brow.

Mackenzie folded her arms. "I have a PhD in mythological studies with an emphasis in death psychology."

The brow rose higher. "An emphasis in what?"

"Death psychology as it pertains to... Never mind. That's not important! You turned my husband into a cat." She leaned in and ground out through clenched teeth. "I saw your eyes glow gold. I saw him change, *Hera*. You can't turn husbands into cats!"

"Yes, I can." She sat down behind her desk. "Although I'm not saying I did."

"Who else then!" Mackenzie slapped her palm down on the gleaming wood. "Who else, HERA?"

"Good question." After a moment, she spread her hands and smiled. Mackenzie thought she looked pleased by the recognition. "All right, you've got me. I turned your husband into a cat."

It took a moment before Mackenzie could find her voice. "Turn him back!"

"He'll turn back when he's tired of being a tomcat. Just like you wanted."

"That's not... I didn't..." She could feel her nostrils flaring. "What if he never tires of it!?"

"Then you're well rid of him."

"That's not your decision to make!"

"Really?" Hera made a moue of disgust. "If your husband prefers being a twelve pound, essentially brainless creature of instinct rather than being your husband, your marriage may not be worth saving."

"That's..." Mackenzie scrubbed at her face. That almost made sense.

"Now that's settled, shall we talk about how you seem to be having no difficulty with my actual identity?"

"Your identity?"

"Hera." Her eyes gleamed gold. "Queen of the Gods. Queen of Olympus."

"My husband is a cat!"

Hera nodded. "That's fair."

* * *

Hungrrrry. He was sooooo Hungrrrry.

He'd spent an amazing night and definitely shown that orange cat who had the faster paw but the sun was up, he had a burr in his tail, and he was so hungrrrry.

Starrrrrving.

* * *

"Did you hear that?" Louise shifted her extra-large coffee to her other hand and cocked her head. "Someone's not happy."

Rick shrugged, sorting through his keys. "Probably Sophie. She's never happy."

Louise glanced up at the *Dinah Grace Cat Shelter*'s only other employee who was too damned tall. The next time, no employees over five six. No. Five four. Four inches was plenty. Why should she get a crick in her neck? "Sophie's also about thirty feet away behind two closed doors."

"So you're saying...?"

"Unless she's found a bullhorn, it's not Sophie. You go on in, I'm going to look around." She took a long swallow of coffee as she walked around the corner of the building toward the sound. People occasionally abandoned animals at the shelter and she needed to be more highly caffeinated if that's what she was about to find. "Puss, puss, puss. Come on, baby. Let's..."

Another wail cut her off.

It didn't sound injured, it sounded...actually, it sounded like Sophie when she was demanding more food than her diet allowed.

"Hey you, come on out. You can trust me..." Her voice trailed off as a large silver tabby galloped up the alley and butted her hard in the shins. "Well, hello. Who are you?"

Up on its hind legs, paws above her knees, greenish-gray eyes stared into hers as it wailed again.

"Are you starving, is that it?" Louise set her coffee on the edge of the dumpster and used both hands to prevent damage as it climbed up her body. No. He. Not it. A hand thrust under his butt for support made it very obvious that he was an intact tom. "Not a stray though are you?" she asked as he rubbed his face against hers. He smelled like a healthy cat and a little like...Calvin Klein Obsession? "You're too clean, too well fed to be a stray." Shifting his weight to her hip, she retrieved her coffee and took another drink, experience keeping it out of range as he tried to head butt the bottom of her travel mug. "Come on, let's go inside and see if you've been chipped, then we can... Enough of that!" Both front paws had been thrust down the front of her shirt and plunged into her cleavage. There'd been no claw contact so far but that was unlikely to last. If she'd been in her usual t-shirt and jeans, there'd have been no problem but she had a Zoom meeting with the board of directors at ten, so in lieu of makeup or styling her hair—because makeup and discreet highlights were so very essential to running an underfunded shelter—she'd made a minimal effort by replacing her t-shirt with a scoop neck sweater. A choice the cat was taking full advantage of.

"I've no objection to carrying kittens in my shirt, but you, young man, are too large, too heavy, and... Excuse me!" Shifting him to a football hold, she pointed his front end away from her body. "Cheeky! If I'm going to get so thoroughly felt up, I'd like dinner first."

* * *

Dinner?

So hungrrrrry.

Legs dangling, body clamped securely to the woman's side, he arced as far as he could toward the warmth. She smelled good. She sounded safe. Her breasts were soft. He liked soft breasts. At the thought of how they'd flexed under his paws, his throat began to vibrate making...a good sound.

Was he purring?

"All right..."

He was unsure about being inside the building. Very unsure about the door closing behind him.

"...we'll see if anyone's out looking for you, then we'll get you something to eat."

He purred louder.

* * *

"You're a Goddess!"

"First among Goddesses," Hera amended.

Mackenzie ignored her. "Find him!"

Hera shook her head. "I'm not a goddess of cats, Dr. Whyte."

"Fine," Mackenzie spat. "Then call Bastet!"

"We're not speaking. It's been eighty-two years and she's still annoyed about the incident with the duck."

"The what?"

"The duck."

"There's a goddess of waterfowl?"

"Probably. You lot have created a number of very niche deities over the years."

Mackenzie took a deep breath. "I don't care about ducks. I don't care about Bastet. I don't even care about ancient pantheons being real and doing jobs they're clearly unqualified for..."

Hera cleared her throat. "Goddess of Marriage."

Mackenzie ignored her. "...I care about my husband. Who is a cat! A lost cat!"

"Did you put up posters?"

"No. I did not put up posters."

"Many lost pets are found by putting up posters."

"Raymond is not my pet!"

"Maybe that's why you're having marital problems," Hera said thoughtfully. "Are you counting?"

"Yes."

"You should..."

"Still counting," Makenzie spat out between clenched teeth.

"Fine."

She got to thirty before she managed to overcome the urge to scream profanity.

And made a mental note to check into scream therapy when all this was over.

"*Can* you find him?" she demanded.

"No more easily than you can."

"Can you find your..." She waved her hands, searching for a better word and finally had to settle for sounding ridiculous. "...magic. The signature of your magic," she added as Hera's perfectly arched brows rose.

"What have you been reading?"

"I haven't..."

An eye roll cut her off. "Watching then."

"Okay. So you can't." Mackenzie could feel her nostril's flaring. "Then you'll help me search!"

"Will I?" Hera tapped her lip and frowned at Mackenzie. Who bared her teeth. Unexpectedly, Hera laughed. "Well, you're not boring, Dr. Whyte, I'll give you that much. All right," she continued before Mackenzie could respond, "I'll help you find your kitty cat, but he still has to turn back on his own."

"That's not..."

"Therapy is about discovering self-awareness," Hera said, as she stood and came around the desk. "The therapist merely helps you help yourself."

"You're not a therapist!"

"And yet when I first saw you, you were Madame Mopey-pants, feeling guilty about everything." Hera smiled when Mackenzie turned and scowled at her. "Now, you're engaging with the world again and blaming me for your problems. I call that progress."

* * *

Mackenzie scrubbed her palms against her thighs, looked left, looked right, then jumped back as a bus thundered by. She had no idea of where to start searching. "Pity Argos Panoptes isn't still around," she sighed. "A hundred eyes would come in useful."

"You'd think, but not so much. A hundred eyes, superhuman strength, one little job, watch the heifer, and Hermes takes him out. Hermes." Hera sniffed dismissively. "He's delivering flowers now."

* * *

"No chip. Not surprised, mind you." Rick set the scanner on the exam table. "If you don't neuter, you're not likely to chip."

The cat was friendly with Rick, obviously used to being handled by both men and women, and not at all hand-shy. In fact, not shy at all. When Louise picked him up again, he rubbed his head against her breasts and purred. "Look at these pads." She held up a foot and waved it at Rick. "Soft and smooth. He can't have been lost for very long."

"Then he probably hasn't wandered far." Rick ran a hand down the plush tail. The cat shot him what Louise could only call a speculative look, then shifted his purr up a notch. "Maybe we should put him back outside and hope he finds his own way home."

Louise passed the cat to Rick. "You're having a little trouble with the concept of shelter. Tuck him in the empty crate by Hiro and Jenny can take a look at him this afternoon."

Rick's brows rose. "You want Dr. Lum to *look* at him?"

The cat's owners were probably out searching for him—he was too obviously a house cat to not have a support staff—but they hadn't neutered him and one tomcat could be responsible for hundreds of kittens every year. Louise looked up at the art-work on the wall. An infinite line of kittens disappeared into the distance, with spay and neuter your pets painted in heavy, angry brushstrokes across the bottom. She'd painted it five years ago and the line of kittens kept getting longer. If their lost cat's owners hadn't called the shelter by the time the vet arrived...

"Louise?"

"Yes, have her *look* at him," she said, starting the coffee maker.

* * *

"When men get older, they fear the loss of their virility. As you have an open marriage, your husband is probably using multiple partners to self soothe."

Mackenzie backed out from under a car and sucked at the scratch on her hand. That tabby had not been Raymond. When the bleeding stopped, she sat back on her heels and glared up at Hera. "Your husband had sex with a woman while he was a swan."

The red sole of a gold Louboutin tapped next to Mackenzie's knee. "Your point?"

* * *

"Well, hello you."

Louise watched Jenny shift the tabby's head away from her breasts and grinned. The cat had a bit of a breast obsession. "No chip, no calls."

"How long has he been here?"

She glared past Jenny's shoulder at Rick, found a neutral expression when Jenny looked up, waved a hand, and said, "Long enough."

Jenny stared at her for a long moment, then she nodded.

* * *

Soft. Warm...

He rolled over on his back and waved all four paws seductively.

"Now, here's the thing..."

Front paws wrapped around the hand rubbing his chest, he nuzzled the space between thumb and forefinger.

"...you can neuter a cat with a general. I started out in a country practice...Yes, I did, who's a sweet boy?"

He licked her wrist.

"When we castrated the calves, we'd gather up all the tomcats, wrap them in towels..."

A small plastic lid hit the table beside his shoulder. The other woman, the first women, the alley woman, picked it up before he could disengage and swat it.

"...a shot, a snip, and no more balls. However, you, city boy..."

He heard an almost familiar buzz. Looked up to see an electric razor.

"...get a general. But first, my lovely, I'm going to have to remove some of this very plush fur."

Wait.

He got a general?

A shot? A SNIP?

* * *

Louise leapt back, heart pounding, and stared at the man sprawled on the exam table. He was in decent shape, had a thick head of salt and pepper hair, and wide, familiar greenish-gray eyes. He was also naked.

And the cat was gone.

"Fuck," she said softly.

Unable to find other words, she sketched questions in the air with both hands. Across the table, Jenny swallowed hard and shrugged.

Pulling a bit of orange fur out from under a fingernail, the naked man glanced from her to Jenny, and back to her again. "I don't suppose I could borrow a phone?"

* * *

Uncaring if the door to the *Dinah Grace Cat Shelter* hit Hera right in the face, Mackenzie slammed it shut and threw herself across the room to the counter. "I'm Dr. Mackenzie Whyte. My husband, Dr. Raymond Whyte, called from here?"

The woman behind the counter ran her hand back through silver hair and narrowed dark brown eyes. She had the look of a woman who'd faced the worst the world had to offer and prevailed. "Your husband was a cat."

"I know."

"A cat."

"It's a long story."

"You think?"

Mackenzie suspected the accompanying gesture was less than polite. She didn't care. "Where is he?"

"In the back. But..."

A hand appeared in Mackenzie's peripheral vision, waving the other woman quiet, and Hera said, "Go ahead, I'll deal with this."

Mackenzie turned far enough to glare at her. "Like that's never ended badly!"

Hera ignored her, smiling at the woman behind the counter. "I imagine you'd appreciate a sizable donation, wouldn't you, Louise?"

Louise folded her arms. "Don't patronize me."

"Trust me, I have never *patronized* anyone. My name is Juno..." Hera cut off Mackenzie's protest with a raised hand. "She's Italian. Go reunite with your husband. Before," she added when Mackenzie opened her mouth, "I get bored and bill you for an off-site consultation."

"My husband...!"

"Learned his lesson and decided he didn't want to be a tomcat anymore. You're welcome."

"We were about to neuter him," Louise pointed out dryly. All things considered, Mackenzie admired her composure.

Hera waved that off. "Carrot. Stick. Whatever." Then she turned a golden gaze on Mackenzie. "Go."

Mackenzie went.

* * *

By the time the Uber dropped them at home, it had begun to feel like a dream. Not a bad dream, just...removed. Unreal. Her husband a cat? Not possible. Raymond had gone upstairs to the en-suite to shower. She'd stared into the hall mirror, trying to piece together what had happened. They'd gone to see Dr. Próta...

Yesterday.

And then...

Her reflection shrugged. Mackenzie went to pour drinks.

They hadn't been able to talk in the car. The things they had to talk about weren't the sort of things that could be spoken of with an audience. But they had to talk. That, at least, she was certain of. A red wine in each hand, she climbed the stairs. The shower was off so Raymond was...

On the bed.

Her brows rose, impressed by his flexibility. She wasn't at all surprised by what he was using it to do.

* * *

A hand on either side of the laptop, Lousie stared down at the shelter's bank balance. They could afford to replace the roof. And the plumbing. "Fuck," she said softly.

* * *

"It's just I might have trouble getting my wife to attend a session. Anna doesn't like leaving the apartment. It's like she's rooted to the spot, you know?"

"Oh, I know, Mr. Norris." Hera smiled as she noted the particulars in her daybook. "And I assure you, I have experience dealing with that kind of thing..."

Casey's

Edward Willett

It was a slow night, partly because it was Monday, partly because of the howling wind lashing the city with sleet and freezing rain. I had the place to myself until *he* showed up.

I saw him out the front window, standing on Dewdney Avenue, staring up at my sign, the downtown office towers just an Impressionist sketch in the distance behind him, past the old railyards. Red light glowed on his face, intensifying as each letter lit up. The light flashed seven times, then went dark, and then the process repeated, as neon tubes spelled out, over and over, CASEY'S.

I thought about locking the door. It would have been a kindness. But he'd seen me, and knew the brewpub was open, and if I ran over and locked the door now it would have been the very antithesis of hospitality, and I'm all about hospitality, even after all these years.

So, I sighed, pulled sleeves over the two tap handles at the end of the bar, wiped my hands on my apron, and put a smile on my face.

The door opened and Jake came in.

He didn't look any older than he had either the first or the last time I'd seen him: his shaggy hair, wet from the rain and sleet, was still black; his face remained unlined. But he looked…tired. He had bags under his eyes. He wore faded jeans and an old corduroy jacket that didn't look nearly warm enough for the weather and, some time since our last encounter, he'd grown a really unfortunate mustache.

He stopped just inside and looked around. I kept my eyes on him. I knew what he was seeing: plain wooden tables and chairs, undecorated walls, a tin ceiling with upside-down-wok-shaped light fixtures hanging from it, a few wooden pillars. The bar was long and well-worn. Aside from the tap handles I'd just covered, there were twelve others. There were no other bottles behind me—no whiskeys or liqueurs or wines. I only served beer, and the food offerings were limited to peanuts, pretzels, or flatbread with a choice of dips: hummus, hummus, or hummus.

"Welcome to Casey's," I said, as the silence stretched on a little too long.

His gaze swung around to me. Dark-brown eyes studied me from beneath bushy brows. "Not what I expected," he said at last. Even after all this time, his voice held a trace of a German accent.

"Really?" I pulled a rag from behind the bar and began wiping down the wood, even though it didn't need it. "What did you expect?"

"With a name like Casey's?" He came over to the bar and sat down on a stool. "Green walls and shamrocks and waitresses with fake Irish accents and nothing to drink except Guinness, Harp, and Kilkenny." He glanced at the tap handles. "Which you don't have at all."

"Casey's is a brewpub. I make all my own beer."

He took another look around, frowning.

"In the basement," I explained.

His face cleared. He ran his hand through his sopping hair and brushed ineffectually at his wet clothes. "Nasty night."

"It is. Why are you out in it?"

"Looking for something. Or someplace."

"Oh?" I said noncommittedly. "Did you find it?"

"No. I thought maybe..." He looked around. "But no."

Short of telling him we were closing for the night—hard to pull off when it wasn't even 7 p.m.—I didn't see any way to get rid of him. And again, that whole hospitality thing. You can't fight your upbringing.

"What can I get you?" I asked instead. I knew I'd have to listen to his tale if I poured him a beer, but by this point I knew I'd have to listen to it no matter what.

He looked at the taps. "What do you recommend?"

"Dark or light? Ale or lager? Hops or malt?"

"Dark. Not too hoppy."

"Got just the thing." I poured him a pint of The Old Sod, a brown ale done in a traditional northern-England style.

He sipped it and made an appreciative face. "Good stuff."

"I aim to please."

"I'm Jake," he said, and held out his hand.

I knew that, of course, but I gripped it anyway. "Ninette. Folks mostly call me Nin."

"You work here by yourself?"

That could have been taken as a creepy come-on, but I knew it wasn't. Even if I hadn't known Jake, I would have been able to tell. It's a gift, I guess you'd say. Plus years of experience, of course.

"Yes," I said. "I own the place."

One of those bushy eyebrows raised. "Bit young for that, I'd have thought."

I smiled. "I'm older than I look."

"Could you…use a hand?"

"Is that what you're looking for, Jake? A job?"

"No." Then he paused. "Well, yes. I guess. I mean, I *need* a job. And I'd be glad for the work. But what I'm really looking for is a job I had once and threw away."

"Want to tell me about it?" I knew he did. There'd been no escaping it once I let him in the door, so why fight it? I pushed a bowl of peanuts over to him. "I'm all ears."

He took a few peanuts, drank some more beer, and began.

"This was…a long time ago. When I was in university."

"What were you studying?"

"History. Ancient history."

"Are you a teacher?"

"I…have been. At least…" Again, he looked confused. Lost, even. "I think so?"

"You're not teaching now?"

He shook his head. "No. No, I've just been…doing this or that. Odd jobs, mostly. Short-term. I move around a lot. Not how I thought my life would go, back then." He drank more beer.

"Things happen. I mean, I never thought I'd end up running a brewpub in Regina."

He made a face. "Never thought I'd end up drinking in Regina, but here I am." He took another swallow of beer. "Good stuff," he said again.

"Thanks. You were saying…?"

"Well, I needed work, so I stopped in at all the pubs near the university to see if they were hiring. Mostly, I got doors slammed in my face, both figuratively and, occasionally, literally. But then I passed this one place I'd never noticed before, even though I'd spent my fair share of time on that street. Just a hole in the wall, but I thought, *What the hell?* and went in."

"What was this place called?" I said casually, as if it didn't matter.

"It was..." His face went blank for a moment. "You know what? I don't remember. Isn't that weird?"

"Weird. So, you went in...?"

"It was long and narrow at the front but opened up in the back, so it turned out to have more tables than I thought. Everything was wood, kind of like this place, only a different color. Just a single bartender behind the bar."

"Man or woman?"

"Can't remember that, either." Jake shook his head. "Getting old, I guess."

"Happens to the best of us. What *do* you remember?"

"The beer. Not the regular beer. The special brew."

"Special brew? What was so special about it? Maybe I could brew something similar."

He snorted. "No, you couldn't." He finished his pint and tapped the glass. "Same again."

I filled it and pushed it back to him. "Why not? I do good beer." I pointed at the pint of Old Sod. "You said so yourself."

"You do." He took a swallow of it. "But that place..." He paused. "Look, if I tell you, you're going to think I'm crazy."

"No, I won't," I said truthfully. "And even if I did, you'd never know. I told you, I'm a good listener."

He searched my eyes. I met his gaze with a friendly smile. His eyes widened momentarily, but then narrowed again as his face fell into a puzzled frown. Then he shook his head and returned to his beer and his story. "Anyway, it turned out the bartender—the owner, I found out—*did* need somebody. I was hired on the spot."

"Wow, that *is* crazy."

He gave me a look. I gave him more peanuts. He took some. "The place had the weirdest clientele," he said as he chewed. "Ordinary people came in, sure. Usually just once, though. They seemed...uncomfortable. But the regulars! Men in outlandish clothes. Beautiful women who looked like they'd as soon slide a dagger between your ribs as talk to you. One guy always carried a hammer around with him, but I don't think he was a carpenter. Another guy, big guy with a beard, only had one eye, but you felt like he saw more with that one eye than anyone else managed with two.

"One skinny little guy was always surprising me—I'd serve him at one end of the bar and then I'd find him at the other end, but I never saw him move. And then on Friday nights, we had the most amazing music, from a guy who played a lyre, if you can believe it. Sad guy, always moping around—something to do with a lost love—but voice of an angel." His own voice dropped. "We may have had one or two of those in there, too."

I raised my eyebrows. "One or two what?"

He took a deep breath. "Angels." He looked around as though afraid of being overheard, but it was still just the two of us. "They weren't ordinary humans, at least."

"Does sound like an unusual place. But tell me…if you thought a couple of the customers were angels, who did you think the others were?"

He hesitated. He took another deep swallow of beer. He put the glass back down on the bar. "Gods," he said at last.

I raised my eyebrows even higher. "Gods?"

"Gods. Well, and a few demigods. Ancient ones. The guy with the hammer? Thor. One-eye? Odin. Fast little skinny guy? Hermes. The player with the lyre? Had to be Orpheus, pining over Eurydice."

"Maybe he was just a big fan of *Hadestown*."

Jake frowned. "What?"

"Never mind. Bad joke. It wasn't out yet."

"What wasn't…?" He shook his head. "Never mind." He finished his second pint and tapped the glass for a refill. "Told you you wouldn't believe me."

"Sorry. Please, I want to hear it all." I drew him another pint. Normally I'd have urged someone downing beer at that rate to take it a little slower, but…like I said, I knew Jake.

He didn't immediately dive into his third pint, at least. "So eventually, I confronted the owner. Who said I was absolutely right and asked if I had a problem with that—almost accusing me of racism."

"Against gods, you'd think the word would be 'deism,'" I put in, "but that already has another meaning. And the equivalent of 'racist' would be 'deist.'"

Jake blinked. "I never thought of that. What *do* you call someone who doesn't like gods?"

"If someone hated gods out of fear, you'd think you'd call that person 'god-fearing,' but a God-fearing person is someone who's very religious, oddly enough. Unless you put it into Greek. So, 'theophobic' maybe?"

Jake was looking a little blurred around the edges. He took another long swallow of beer, which wasn't going to help. "Whatever," he said impatiently. "The point is, I wasn't. I didn't care if they were gods. I thought it was cool. Studying ancient history, remember? I said I was perfectly fine serving gods.

"'Well, now that you know,' the owner said, 'there are a couple of rules. The first one is, *no asking for favors*. And no accepting them, either. Somebody wants to tip you, say, half of Norway, you tell him "no." But be polite. For the guests, there's a strict no-smiting rule, but it is a bar, and sometimes even a god can drink a little too much.'

"'Of course,' I promised.

"The owner looked skeptical but went on. 'Now you know the truth, I'm going to let you draw the Special.'

"'The Special?' I asked.

"The owner nodded and took me down to the end of the bar where there were two taps, covered with sleeves."

I very carefully did not look down at the end of *my* bar.

"I'd figured they were out of order, but now the owner pulled off the sleeve on the tap on the right," Jake went on. "That tap handle was pure gold, I'd swear it.

"'This is Ambrewsia,' the owner said. 'The Brew of Knowledge. The beer of the gods.'

"I reached out to touch the handle, but the owner slapped my hand away. 'One more rule! Under no circumstances are you to drink Ambrewsia yourself. Not even a sip. Understand? It's not for humans.'

"'I understand,' I said. I looked at the other covered tap. 'What about that one?'

"'That one, I draw,' the owner said. 'The other beer I make, that's for humans. It's good stuff, it makes them happy, and even makes them healthy, which you can't say about most of the beer made these days. But this stuff is not for them, and it's not for you. Do you understand?'

"'I understand,' I said. What was there to not understand?

"'And you promise to obey?'

"'Of course,' I said, because it seemed simple enough.

"But that was before I drew Ambrewsia for the first time.

"It was the spring equinox. This customer…a scary-looking fellow… said he'd just dropped off his wife for an extended stay—he seemed glum about it—and wanted a pint before he headed home. I brought him his beer, but it was all I could do not to down it myself the minute it hit the glass. Golden as a summer sunset, or a field of ripe wheat, or… or…"

"Gold?" I suggested.

"Exactly!" he said. "And it smelled like every good thing I'd ever eaten or drunk or imagined. It smelled like Christmas and home and birthdays and Mom's cookies. It was…"

"Ambrosial?" I suggested.

He hiccupped. He'd been working on that third pint while he talked. "Perfect! Perfect. You know all the good words."

"So, let me guess. Eventually, you forgot your promise and drank."

His face fell. "Yes. Just a couple of nights later. I was serving this big guy, so big he reminded me of an elephant somehow. With him was a woman. I couldn't quite get a good look at her. Her face was shadowed by this huge hat, and the hat was moving, like there was something under it that was alive. Creeped me out.

"The owner gave me two pints to take out to them, Ambrewsias, both of them. Turned out, though, the woman had changed her mind. She wanted an ordinary lager. I was heading back to the bar with the Ambrewsia when I suddenly realized I had a pint going to waste. I picked it up and took a sip, just a sip, to see what it tasted like. And…" His voice trailed off and he hiccupped.

"And?" I said gently.

He shook his head. "It blew my mind," he said softly. "I knew stuff, just for a minute, stuff I'd never known before, stuff I never even knew about before, like why dark matter is an illusion and where the openings into the multiverse are and whether Schrödinger's cat is alive or dead and how often you need to change the oil in a 1932 Ford Model A. Everything. Just for a minute.

"Then it was gone. And there was the owner, staring at me with folded arms, standing in front of the Ambrewsia tap and the one beside it, the one still in the sleeve. And just enough of all that stuff that had blasted through my brain in the seconds it took to swallow that mouthful of Ambrewsia remained to tell me that beneath that second sleeve, the tap handle read, 'Brew of Life.' And that if I drank that, I would live forever. I'd be a god, too, or at least a demigod."

"Probably more like a hemi-semi-demigod," I said. "But go on."

He blinked blearily at me. Pint three was pretty much gone and it seemed to have hit him hard, all at once. He tapped the glass. I filled it a fourth time. "'Let me drink,' I shaid…said. 'No,' the owner said. 'Yes,' I said. 'No!' 'Yes!' 'No!' 'Yes!' 'N—'"

"I get the picture," I put in hastily because he'd gotten into a rhythm and I wasn't sure he could snap out of it. "So then what did you do?"

"Tried to shovel…shove…my way past the owner." He drank again.

"You tried to muscle the owner of a place that serves beer to gods?" The situation seemed to call for a little incredulity, so I dribbled some into my tone.

"I know, I know. Shtup…stupid."

"I'm guessing you didn't get the Brew of Life."

"No. Nosshure what hip…hap…happened. Suddenly on my ash on the street."

I frowned. "On your…?"

"Yeah," he said morosely. "And the pub was gone."

"It vanished?"

He nodded. "Gone!" He banged his hand on the bar for emphasis. "No door. No…thing. With words."

"Sign?"

"Right! No sign." He banged the bar again. "Nothing. Nobody never heard of it." Bang! "Never!" Bang! "Never been there."

"Wow. That's weird."

He chugged the last of his fourth pint and got unsteadily to his feet. "How mush?"

"On the house. That was a much more interesting story than I normally hear. And it's not like I'm run off my feet tonight."

"Thanksh!" he slurred. He staggered toward the door, which just then swung open, letting in both a blast of icy wind and a pro-basketball-player-sized man with golden hair and eyes to match, eyes that narrowed to slits as he turned and watched Jake stagger out into the sleet-scoured street.

I sighed and, as the new arrival made his way to the bar brushing ice off his shoulders, pulled the sleeves off the two taps I'd covered before Jake came in. "Wasn't that what-his-name?" the new customer asked.

"Jake. Yeah, that was him. He turns up every ten years or so. Doesn't matter where I am."

"Powerful stuff, your Ambrewsia," the new guy said. "Of which I'll have a pint."

"Sure thing, Uriel." I filled the angel's glass.

"I could make sure he never bothers you again, Nin. I've got a spare flaming sword in the trunk of the car and I could assign someone to guard your door for all eternity. Worked in Eden. No humans wander in *there*."

"No." I put a coaster down in front of Uriel and set the pint of Ambrewsia on it. "It wasn't really his fault. He was just in the wrong place at the wrong time. I didn't even know why I hired him back then. I thought I was just getting lonely after four or five thousand years of brewing beer and being hospitable. And I was hoping maybe having a human around the place would bring in more mortals…or bring them in more than once. They always seem to be uncomfortable around you god types, but they appreciate a good pint, too."

"First of all, I'm not a god." He glanced up. "And the boss frowns on that kind of talk, as you well know." His eyes came back to me. "And that's not why you hired him. It was just your turn."

"My turn to offer the bargain. Yes, I know that *now*. But I didn't know it *then*. I was being played, too." I very carefully did *not* glance up.

Uriel shrugged. "Every thousand years, a human gets a chance to fix that whole Eden error. You give them one simple rule to obey. 'You must not eat from the tree of the knowledge of good and evil.' 'You must not drink the Ambrewsia.' And next thing you know, they're scarfing down the fruit or draining a pint and you've got to kick them out before they grab the fruit or the beer or the what-have-you of life and live forever. And every thousand years, the humans fail the test. Poor saps can't seem to help it."

"I still feel bad for Jake," I said, and left it at that.

I didn't tell Uriel—I've never told any of my regulars, though I suppose Uriel's boss knows—the one little detail Jake left out of his story, because he never knew.

When I poured the two beers that night, only one of them was pure Ambrewsia. That was always Ganesh's choice. But Medusa, his date (their relationship ultimately didn't work out) normally ordered a half-and-half: half Ambrewsia, the Brew of Knowledge, half Immort-Ale, the Brew of Life.

And it was Medusa's pint that Jake sipped from.

Jake came into my bar for the first time in 1850. It was in Heidelberg then. And like I'd told Uriel, every ten years or so, he'd turn up again, wherever I happened to have set up. He'd come in. I'd pour him some beer. He'd tell me his tale. He'd leave without recognizing me or my pub, but that was my signal to vanish from wherever I was and set up somewhere new, because if he found me in the same place twice, he just might remember more than I wanted him to.

We'd been doing this dance for coming up on two centuries. Were a few sips of half-and-half Ambrewsia/Immort-Ale enough to keep Jake alive forever? I didn't know. No human had ever drunk it.

What I did know was that Nin Casey's brewpub was about to vacate its Dewdney Avenue location in Regina, Saskatchewan.

I looked out the window at the sleet, driven horizontally by the wind through the red glow of my sign. "Somewhere in the Caribbean," I said out loud.

Uriel blinked. "What?" Then his confused expression cleared. "Oh, right. Well, I guess we'll all find you."

"You always do." Jake was gone now, but I stared out the window at where he'd been standing. *And so will he. But not for a while.*

"You're in luck," I told the angel. "All drinks on the house tonight. Going-out-of-business sale."

Uriel lifted his beer in salute. "You're a good goddess, Nin Casey."

"'Making glad the hearts of men and gods since 2500 BC,'" I said, quoting my business card.

"I'll drink to that," said Uriel, and did.

The Teotl of Gaming

Daniel Roman

•

Macuil laid his cards face-up on the table and flashed his best shit-eating grin.

"Royal flush."

A round of groans went up from his opponents, six men and women in various states of fancy dress and inebriation who'd made it their night's mission to lose as much money as possible. The dealer's cool gaze drifted from Macuil's cards to the mountain of chips in front of her.

"Congratulations, sir," she said flatly.

Macuil's grin widened as he began raking the chips to his side of the table. "What can I say? I have really good luck with games."

To the dealer's credit, she hardly missed a beat before suggesting another round. The other players nodded, shooting glares at Macuil as he arranged his fortune of winnings into neat stacks.

He allowed his eyes to wander over the other gamblers, tapping a finger against the side of his tequila glass. Then, he slid his chair back on the fine Venetian carpet, downed the rest of his drink, and rose.

"I think I've had enough, actually. Always good to know when to quit."

How fast groans of disappointment could transform into shouts of outrage. He paid the other players little mind, his focus all on the dealer, and the cold look she shot over his right shoulder.

"You have to give us the chance to win back some of our money!" roared the card shark with the buck teeth and gray cowboy hat.

"I gave you that chance thirteen rounds ago, friend," Macuil answered. Using every ounce of coordination he could muster, he hefted his hoard of chips in both arms and went left—away from the bouncers he knew were fast approaching. Luckily for him, he was *quite* coordinated, easily cutting through the thickest parts of the packed casino despite the commotion his lavish burden caused.

The chips clinked like rain on a tin roof when he unloaded them onto the payout counter. The kid working it stood there slack-jawed, his eyes bulging out of his head.

"Wow," he exclaimed, and just like the poker dealer, his voice was much flatter than the word warranted. "This is…a lot, sir. More than I have on hand. I'll have to go back to the safe."

Macuil waved away that idea. "No time for that, I'm afraid. I'll just take however much you have on hand."

The clerk blinked, lost for words. His eyes darted to the crowd behind Macuil.

"*Now*," the god said. "Or I'll get a manager out here to set you straight."

The clerk jumped. "Of course, sir."

As the young worker ducked behind the counter and began rummaging, Macuil turned and leaned against it so he could watch the bouncers make their way toward him. Half the bustling room still separated them from the payout counter—fifty yards, at least. *More than enough time*, Macuil thought.

It wasn't that he had anything against gambling—quite the contrary, it was one of his favorite vices. He could hardly call himself the God of Games if it wasn't. But casinos weren't a *fair* game. They were designed to fleece people, not provide an honest contest. The house always wins, as the saying goes.

That was one of the reasons Macuil had never invested in any such establishments himself, despite the fact that he often enjoyed their atmosphere, drinks, and company. There was nothing worse than a rigged game. Once upon a time, he punished people with venereal diseases for that sort of bad faith overindulgence. But how did you give a casino a venereal disease?

If you wanted to hit these sorts of places where it hurt, there was only one way to do it. Go for the wallet.

"There you go, sir. One million dollars. I, uh…*congratulations*, sir."

Macuil spun back around and was greeted by a smile so forced it looked like the clerk's teeth might crack at any second. A hefty leather bag sat on the countertop between them. When Macuil popped it open, the heady musk of fresh money wafted from the stacks of hundred-dollar bills within. He snapped the bag closed.

"Thank you very much, my friend." He plucked the yellow sinicuichi flower from the lapel of his shirt and laid it on the counter. "Give my regards to the owner of this fine establishment."

With that, Macuil gathered up his winnings and waded back out into the throngs of gamblers. The bouncers had spread wide across the room, cutting him off from the exits in an attempt to corral him between them. So he made straight for the empty bathroom. Inside, there was a small, grimy window high up on the wall of the second stall. Macuil closed and locked the stall door behind him, climbed up onto the toilet, and let himself out.

Hot, dry air immediately flooded his nostrils as he landed in the alleyway outside the casino. At one end of the alley, cars flashed by in a never-ending stream. Macuil went the other way, to the deserted backstreet. As he rounded the corner, shouts drifted to his ear from the open bathroom window. He smiled to himself, hefted his bag, and kept walking.

A black Honda sat parked a block to the west. Macuil let himself into the backseat, sinking into the soft leather. Mariah looked at him in the rearview as the engine roared to life.

"I was starting to think you might not show."

"Me? I'd never stand you up like that."

The cabbie snorted as her eyes went back to the congested Vegas traffic. "You know, there are safer ways someone like you can spend a night."

"True," Macuil admitted. "But I need to do this. I suppose you could say it's my duty."

"It's your duty to win enormous sums of money from casinos and sneak out before the bouncers catch you?"

"Exactly! And to have fun while I'm doing it."

Mariah shook her head and laid on the gas as she hit the on-ramp for the highway. "Whatever you say, boss."

••

By the time the Honda was crossing into northern San Diego, Macuil's good mood had all but vanished. He found himself wishing Mariah wasn't such a damn good driver as she navigated the streets to their destination in record time. Five hours had passed since the Mesa House Casino, but to Macuil it felt more like five minutes.

The car rolled to a stop. He averted his gaze from the window, patting the bag beside him.

"You remember where to take the money?"

Mariah turned in her seat to look at him. "Same place as last time, right? 13 Coral Crest Way?"

Macuil nodded. "Precisely. Well…thanks for the lift, Mariah."

"Always interesting, Macuil."

He got out of the car and waved over his shoulder, listening to the Honda pull away as he started walking. At which point, he could no longer avoid looking at the inevitable.

The headquarters of Five Flower Entertainment sprawled before him, a shining complex of girded steel and shimmering plexiglass. Macuil's brainchild, and the company behind the most wildly popular video game ever to grace computers: *The Untouched Land.*

The software engineering company had a vast campus, replete with a gym, recreation area, café, dormitories, and—his personal favorite—a lounge with more than fifty thousand board and video games for the company's employees to enjoy. It was a veritable paradise to the person who loved a good game of…well, pretty much anything. The workers had taken to affectionately calling it the Game Sanctuary.

Much as he might wish to go straight to his personal penthouse or the Sanctuary, he knew he had a responsibility to check in with the senior staff meeting currently underway. *Responsibility.* Had any word ever tasted so bitter?

The security guards at the front door gave him a nod of respect, which he returned as he strolled through the sliding glass doors and into the cooled interior of the complex. More greetings at the polished mahogany desk which dominated the building's foyer. His face was well-known at Five Flower…which was only appropriate, seeing as the company *was* named after him.

Macuil went into the elevator and pressed the button for the top floor. He took in a long, deep breath through his nose as the metal box rose through the innards of the building.

Sound from the meeting room assailed him the instant the doors inched open. Macuil arched a brow, said hello to the receptionist, and went to see what the fuss was about.

To his surprise, what was taking place looked less like a staff meeting and more like some kind of…*party*. Balloons carpeted the ceiling and a platter with little sandwiches and bottles of soda lined the middle of the table. The conversation quieted as Macuil entered the room and every head turned toward him.

Macuil's personal liaison, a blazer-wearing, sharp-talking woman named Jensen, was the first to recover. "Mr. Shoctul! What a pleasant surprise! We didn't know if you were going to make it for the big news."

"Oh? What news is that?"

Though she had a reputation for unwavering professionalism, even Jensen couldn't keep the grin off her face. "Creature design has finally figured out how to get the new organic monster routing to work properly."

"Really?" Macuil felt a surprising pang of excitement...which promptly died at Jensen's next words.

"All 8,314 possible routes have been tested and accounted for. That was the last kink we had to iron out before the launch on Friday," she said, beaming. "We have a *working expansion*!"

"Is it really organic if you can tell me how many possibilities there are?" Macuil muttered.

There was an awkward silence. Puzzled looks, exchanged. Jensen's smile slowly withered.

Mictlan. I'm supposed to be the god of parties and here I am sapping all the fun out of the room. He laughed, a little too loudly. "I'm just teasing, Jensen. That's wonderful news. You should all be very proud!"

That did the trick. A cheer went up from the company's division leaders, almost like they were children who'd just received the nod of approval from a discerning parent. Conversation resumed.

Macuil watched the celebrating humans and gave the appearance of joining in as best he could. As soon as it was appropriate, he excused himself.

•••

A single pane of plexiglass made up the entire western wall of the Game Sanctuary, allowing the beautiful San Diego sunsets to paint the room's innumerable shelves in a brilliant orange glow. Those shelves were filled with board games beyond count, stored in boxes of a thousand different colors and sizes. The bookcases behind the 120-inch flatscreen were lined with neat stacks of video games from dozens of different consoles. Ten computers sat arrayed in two rows of five facing each other, optimized for competitive gaming.

A twelve-foot-long oak table occupied the room's center and it was there that Macuil set up shop. In spite of the Sanctuary's open-door policy, he had the place completely to himself. The breathtaking sunset had long passed. Even the resident programmers who liked to combat their insomnia with night-owl game binges had gone off to collapse in their beds.

Yet Macuil remained, staring blankly at the gameboard in front of him. Plagued by the same damn question that consumed him whenever he set foot in the F.F.E. headquarters of late.

Why am I so unhappy?

He leaned back in his chair and forced his rheumy eyes to focus on the board in front of him. A stylized X stretched from corner to corner of the square playing field. Two piles of six red and blue stones each were arranged at the sides of the board and, in its center, a handful of beans used as the dice. Patolli was the first board game Macuil had ever inspired, back when he had still been young and wide-eyed at the possibilities of this lush world. It was simple compared to most of the things he'd created in his long life…but there was something about it that made him feel at peace. Reminded him a little of who he was, maybe.

When he first discovered that humans had invented video games, Macuil had been immediately hooked. It seemed a limitless frontier… but even he couldn't have predicted just how much power it would give him. With the advent of massively multiplayer online role-playing games—MMORPGs—he discovered an opportunity for true security in this new world that technology and globalism had built. By that time, several of the other gods who Macuil had once reigned alongside had already faded, unable to adapt to the world's changes. When the last of their worshippers died, they simply went with them. The Aztecs who once venerated Macuil and his brethren might have been scattered from the bastion of their once-proud empire, but by tapping into the common love of games shared by all people, Macuil had found a way to survive.

In essence, he'd traded the roving ways of his youth for a steady paycheck of worship. Of all the different types of games in the world, none were played with as much dogged loyalty as MMORPGs.

His enthusiasm for the medium only deepened once he learned how to do the coding behind it himself. Whenever a new form of entertainment rose to prominence, Macuil liked to take an active hand in its design—a stance he'd held for as long as he'd served as the god of such things. That's why Five Flower Entertainment wasn't *just* a video game company—it also had branches in board games, tabletop RPGs, and sports stadiums. Movies and music. All entertainment was Macuil's domain, and *The Untouched Land* was its bravest frontier.

Over time, however, those strings of code became more like the bars of a prison. For some reason he'd never been able to put his finger on, *The Untouched Land* just didn't satisfy him like it used to…and it was becoming harder and harder to return from escapes like the previous night's jaunt to Vegas.

Every game has a shelf-life. Maybe The Untouched Land *has simply run its course,* he thought. *Sometimes the things you do just don't go as planned. Remember* Monopoly*? You inspired it out of spite, a lesson against human greed...and instead it became a ridiculous success that's brought in almost a century's worth of worship.* Macuil chuckled to himself, feeling the tiniest bit better for imagining all the fist fights and family feuds *that* particular experiment had spawned.

Yet still, he sat over his Patolli board as the hours whiled away.

Maybe I'm trying too hard, he admitted to himself at last. He'd been planning to sit on his feelings until he figured out how to make *The Untouched Land* exciting again, but maybe what he needed was to get back out and honor some of his other duties. *After all, aren't I the deity in charge of partying and dancing, too?*

Finally, achingly, he rose from his chair. It was a quarter past three in the morning—not too late to find a good time in San Diego, if you knew where to look. Macuil went to his penthouse, changed into gray slacks and his favorite shirt—the silver button-down with the purple morning glories on it—rolled a fresh cigarette of loosely packed tobacco, and took the elevator to the complex lobby.

The night guard sitting at the desk gave Macuil a tip of the hat as he strode out of the elevator, but their conversation didn't extend beyond weary hellos. Everyone who worked at Five Flower Entertainment had grown used to the unpredictable comings and goings of their company's CEO.

Outside, the night was filled with the distant rumble of waves and droning of the occasional car. Macuil lit his cigarette and took a full, deep drag, blowing out some of his tension along with the smoke. Then, he started walking.

He didn't make it very far.

As he rounded the corner to the next block, a huge, bald man wearing a pinstripe polo shirt that looked ready to bust at the seams came into view. He was leaning against a gray sedan, enjoying some time with a cigarette of his own. When he saw Macuil walking by, he flicked the butt on the ground and came toward him.

"Hey. You McCool?" he asked, in a voice that sounded like a bag of rocks being dragged behind a truck.

Maybe it was the fact that the man butchered a name which had already been simplified to appease an indifferent people. Maybe it was the insolent way the human strutted about, or frustration from staying up all night racking his brains for an answer to a problem that probably didn't exist. All Macuil knew for sure was that when he heard the man grind up what little remained of his once proud title, he grimaced so hard his cheek cramped, his buzz instantly died, and the words came spilling out.

"My name is Macuilxochitl, *human*. Can I do something for you?"

The big man straightened his offensively outdated shirt. "Sure can, Mr. McCool. I'm here on behalf of someone who'd like very much to have a conversation with you."

Macuil's brow furrowed...then crumpled even harder when a fist the size of a ham slammed into the side of his face.

He went down hard on the concrete, the coppery taste of blood in his mouth. Blinking, Macuil spat a thin string of crimson onto the sidewalk. He stared at it, his eyes widening.

Then he burst out laughing.

"You hit me! No one has done that in...Huitzilopochtli only knows how long!"

"Shut your mouth and get up," the beefy stranger ordered. He yanked Macuil up by the front of his shirt to dispel any confusion about the meaning behind his eloquently worded request.

"Where are we going?" Macuil asked.

The bald man growled, as if that was all the answer an articulate person should need. He reached into his pants pocket with his free hand, pulled out a set of smart-keys, and clicked a button. The trunk of the sedan popped open.

Macuil's eyes widened even farther. "I get to ride in the trunk?"

"I said shut up!"

In that moment, he felt his captor's body tense in preparation for motion. Had he wished, he could have effortlessly slipped through the man's fingers. No mortal could hold him if he wished to escape.

But...damn it, this was the most exciting thing that had happened to him in years. Maybe centuries!

So he let the ham-fisted kidnapper throw him into the trunk. He didn't fight when the cell phone was taken from his pocket. He didn't even bite off any fingers when the idiot fumbled with the gag.

"Can you at least pick up my cigarette?" Macuil managed, before his kidnapper stuffed the cloth into his mouth.

A scowl twisted the bald man's face. The trunk slammed shut.

Macuil lay in the cramped space, his breath loud in his ears. *Well, at least my night won't be boring.*

The car started, the soothing sound of tires on pavement cutting an urban lullaby to keep him company on the trip. And in the darkness,

Macuilxochitl's thoughts returned to the last time he had tasted his own blood in his mouth.

One of the last times he had felt *truly* alive.

•
•••

Even Tlatoani Motecuhzoma had come down from his palace to watch the game. Surrounded by a retinue of warriors bedecked in quetzal feathers, the ruler of Tenochtítlan howled his support as passionately as the peasants watching from the outskirts of the tlachtli. Their cheers were deafening, thunder against the stone of the city.

Fire surged through Macuilxochitl's veins, his feet pounding across the dirt lane in the middle of the tlachtli. The heavy rubber ulli bounced through the air, propelled by the hips of players who dove headlong to save it from touching the ground. Many glorious ullamaliztli matches decorated the history of the Mexica people…but never had there been one quite like this.

Macuilxochitl moved among the humans, taking his team on the offensive. "Xipilli!" they shouted, invoking his human alias to call for the ulli. He was the wind…yet Huitzilin was the eagle, soaring upon the swells. His lithe form moved with an agility that seemed supernatural even to Macuilxochitl, rolling and sprinting down the tlachtli.

The ulli flew into the air, launched by a sliding hip strike from one of Huitzilin's teammates. It sailed toward one of the goal rings that hung suspended from tlachtli's walls.

Macuilxochitl moved to intercept, but the eagle was there. Huitzilin's shoulder connected with his jaw, snapping his head around and sending him careening onto the slanted stone. He rolled, scraping the skin from his arms, tearing loose one of his deerskin kneeguards. His head whipped up, searching for Huitzilin.

For a stunning moment, it was like watching Huitzilopochtli himself. Huitzilin went low, catching the ulli with his hip. Pushing off the ground, he bumped it high enough to get an elbow underneath, knocking it yet further ahead. The human stumbled with reckless momentum, leaping, turning in midair to meet the ulli with his hip a second time.

The heavy rubber ball hit the rim of the hoop, teetering backward.

Huitzilin hit the ground, cracking his head against the wall beneath the goal. He spun, pushing himself up with a roar, one hand to the ground, the other elbow slicing upward.

The slap of hide elbowpad hitting rubber ulli was startlingly loud, echoing as the crowd held their collective breath.

The ulli slipped through the ring of the broad stone hoop.

Cheering, loud enough to shake the sky. The stone city of Tenochtítlan bore witness, carrying the sound of the people's tearful ecstasy for miles.

Macuilxochitl slowly rose. Belatedly, he realized there was a coppery taste filling his mouth. His own blood. Numbly, the God of Games watched his challenger parade around the ullamaliztli tlachtli, the spectators spilling onto the court to celebrate his victory.

Macuilxochitl barely heard them. Already, the teotl—the energy*—of those who honored him flooded his soul. Gambling on the outcome of the game had been fierce. Men won and lost their livelihoods; women, the beautifully dyed clothing and baskets they had spent weeks weaving. Livestock changed hands. Rare stones and special tools. The betting had been so outrageous that there were even those who had to sell themselves into slavery to pay off their debts.*

All for the glory of the game. For ullamaliztli…and the god who presided over it.

When the tlatoani came down from his platform, the crowd finally quieted. He was accompanied by a priest wearing a white and blue xicolli, as well as his retinue of feather-clad warriors. Each of them held a bow and bore a quiver at their hip. The ruler of Tenochtítlan stood at the center of the tlachtli, his chin high as he addressed his people.

"This day, Huitzilin of Texcoco has proven himself to be the master of ullamaliztli. He played so well that not even Macuilxochitl himself would have been able to best him!"

Another round of cheering. Macuilxochitl bit his lip. If only the humans knew just how true those words were.

Tlatoani Motecuhzoma motioned for Huitzilin to step forward. The ulli player did so with a tear of joy in his eye. Macuilxochitl could hardly begrudge the man his pride. Huitzilin had just played the best game of ullamaliztli he would ever play. Defeated a god, though he did not even know it.

The tlatoani's priest raised his bone rattle-stick to the sky, shaking it in an even, calming rhythm. "We thank you, Macuilxochitl, for blessing Huitzilin with such prowess," he intoned. "Now…we offer his life to you. May his power become your power!"

Huitzilin straightened, his chest puffing out. Sacrifice was the greatest honor an ulli player could earn and Huitzilin had earned it well.

The tlatoani's warriors raised their bows and fit nock to string. The priest uttered the final words. Tlatoani Motecuhzoma wished the ulli player well on his journey. Huitzilin raised his face to the clouds, lifted his arms, and screamed his thanks to the God of Games.

Bowstrings twanged and five obsidian-tipped arrows punched through Huitzilin's body. One took him in the forehead, spraying blood across the tlachtli as he collapsed to his knees. His bloodshot eyes rolled downward from the heavens…rolled downward, and locked with the gaze of Macuilxochitl.

Huitzilin slumped over in the dirt and lay still.

A collective sigh escaped the crowd. Macuilxochitl breathed their relief, their reverence, in through his nose. Strength infused him as his chest swelled with air, with the teotl of Huitzilin of Texcoco, an ulli player truly without equal. His bones creaked from the strain of supporting his might, as the denizens of Tenochtítlan bolstered him with their worship.

When Macuilxochitl released the breath, he was whole.

••
•••

The car ground to a stop.

In the darkness of the trunk, Macuilxochitl came suddenly alert. One of the doors slammed shut, rocking the vehicle. Voices exchanged words. Footsteps approached, crunching on dirt.

When the trunk screeched open, Macuil was lounging with his head propped up on his bound hands, doing his best to smile around the gag in his mouth. The slab of beef wearing the pinstripes was not impressed. He hauled Macuil out of the trunk and shoved him roughly to the ground.

The sandy, rocky ground. That, as much as anything else, told Macuil exactly what sort of trouble he was in. Or would have been in, had he been human.

As things stood, the idea that the six men surrounding him in the dark of the desert night could do anything to harm him was laughable at best—insulting, if it were a day when he was feeling mercurial. Luckily for them, he was far too curious to be wrathful.

He didn't have to wait long. After exchanging a few words with the bodybuilder who'd given Macuil a lift in his trunk, a lanky guy sporting a broad forehead and a loose green button-down stalked over. A handgun hung at his hip.

The man had Macuil's phone in one hand. Slowly, purposefully, he tucked it into his shirt pocket and drew the gun. He used the barrel to pull down Macuil's gag.

"*Ah,*" Macuil yawned. "Thank you. Not the most comfortable."

The gangster stood there, tapping the pistol against his thigh as he took in the sight of Macuil bound in the dirt. Then he dropped a crumpled sinicuichi flower on the ground between them.

"Everett over there tells me you're called McCool. That's a real fucking stupid name and I don't feel like saying it, so I'm going to call you Mac." Macuil grimaced, but the man carried on as if he hadn't noticed. "You took a lot of money from me the other day, *Mac.* The Mesa House. One million dollars. I want it back. You make that happen, there's a chance you get out of this alive."

Macuil couldn't help himself. He laughed.

The gun rose, until the barrel stared him right in the eyes. "I'm not known for my patience," the gangster warned. "The next time you laugh, or crack a joke, or so much as fucking smile, you're dead. Give me back *my money.*"

Macuil raised his empty, bound hands. "I'm afraid that's just not possible. I donated it. To charity."

"You did *what?* Donated it…to who?"

"Gamers Without Boarders."

A disbelieving pause.

"What the fuck is Gamers Without Boarders?"

"They bring board games to kids in third world countries. It's their mission to make sure no kid grows up without games."

"You donated a million dollars…to a *board game charity?* Not even the Red Cross or something? What the hell is wrong with you?"

"We all have our priorities, Tony. Don't judge mine and I won't judge yours."

The man started as if he'd been slapped. "The *fuck* did you just call me?"

"Tony. You gave me a nickname, so it's only fair. You look like a Tony. First, you're clearly a gangster. Second, you've got the receding hair going on and—"

Fire sliced across Macuil's cheek; thunder raged in his ears with the gun's retort. His head jerked around. Ringing. He blinked, pain spreading over the side of his face where the bullet had grazed him.

The gun hovered in front of his forehead and, for the first time, Macuil felt…*uncertain.* If it were the time of the Aztec, no human would have been able to harm him in such a manner. The weapon simply would not have pierced his skin.

But this wasn't the time of the Aztec. This was the age of commerce and industry, in a country which worshipped no gods, in a desert where bodies were never found. Macuil's eyes drifted from the smoking barrel of the gun to the man who wielded it.

"You like to play games?" the gangster asked. "Fine, let's play one. You win, and you keep breathing a little longer. You lose, and I blow your fucking brains out."

He took a step back, no doubt so that said brains wouldn't get on his expensive shoes, and took aim.

"What number am I thinking of?"

Macuil did his best to keep a neutral expression. *A game? More like an opportunity.* He tried to swallow, to gather his confidence…but his mouth was bone dry and his face ached something fierce. *Then again, this guy is clearly going to shoot me either way…and I can't be sure what will happen if he tries to put a bullet in my brain. The rules of this world, they've all changed…*

Yet, fear or no, Macuilxochitl would be a gambler till the end of his days. He guessed. Of course he guessed.

Tony barked a laugh. Nervously, his squad of cohorts chortled along.

"What the fuck are the chances of *that*?" he asked, shaking his head.

Macuil shrugged, testing the strength of the tape around his wrists. "I have really good luck with games. And I suppose you could say thirteen is something of a lucky number for my people."

"You don't say?" Tony asked. "Well, I guess that makes you an unreasonably lucky son of a bitch. Can't be having that, now can we?"

The strangely conversational tone was all the warning Macuil got before the gun went off. *Here goes nothing,* he thought, feeling detached as the flash blinded him.

Ringing, ringing in his ears.

Screaming…

Blinking, Macuil realized he was still on his knees. But Tony…Tony was stumbling backward, clutching his hand. Blood gushed over his wrist, pouring from the stumps where his first three fingers used to be before they were blown off by the misfire of the gun. The pistol was on the ground, forgotten in the chaos. Macuil's phone was beside it.

A magnificent, shit-eating grin stretched across his lips.

"Still got it!" he shouted. "That's what you get for trying to cheat the God of Games, dick!"

Whether Tony and his goons heard him, Macuil didn't wait to find out. His wrists tore through the tape as if it were nothing. He snatched up the phone. Then he was moving.

For a heartbeat, he was back on the ullamaliztli tlachtli. Macuil dashed forward, leaping across the sand and behind the rocky abutments which decorated it. Gunfire rang behind him, throwing up plumes of dust. Tony's screams of "Get him!" accompanied the shots…but in the dark, in the wild, the humans had no chance at all of catching Macuilxochitl.

He slipped away into the night, leaving the shouting and gunfire far behind.

•••
•••

Once he'd put some distance between him and the thugs, Macuil slowed to a comfortable pace and allowed his feet to carry him through the desert. He had no real way of knowing where he was going—only the stars to indicate that he was heading west. West meant ocean, eventually. At least he didn't have to worry about food or water.

The moon rose to its zenith; fell beyond the horizon. The sun took its place, soaring high overhead to bake the sands.

Macuilxochitl walked.

Unfortunately, long journeys by foot were a breeding ground for thoughts he'd much rather distract himself from with a good game. But there were no distractions in the desert. Only his problems.

He'd been kidnapped, his blood drawn…by *humans.* Since he'd escaped, that didn't particularly bother him—quite the contrary. It had been more exciting than anything he'd done in ages.

That was the problem.

Despite the fact that Macuil was stranded in the middle of the desert with only cacti, rocks, and the occasional skink for company, that familiar feeling of existential dread was creeping back in, just like it always did when he was on his way back from a moonlit adventure. On his way back to Five Flower Entertainment, and *The Untouched Land.* His prison.

When did it become that way? There was a time when I thought The Untouched Land *was my magnum opus. But now whenever I so much as think about it, or even the building that houses it, I get this…this tetziltlalpilli in my stomach.*

He rubbed at his belly, as if that could do anything to help. His flowery shirt was soaked through with sweat, but neither the cooling sensation nor the gentle entreaty of his massaging fingers could do anything to relieve his discomfort.

"That's because the discomfort is in your soul," a voice whispered inside his head.

Macuil frowned. The voice was…familiar. It sounded almost like his own, but the words had the smack of someone else behind them. Someone Macuilxochitl hadn't seen or heard from in a very, very long time.

He scanned the surrounding dunes, not knowing exactly what he was looking for, but trusting that he'd know it when he saw it.

And so he did.

Hidden among the tuberous branches of a nearby coastal cholla, a hummingbird flitted about. Its little turquoise wings moved so swiftly they were a blur; its beak, long and curved, housed a slender tongue that slipped out to taste the juice of the cactus' flowers.

Macuil whistled. "Well, well. Long time no see. And without even bothering to write and let me know you were coming?"

Rather than answer, the hummingbird zipped away.

Macuil realized he was clenching his teeth. A hummingbird in a desert. Good old Huitzilopochtli never was the most subtle. He'd once used a trick just like that to lead the Mexica to the place they came to call Tenochtítlan. Which he never let anyone forget, of course. If he thought condescending to Macuilxochitl in such a manner was going to produce similar results, he had another thing coming.

"Fuck off, Huitzilopochtli. If you wanted to give me advice, you could just come talk to me instead of using cryptic signs like an asshole."

Macuilxochitl started walking again. *Let the old sack suck on that.*

He'd hardly made it two steps when he stopped short, eyes widening.

A bark of gunfire rang out in his memory. The roar of the crowd at the tlachtli. Unpredictability…and the genuine elation which followed it.

"That's it," he whispered. "That's what's missing."

His eyes drifted back to the cactus where the hummingbird had been. "Touché, Huitz. Touché."

Shaking his head and chuckling to himself, Macuilxochitl hoofed it over the next rise, and continued on his journey.

* * *

It wasn't much later that he finally came across a road. He plucked his cell phone from his pocket. In the desert, without a signal or landmarks, the bauble of technology had been useless. But now that he had something to go on…

A minute with the GPS app gave him a location. He swiped it to the side, then pulled up his contacts and made a call. The ringtone cut off with a click as it connected.

"Hello?" said Mariah's voice.

"I need a No-Questions-Asked pick-up," Macuil replied.

Silence on the other end.

Then, "Ok. Sure thing, boss. Where are you?"

Macuil told her. Then, as an afterthought, added, "Make sure to bring some coffee. And maybe water, too."

It was going to be a busy day.

•
•••
•••

Two hours, three cups of coffee, and a bathroom break later, Macuilxochitl strode through the sliding glass doors of Five Flower Entertainment with his head held high. The lobby was abuzz with groups of people coming and going, all chattering excitedly. More than a few stopped as he passed, gawking at the dirt and spatter of blood on his otherwise stylish outfit. He passed the blinking receptionist with a nod and called for the elevator.

"Mr. Shoctul! I was beginning to think you might miss the release."

Macuil turned to find Jensen behind him. His company liaison arched a brow when she caught sight of his disheveled state, but was tactful enough not to comment.

"Wouldn't dream of it," Macuil said. "Everything still on schedule?"

"Indeed. QA wrapped its final inspection early this morning. At midnight, the newest expansion for *The Untouched Land* will go live…and destroy every record the game has set to date."

"That's good. Thanks for the update."

The hint of a frown slipped past Jensen's unshakeable reserve. From her, that was akin to shouting her shock over his lack of enthusiasm from the rooftops.

"Of course, sir," she said hesitantly. "Will you be attending the release party tonight?"

The elevator dinged. Macuil went in and gave her an apologetic shrug. "I doubt it. Long night."

For once, his assistant didn't bother to hide her disappointment. "If you feel up to it later, you should come celebrate with us. It would mean a lot to the staff."

"I'll think about it. Goodbye, Jensen."

As the doors slid closed, Macuil was left wondering if he should have said anything more. But then he was traveling upward and that concern sloughed off his shoulders. The elevator was quiet, and that let Macuilxochitl's mind become quiet.

When the chime rang for the fifteenth floor, his eyes slid open and he walked purposefully down the long hallway to his penthouse. Noonday light spilled in through the apartment's wide windows, blanketing the floor in warmth. Macuilxochitl took off his shoes and socks. He always thought better when his bare feet could touch the ground. He padded across the soothingly hot tiles, past the chic leather chairs and high table that occupied most of the small space. The dresser beside his bed held row upon row of neatly folded clothes, though he couldn't for the life of him have said who did the folding. He changed out his dirty slacks with a fresh pair; his favorite flowery button-down for another, light blue petals drifting upon a beige field.

Refreshed, he grabbed a bottle of water from the fridge and went to the cutting-edge desktop computer in the corner of the room. The work station sat arrayed on a beautiful mahogany desk that was easily the most expensive piece of furniture in the penthouse. With a click of the power button on the tower, the computer hummed to life and a black loading screen with the letters *TUL* filled the display. Less than twenty seconds later, the portal for back-end maintenance to *The Untouched Land* greeted him.

Changes Macuilxochitl made on his personal terminal wouldn't go into effect until he gave the final override command prompt...but from this computer, he could access the entire code library for the game. *The Untouched Land* lay open at his fingertips.

Macuilxochitl lounged back in the comfy leather office chair, took a long, deep breath, and cracked his neck.

Then he got to work.

The first thing he attacked was the monster encounter and loot drop algorithms. Video games might boast a nearly infinite number of combinations for such trappings, but in reality, they were just as rigged as the Mesa House Casino. The employees of Five Flower Entertainment could go in at any time, adjust any of the rates at will. It was done out of 'consumer convenience'...but what it *was* was a lie.

Macuilxochitl wanted the game to feel more lifelike. More *honest.* One minute, you could be minding your business, the next you might round a corner and come face-to-face with three hungry dimetrodons. Or be thrown in the trunk of a car by gangsters. The point was that life had true spontaneity and his game, which was meant to simulate a virtual life, did not. That had to change.

Of course, he'd have to leave some traps in the code to foil the GMs as well. F.F.E. called them Game Masters, but really they were more like Game Police. He'd never been overly fond of police, nor they of his pursuits. If his newly polished designs were to have any sort of permanent efficacy—if they were to lead the GMs on a merry chase—then the randomness he'd inserted had to evolve...*randomly.*

Macuil grinned. *Now* that *is an inspired idea*, he thought, as his fingers flew across the keyboard.

The foundation laid, he quickly made another two dozen or so minor alterations to the game, cementing that sense of surprise into the DNA of *The Untouched Land* as best he could. It wasn't enough to totally satisfy him...but it was a first step. And wasn't that where anything worthwhile began?

By working his changes into the game, Macuilxochitl ensured that the teotl of gamers everywhere would continue to grow like maize beneath the midsummer sun. Whenever their characters died, whenever they lost a dice roll for an epic piece of gear, whenever they lagged and fell off a cliff and threw their hands up in outrage—his spirit would be bolstered. Now, with random creatures spawning across the map and totally randomized loot tables, that teotl—that *spirit*—would be that much stronger, because there would be that much more emotion behind it.

At last, a single line of text floated across his screen.

FINAL OVERRIDE NECESSARY. ARE YOU SURE YOU WISH TO PROCEED?

Stretching muscles that had grown stiff as boards, the God of Games leaned back in his chair and groaned. The sun had set while he'd been consumed by his work and now the only light in the penthouse was the electric glow of the monitor. The release party downstairs would have finished, the employees of Five Flower gone off to their families or other late-night endeavors.

Some small part of Macuilxochitl felt a little guilty for what he was about to do to them. They'd view this as a cataclysm; the entire company would go into crisis mode for months, if not years. But in time, they might come to appreciate the beauty in what he'd done.

And if not? Well...that was their problem—a *human* problem. Macuilxochitl had spent far too long worrying about such things. He had no doubt what he was doing was right.

Perhaps the key to surviving humanity's changing world wasn't to try and blend into it...but to know when to step away and show the humans a better path. Hadn't that been the domain of gods for as long as there *were* gods? It was as true now as it had ever been, Macuilxochitl had only forgotten it for a time, lulled into a false sense of security by the glittering lights of his digital masterpiece.

No more. There were so many games out there that not even the God of Games himself had tried them all. It was time to stop pretending to be a human, at least for a while, and go find them. To bring a sense of spontaneity back into his own life, for that was always when he'd been the happiest, and best able to serve those who worshipped him.

Slowly, gloriously, Macuil's best shit-eating grin stretched across his lips. The giddiness he always felt before a long journey was settling into his bones.

He hit the ENTER key.

Macuilxochitl rose and took a last moment to look around his penthouse, to think about the life he'd built in San Diego. He found that he wouldn't miss it. And even if he did—he could always create something like it again. One of the perks of immortality was that you never lacked for second chances.

Whistling to himself, Macuilxochitl closed the door to the penthouse behind him, walked out of Five Flower Entertainment, and didn't look back.

The House of Life

Jennifer Dunne

Anna Carlyle shouldered open the back door to the Cat Sanctuary where she was assistant manager and placed the Havahart trap on the counter. As soon as she let go of the handle, the thin calico cat inside, who had been crouched silently against the floor of the trap, began yowling and throwing herself against the wire walls. The trap tipped over on its side, rolling the calico, but didn't open.

Bastet, known to the humans who worked here as Bess Tate, came running from the front of the sanctuary. She immediately started cooing and murmuring to the terrified animal.

She put one of the towels on the counter, then opened the door of the trap and gently lifted the calico out. The cat settled, glancing up once, then bowing its head. The humans who met Bastet saw only another of their kind, a graceful middle-aged woman dressed in dark brown faux suede jeans, brown ankle boots, and a camel-colored turtleneck with the silhouette of a cat embroidered on the turned down collar. If they noticed the thin scar from her nose to her upper lip that gave her features a slightly feline cast, they were too polite to say anything about what they considered a deformity. But the cat was wiser than the humans, as cats often were. Humans may have abandoned her worship, but the cats never had.

Great goddess Bastet, the cat pleaded. *I only entered the trap to get food for my kittens. Please, do what you will with me, but save them.*

Bess ran her hands lightly over the cat, using her powers to assess her. She found nothing more serious than malnutrition.

"This cat's teats are swollen with milk. Where did you find her?"

"The alley between 8th and Pine," Anna answered. "We've gotten calls for about a week that a cat's been lurking there."

"She was lurking because she didn't want to go too far from her kittens."

They are hidden in a secure nest, by the stairs to the food building, the cat offered.

"There's a restaurant on that street, isn't there?" Bess asked.

"Marconi's Italian."

"She probably hid the kittens near there. The ovens would keep the wall warm and the trash would be a good source of food. It's closed today, right? Most Italian restaurants are on Mondays."

"Yes. You think that's why we were finally able to trap her? No tasty trash?"

"It seems likely. I'll go over and try to find the kittens. You watch the sanctuary."

"Sure thing, boss. I'll get the mother cat settled in one of the transient cages until you come back with her kittens."

Thank you, great goddess, the cat said, and closed her eyes, giving herself into the care of the human woman that served Bastet.

* * *

A short time later, Bastet had loaded the four tiny balls of fluff into a towel-lined shoebox. Their eyes were open, but they still had a slight curl to their ears, so they were probably about two weeks old. Even as infants, they'd known better than to hiss or claw at their goddess, so she hadn't seen their teeth.

She put the shoebox into the front seat of her BMW and carefully belted it in place. She'd chosen the car for herself as part of her cover identity as a doctor specializing in women's fertility issues and was surprised to find herself growing fond of it. She had to admit she did like the hundreds of horses controlled by its engine, rather than the single horse that had pulled her chariot in ancient Egypt. There were advantages to being able to move speedily, especially since showing up in a car caused far fewer questions than transporting herself through the aether. It was also far less exhausting.

As she settled behind the steering wheel, the rattling chime of a sistrum interrupted her thoughts. A petitioner! Bastet passed her hand across the display screen on her dashboard, transforming it into a scrying portal. A thin, brown-haired woman sat on a king-sized bed, eyes closed and a crumpled paper clutched in her hands.

"Please, let me have a baby," she whispered.

Not a direct petition to the goddess by name. Most of those came from neo-pagans who felt they'd been wronged, calling for Bastet's lion-headed avenging aspect. But a generic request to "the powers that be" from one of the people in this city would come to her if it related to her primary human area of influence of motherhood and fertility.

For centuries, she had been trapped in her feline form, sustained by the worship of the cats. It wasn't until the popularity of the "King Tut" museum exhibition and the thousands of copies of her statues it sold that she'd been able to reclaim her human form. She'd immediately forced Demeter and Persephone to concede the city, since fewer and fewer people read their stories in the original Latin or Greek, weakening them. But she wasn't strong enough yet to challenge them for the entire country.

Bastet focused on the image on the paper, backing up the scene until before the paper had been crumpled into a ball, and saw the fertility results of Caroline and Mitch Sanbourne. She flipped open her cell phone, another wonderful invention that reduced a goddess's need to be constantly sending visions to people, and speed-dialed her assistant at her fertility clinic.

"House of Life fertility and genetic screening clinic," Seshat answered.

"Cee, it's Bastet. We have a petitioner. Caroline Sanbourne." She spelled the name and heard the rapid tapping of computer keys in the background.

"Got it. The search engine stalking program we got from Onuris will place our ads prominently on her screen as soon as she logs onto a computer."

"Excellent. Let me know when she schedules a visit." Bastet turned off the phone and placed it on the dashboard. The scrying portal had returned to the factory-standard display.

Bastet smiled as her finger brushed across the car's GPS controls. Onuris, the god of hunting, had made a surprise resurgence in recent years. The number of people who muttered, "Please, let me find..." while using a web browser had woken him from his Christianity-induced slumber, and the number of pleas from people given bad directions by their GPS devices had only increased his strength. As the most powerful member of their pantheon in this hemisphere, she'd helped him get acclimated to the modern world. After he'd settled in as a computer programmer for a Silicon Valley startup specializing in searching the internet, he'd repaid her kindness with the ad-hunting program.

A tentative squeak rose from the box on the passenger seat. Bastet turned her attention to her loyal worshippers.

"Don't worry, sweet babies. I haven't forgotten you. I'll take you to your mother. Time enough to help the human after I help you."

* * *

A week later, Bastet paused outside the House of Life fertility and genetic screening clinic, considering it as a new patient might. The office was a modest storefront on a relatively unused one-way street downtown, with inspirational posters of green shoots poking up from desert wastelands papering the front windows.

"Using technology to help life thrive," one poster proclaimed. Another suggested, "Despite appearances, nothing is truly barren."

The optimistic, can-do attitude and clean but low budget look appealed to the women who petitioned her. They found it far more approachable than the sterile, high-tech appearance she'd originally copied from other fertility clinics. Not surprisingly, her client base was growing rapidly, even among women who normally petitioned other gods for assistance. Once they walked through that door, she was free to help whomever she wanted.

Each set of parents who thanked her daily in their thoughts for their "miracle" child increased her power, making it that much easier to help the next. Her success rates were now more than double those of standard fertility clinics, forcing her to invent a number of increasingly creative excuses to explain the discrepancy.

Pushing open the door, she entered a scene that resembled a high-end spa, rather than a fertility clinic. Vague scents of incense – a floral mix she got from her son – and the soft sounds of New Age bells made her clients feel even more welcome and relaxed. The firm's name was spelled out in brass letters hovering above a water wall directly in front of her. To her right was a waiting area with plush velvet couches and a buffet table of fruit waters and herbal teas. To her left was a receptionist's desk situated between two closed doors. The receptionist, Lydia, was a young Egyptian woman in a pastel kaftan and head scarf. Bastet had been worried about being recognized by her countrywoman, but Lydia had only laughed at the coincidence of cat-loving Dr. Elizabeth Tate's name sounding so similar to the Egyptian goddess of cats.

"Good morning, Dr. Tate."

"Good morning, Lydia. Who do we have on the schedule today?"

"A new patient consult, Caroline Sanbourne, at ten. Then the Rosens are coming at eleven to review the genetic profiles of their embryos before selecting one for in-vitro."

Bastet smiled. The Rosens would be pleased with their choice, no matter which of the viable embryos they selected. With her blessing, any one they chose would produce a healthy child.

Opening the door to the left of Lydia's desk, Bastet entered her office. She'd started with only the obligatory framed diplomas confirming that Elizabeth Tate was, according to various and sundry licensing bureaus, fully qualified to practice reproductive medicine. Once she understood how the bureaucracy worked, it had been easy enough to give the administrators a vision of her name and qualifications as part of the list of newly licensed doctors they were entering in their database. Modern people believed everything they saw.

From that basic beginning, she'd added various pieces of artwork that had been given to her by grateful parents, as well as by people who had adopted cats from the cat sanctuary. As a result, these featured mainly a variety of mother cats caring for kittens, as well as a proud image of a tuxedo cat that said, "Nothing is truly black and white…except maybe your cat."

She took her white lab coat off of the hook and shrugged it on over her soft chiffon cowl-neck blouse in an abstract pattern of gold and brown. She hated the coarse lab coat, preferring to wear sensuous clothing that was a delight to the touch. But modern patients distrusted doctors who did not wear lab coats. At least the gold embroidered "Dr. Bess Tate" on the left chest elevated the look a little bit.

She sat down behind her desk, arranging the blotter and pen holder at just the right angles. When she felt the office was as soothing and encouraging as it could be, she pressed the button on her phone that would tell Lydia she was ready to receive their first client.

A moment later, Lydia opened the office door and ushered inside the woman from the scrying portal.

"Please, have a seat." Bastet gestured to the pair of gold-velvet chairs pulled up in front of her desk. "How can I help you?"

Caroline sat on the edge of the left-hand chair, and put her handbag on the other. She rummaged inside for the printout from her doctor, a slight tremble in her hand causing her to knock over her bag and spill its contents. Apologizing profusely, she stuffed everything back into the bag, then produced the papers for Dr. Tate.

"My husband and I haven't been able to have children and the other doctors we've seen haven't been able to find any reason why I can't conceive. I'm hoping you'll find an answer they didn't, Dr. Tate."

"Bess, please." She quickly glanced over the pages, because Caroline expected it, then placed them to one side on her desk. "You and your husband both want children?"

That was the one scenario she could not solve. If it was going to be an issue, she needed to know now.

"Yes, very much so. I just didn't think he needed to take time off work for an introductory meeting."

"This is more than just an introductory meeting. Your previous physicians sent over your lab test results and their conclusions for my review. As your doctors have already told you, there is no physical reason you should not be able to get pregnant. We just need to give nature a helping hand."

When that helping hand came from a goddess, nature rarely refused to go along.

Caroline released her breath in a deep exhale.

"What would be involved in that helping hand? And how much will it cost?"

Bastet could feel Caroline's worries growing again. That would not do.

"The procedure is simple enough." Not as simple as petitioning Bastet to use her powers to ensure a pregnancy, but more acceptable to the modern woman. And because of that pesky detail of human free will, they had to believe she could help them before she actually could. "I'll give you a nasal spray to take every evening, that will boost your hormone levels and encourage your body to produce multiple eggs. We will harvest those eggs, in a simple outpatient procedure, and have your husband donate sperm. Since your husband's sperm does not have issues, we'll let them fertilize the eggs in the usual way, rather than injecting them into the eggs. Then, my lab assistant will culture the resulting embryos. Are you with me so far?"

"Yes. I looked up IVF online before coming here. A lot of the articles talked about needing to have my husband give me daily hormone injections."

Bastet shrugged. "Both injections and nasal sprays have comparable efficacy of hormone delivery. I find that taking a spray is much less stressful for prospective parents than dealing with needles. They tend to worry about the pain or not doing it correctly, and worry is counterproductive."

Caroline nodded and settled more firmly into her seat. Good. She was starting to relax and get comfortable. The more she relaxed and trusted Bastet, the easier it would be to overcome the fears and insecurities that were preventing conception.

"Once we have a full set of embryos, we'll test them with two types of genetic screening. The first screens out gross genetic unviability. Some 60-70% of embryos fail to get the correct number of chromosomes. It's possible this is why you haven't gotten pregnant yet. Your husband's sperm may have successfully fertilized your eggs, but the resulting embryo wasn't viable."

Caroline's expression turned distant and, after a moment, she nodded to herself. No doubt she was thinking back to times in the past when her period was late and she had briefly hoped she was pregnant. Bastet found women were more comfortable discussing potential genetic defects in the context of their bodies naturally refusing faulty embryos. Talking about DNA and gene sequencing seemed too much like science fiction and raised the specter of Frankenstein's cobbled-together creations, as she'd learned from one of her early petitioners. Bastet continued with her spiel.

"The second type of genetic screening we do is not usual for fertility clinics. We screen the embryos against a wide range of known genetic issues, so that we can select only the healthiest embryo to implant." Their method of screening used Seshat's divine power, but clients didn't need to know that.

She paused and waited until Caroline nodded, accepting a belief that her baby would be healthy. Bastet lifted a hand and gestured at the thin scar running from her nose to her lip. "Keep in mind, however, that not all birth defects are genetic in nature. I myself was born with an easily corrected cleft lip, which is one of the reasons I became interested in obstetrics."

"I already cut out caffeine and drink plenty of orange juice. I'll do everything I can to ensure a healthy baby."

Bastet smiled. "I'm sure you will. And I'll give you some strengthening herbal teas as well. The implantation is another simple outpatient procedure. I recommend that you get it on a Friday, so you can rest over the weekend and have the greatest chance of success. After that, it's a standard pregnancy and delivery."

"That just leaves the question of cost. Those extra genetic tests and supplements don't sound cheap." Caroline bit her lip.

"Have no worries on that score." Bastet put a little bit of her power into the words, ensuring that Caroline truly did not worry. Worry was counterproductive to conception. And Bastet had known the location of enough buried golden statues not yet found by Egyptologists that she'd been able to establish secure funding sources for tens of thousands of pregnancies, as well as her cat sanctuary. "We work with a wide range of insurances and philanthropic organizations to ensure that anyone who wants a child is able to afford one. Have you any other questions?"

"No, I don't think so. Other than, when can we start?"

"I'll have my lab assistant draw some blood to determine exactly where you are in your cycle and how much additional hormone we'll need to give you. If you're ready, we can begin now."

Caroline paused, then nodded decisively. "I'm ready."

Bastet led her out of the office, into the reception area, then through the other door into a more traditional-looking medical facility, a long hallway with doors on either side. Some led into examination and procedure rooms, while others led into high-tech lab areas with inexplicable glass and metal machines. These were Seshat's domain, where she had translated her traditional roles of recording and measuring lives into the modern world. She used computers instead of palm leaves, but the result was the same. As usual, all that could be seen of her was her dark brown hair pulled into a ponytail atop her head, fastened with a clip bearing her traditional seven-pointed star. She was peering intently through the eyepieces of a machine and making notes on a clipboard.

"If you have a moment," Bastet said softly. "I'd like you to meet our newest client, Caroline."

Seshat jerked upright, then bounded out of her seat, sending her stool rolling wildly across the room. Compared to Bastet's calm, refined elegance, Seshat vibrated with barely-leashed intensity.

She circled around her lab station to shake Caroline's hand vigorously. Her leopard-patterned lab coat had "C. Schött" embroidered on the chest, almost but not quite covering a garish t-shirt for a heavy metal rock band. Bastet sighed and forced herself not to roll her eyes. She did not want to endure another lecture on the mathematics of modern music. Instead, she went to the storeroom down the hall to get a box of her special herbal tea for Caroline, a proprietary blend infused with her power. That much at least hadn't changed in all the centuries since she'd been Egypt's second most important goddess.

Seshat glanced up and down Caroline's length with a broad smile.

"Oh, I'll take the measure of you right enough," she said, bobbing her head in time to the beat dimly sounding from the air-buds in her ears. "Nothing to fear, just a little pin prick."

Caroline let Seshat pull her toward a counter and a molded plastic chair. Seshat kept up a steady stream of chatter, further lulling her into obedience. Caroline dutifully rolled up her sleeve and sucked in her breath at the unexpected chill of the alcohol wipe against the inside of her elbow.

"A little cold, that's the alcohol evaporating, no worries," Seshat said. "Make a fist, quick and easy, one and done, and there you go."

Caroline blinked. Seshat was pressing a cotton ball to her skin, a needle containing a vial of blood in her other hand.

"That's it?"

Seshat wrapped a length of self-sticking stretch tape around Caroline's arm to hold the cotton in place.

"That's it for now. Don't lift anything heavy with that arm for the rest of the day. Go with Bess, now."

Caroline stood and looked over her shoulder. Bastet was waiting in the doorway, liking how the golden light from the hallway spilled around her like a halo. Image was important.

She held out a small white box to Caroline. Gold foil letters spelled out "The House of Life" on the top of the box.

"Here is the strengthening tea I mentioned. I'll call you when we have your results, and we can set up a time for you to pick up your hormones. Bring your husband. I can answer any questions he may have at the same time."

Caroline took the box, her fingers brushing Bastet's hand as she did. Bastet let her power flow across the connection, ensuring that the next eggs Caroline's body produced would be vibrant and strong. Caroline gasped and pulled back the box.

"Static electricity from the machines," Seshat hurried to explain. "That's why the floor inside the lab has rubber mats."

Caroline nodded and absently rubbed her finger tips. "I'll be more careful in the future."

Bastet smiled and ushered her out of the lab back into the soothing environment of the waiting area. "You're going to have a beautiful baby."

And it wouldn't take too many more mothers like Caroline before Bastet could start opening Houses of Life in other cities. It didn't matter if women asked for help from "Bastet" or "Bess Tate". As long as they asked for her, she'd help them, and Demeter could take a long vacation with her daughter in Hades, because she'd no longer be needed. There was a new Top Cat taking control.

Fire Sale

Jean Marie Ward

"It's in the handbook: the senior maenad decides who drives the truck." Dionysus Liber Amoungios spoke patiently into his phone, strangling the urge to roar like a wounded bull. Human employee training was like housebreaking a puppy. Anger—especially the helpless grieving rage tearing him apart—only got in the way.

"But Gini drives like a maniac!" maenad trainee Missy Gunnels wailed in his ear.

He glanced at the muted television on the other side of his office in a former Petaluma bank. The harried anchor segued from a clip of the inferno consuming the Inn at Blue Oak to an aerial view of traffic fleeing the Glass Fire. Dionysus' chest contracted painfully. The sprawling wood and stone resort had been his Napa Valley home and base of operations since he arrived in a bald-tired VW bus in the summer of '67, fifty-three years before.

"Gini won't be speeding anywhere today. One-Oh-One is bumper-to-bumper all the way to the bay," he rasped. His throat felt as tight as his chest.

"You didn't see her driving the bike lanes on the way to the bottling plant. What if a cop caught her? She can't flirt her way out of everything, you know."

Don't bet on it, he thought. "Don't worry about what-ifs. Focus on the job. The future of Liberami Winery depends on getting that hand sanitizer to San Pablo by three this afternoon. Do you really think Gini would jeopardize that?"

"Noooo." Missy admitted in a small voice, stretching the negative into four distinct syllables.

He heard them all. He shouldn't have. If Missy was calling from inside Santa Rosa's Verdeante Bottling plant, she would've been talking over the whirr-whirr clack-clack of the production line. Outside, she would have been competing with the shouts and beeps of loading cargo. But all he heard was Missy.

"Where are you calling from?"

"The truck."

Liberami's cool trucks were top-of-the-line three years ago, but they weren't soundproofed. He side-eyed his phone. "Where in the truck?"

"The back. It's the only place I can hear myself think. But you know what? It's kinda nice. It's like seventy degrees in here, and with the rear door pulled down, you can't smell the smoke. Solid too." He heard rapping, presumably her knuckles on the insulated chamber wall. "I bet this is the safest place in the whole truck. You know, if I rode back here, I wouldn't have to see Gini's driving."

"Stop right there."

"But it's the perfect solution—and safe! I secured those pallets myself."

"I don't care. You're not riding to San Pablo in the back"—*because my insurance doesn't cover puppies…people riding in the back of the truck*—"because I need you in the cab. Gini's a good driver. But she does like to speed. I don't want her treating the fire traffic as a challenge. I'm depending on you to make sure she doesn't get pulled over. I know it's asking a lot, but if we don't get the cash from San Pablo to Goldhen Trust by five, I'll lose Liberami, and the vineyard association will go down with me. Thousands of people could lose their jobs. In the middle of a pandemic."

"Thousands?" She squeaked. In addition to her puppy-like enthusiasm, the twenty-three-year-old still retained her youthful idealism. And he was a god, not a saint. He had no scruples about playing on her sympathies for the greater good.

"Thousands," he assured her. His desk chair creaked beneath his bulk as he leaned back to catch the gust of cool air blowing from the overhead vent. "Between the smoke and the chemicals they're throwing on the fires, the grapes that survive won't be fit to press. The growers need a new product, one that capitalizes on the organic methods they've instituted over the past twenty years. If the sanitizer deal falls through, wineries will go bankrupt. Owners will be forced to sell and speculators will move in. You know what that means."

Well, *somebody* did. As soon as he said it, the lights went out, taking the AC with them. Horns blared outside the bank.

"Power's off," he said, interrupting her reply. He moved to the window and nudged aside the blinds. No lights glowed in the stores on the other side of the parking lot. The black-out extended to the neighboring street. *Not good.* Garden variety, conservation outages didn't start until late afternoon. It was half past ten. The fires must be getting worse. His thoughts flew to his family. Were they all okay? Were they safe? When he talked to his wife a half hour ago, she told him everyone had evacuated and was sheltering with relatives or in motels closer to San Francisco. But she was as closely affined to the Napa terroir as he was. What if she'd decided to go back?

Worst case scenarios buzzed in his head. Missy bleated in his ear. His office phone trilled, its buttons bright in the gloom. *Ariadne?*

"Hang on. Got another call." He hit the desk phone's speaker button. "What's up?"

His assistant Pia Jose caroled, "Get your mask on, Denny. You got company: Emily Ulmaker from Maxwell Ernes."

"Maxwell Ernes?" He repeated, certain he'd heard wrong. "Ernes as in the hedge fund?"

"Yep."

"What's an Ernes rep doing here?" In the middle of a fire zone. In the middle of a pandemic. Not that he didn't need capital stat, but… "I don't know anybody at M.E."

Pia didn't answer. He didn't expect her to. Puppies survived on cute. Experienced assistants routed all their calls through their headset, so nobody heard their bosses flail. Meanwhile, Missy babbled as if "I got another call" meant something different in her world.

"Not now," he told her. "I'll call you back."

"No!" she yelped as he disconnected. He tossed the phone on the soil reports stacked next to his inbox. Missy would be fine even if Gini did drive off in a huff. They both had phones. The doors to the cargo compartment had emergency latches. She wouldn't freeze either. The sanitizer didn't need to be chilled. They were only using the cool truck to protect it from overheating and windblown cinders.

"Denny?" Pia asked.

Hedge fund. Right. He scraped a hand over his hair. He needed to make nice to the money person. He owed it to Ari and everybody else depending on him.

He hoped his wife was all right. She had to be all right.

"Give me a couple minutes," he said. "And see if you can get in touch with Ari. I'm worried about the black-out."

"On it."

He hadn't cleaned up this fast since his current incarnation was a bachelor. By the time Pia reached his sanctum door, the blinds were angled to lighten the gloom without losing the shade. The messy altar of his desk was almost tidy, with yesterday's depressing yield projections safely buried in his inbox under his closed laptop. A Liberami-branded cloth mask—superfluous to a god who couldn't get sick or transmit disease but necessary for appearance's sake—covered his nose and mouth. His purple Hawaiian shirt and ratty deck shoes stayed. As much as the fox ears and tutus worn by his street maenads, his laid-back style was part of the Liberami brand.

"Come in," he said, rising from his chair.

An expensive blonde wearing a gray mask blazoned with crystal-beaded dollar signs strolled into the room. Champagne-colored highlights polished her sleek hair. Her tailored suit was ivory silk. A slim folio case of gray kidskin dangled from her left hand. Matching high heels magnified the swagger of her stride. But the pricey packaging failed to disguise the pissoir taint of old paper and ink, the bloody tang of pennies pried from a broken hand or the rotten egg taste of sulfur coating his tongue. An iceberg the size of Greenland settled in his gut.

Pia made socially distanced introductions from the threshold and exited, closing the door behind her. Abandoning all pretense of civility, Dionysus dropped into his chair without inviting his guest to do the same. "Mammon," he said.

An infernal gleam sparked in the blonde's gaze, overlaying human blue eyes with the image of sideways pupils bisecting yellow orbs devoid of white. "Dionysus," Mammon responded in an incongruously pleasant soprano. "Long time no see. How's the wine business?"

He flicked a thumb at the windows. "Check it out. We've got people lined up around the block for four-shot wine flights and curbside pick-up. Our contactless tastings have made headlines from Seattle to LA. And we still sell no wine before its time."

"That slogan was cheesy when Orson Welles used it fifty years ago."

"Shows what you know. Welles was a genius. He was a great actor, a great director, and the first Golden Age movie star to leverage his celebrity into an income stream."

"Is that what this is about?" A French-manicured forefinger twirled a circle encompassing his graying—*tarnished silver*—hair and the spade-shaped beard jutting below his mask.

This was about being too busy trying to salvage some profit from a plague year to visit a barber. But he'd bite off his tongue before admitting it to Mammon.

"Just following Aristotle's advice," he said, "emulating the qualities of someone I admire."

"An aging fat man perpetually strapped for cash? I arrived just in time."

She—since the god currently presented as a woman, the feminine pronoun seemed apt—scanned the drab room. Liberami had leased the bank and its double-barreled drive-thru bays to move inventory normally sold in bars, restaurants, and winery tastings. The customer-facing teller windows and outside kiosks boasted a certain retro charm. But the backroom office space was furnished with Blue Oak cast-offs. Now they were all that remained of his home. Loss gutted him all over again.

The only exceptions to the utilitarian vibe were the console table under his TV and the high-backed armchairs in front of his desk. Crafted from thick, ancient grapevines salvaged from the wreck of an estate that previously bordered Blue Oak, their twisted limbs served as a constant reminder of his purpose and connection to Mother Earth.

Satisfied he wasn't hiding anything better, Mammon perched on the seat of the grapevine chair closest to the door. Dionysus's mobile beeped as she arranged the leather case on her lap. He glanced at the screen, hoping it was Ari. It was Missy. Again.

Mammon repositioned his nameplate to the side and centered a sheaf of carefully aligned, official-looking papers on the desktop. Her oddly formal gestures recalled temple offerings from ages past. *An offering from Mammon? Fat chance.* He crossed his arms.

She stiffened. "As currently structured, Liberami is underfunded and undervalued. I can fix that. Sell to me today and you'll retain full control over all production deriving from your terroir. I'll even add a provision designating you corporate spokesman. That way you can make all the commercials you want."

Dionysus laughed, a deep *ho ho ho*. He was trying for a rolling Wellesian bass, but even inside his head, it sounded more like Santa Claus.

Mammon pinned him with her double-exposure stare.

"You're serious," he said. "In all the centuries we've known each other, when have I ever sold you anything but booze? I've seen how an investment winery operates. The first thing they do is replace all the old vines with ruler-straight rows of immature grafts. They replace people who've worked the land for generations with migrant labor who can't tell red berries from green. They foul the soil. They kill the bees. Then they try to fix everything by pouring more chemicals down those damned straight rows and poison everything in their path."

Golden goat eyes twinkled at his snarl. "So you sued over the damage to your southern terrace. You still had to buy the owners out—admittedly at a bargain price. But then you went and sank all that money in an artisanal brandy venture."

"You make it sound frivolous. If I hadn't taken those bastards to court, they would have destroyed Blue Oak and a dozen other vineyards besides. As for the brandy, those stills are this year's MVPs. You can make high-proof alcohol out of any organic material, including smoke-tainted grapes."

It was Mammon's turn to lean back. "You're mortgaged up to your old man's hairline, and the last quarter payment on your loans is due today. In cash."

"What's it to you?"

"An opportunity. The sale of Goldhen Trust to Maxwell Ernes was finalized yesterday and I am Maxwell Ernes. Your bank belongs to me. So do your loans."

"Is that supposed to scare me?" He snorted. "You forget, I've dealt with pirates before. Your ransom will be delivered in full to Goldhen's Petaluma branch by closing time."

"Only if you deliver a full truckload of organic hand sanitizer to the San Pablo National Wildlife Refuge no later than three."

"Covered."

He couldn't see her smile, but he felt it, like an antelope feels the rushing wind of a leopard's leap. His body responded like prey. His heart sped. Hairs lifted across his nape.

His phone rang, breaking the spell. He glanced at the screen. Gini's number, not Ari's. Shit. She and Missy must have gotten into a fight.

"You want to answer that," Mammon purred.

He wanted to let it go, but she sounded too damn smug. He raised the phone to his ear. "Yeah?"

"Denny," Gini cried, "thank God you picked up. The truck's gone!"

* * *

No matter what kind of argument they had, Gini would never drive off without her trainee. And if she did drive off without her trainee, she'd never leave without calling. And if she drove off without calling, she still would've floored the gas pedal on the turn out of the parking lot.

Missy tried to explain this to Denny. She wanted to deliver the sanitizer and save the winery, not because he was the godfather of Napa's organic wine industry, but because he deserved a break. He was a nice guy and a good boss, nothing like the Doc Ock wannabe they had for a principal in the school where she used to teach. Denny didn't perv on the staff or pretend he was royalty because he owned a winery and a resort. But let a potential investor show up and even the best manager's eyes light with dollar signs. After that, if you don't ding like a cash register, *faggetaboudit.*

Only she couldn't. She was busting her butt on a metal toolbox in the back of a locked truck heading west through Santa Rosa when she and Gini should have been driving south. A shudder that had nothing to do with cold wracked her sturdy, athletic frame. She hugged the back of her tutu tighter around her shoulders and tried to fit the cable from the charger she kept in her fanny pack into the socket of her phone. Her shaking hands refused to cooperate.

She dropped the phone on her tulle-covered lap and took a few deep breaths. She was perfectly safe. Everything she told Denny about the cargo compartment was true. The insulated walls could survive almost any wreck. The looming, plastic-wrapped monoliths secured to either side of the truck wouldn't shift or fall. The two-foot-wide corridor between them, and the clearances above and behind them, ensured she had hours of air. The hatch's panic switch didn't just protect her from suffocation; it meant she could escape anytime. Between traffic lights and the fires, the runaway truck had yet to hit twenty-five—when it moved at all. She could jump whenever. This minute even.

And the truck, and the winery, and who knew what else would be lost. All those families. All those jobs. When the world was on fire and dying of Covid-19.

She wasn't Wonder Woman, though she was almost tall enough. She didn't have bulletproof bracelets or a Lasso of Truth. But she had location sharing on her phone and, with the charger, enough power for twenty-four hours of continuous operation. Scouts had nothing on Air Force brats when it came to being prepared.

This time the plug slid home. She exhaled in relief. Time to message Gini.

Preparedness first, the lessons of her childhood whispered. Gripping the phone and battery pack in one hand, she knelt on the chill floor and opened the toolbox. You never knew when you might need a big-ass flashlight. Remember *The X-Files.*

* * *

"No," Dionysus barked into his phone. "Missy first!

"This isn't a training run." Gini's voice rose with frustration. "It's a crime. We need the cops. They're the only ones who can find the truck."

"*Find. Missy. Now.*"

His bellow carried only the faintest echo of his god voice, but the ether trembled. Gini gasped, shaken. Silenced.

He hung up before she recovered. He felt bad about it. She didn't know what he was. Except for Ari, none of his human associates did. But he couldn't waste time on persuasion. He'd checked his messages while they were talking. Missy was still in the truck. He couldn't explain himself, either, not with Mammon drinking in every word.

"Trouble?" the money god cooed. The corners of her inhuman eyes creased with glee as she lounged in her throne of polished vines.

She was in this mess up to her diamond-studded earlobes. All the helplessness and fear he felt for his wife, his home, for the soil that gave him life and every living thing depending on him combusted in fury. He braced his knuckles on the top of his desk and lowered his head like the charging bull that was his totem and the symbol of his ultimate sacrifice.

"*You knew about the truck.*" he growled. The power behind it boiled away the dampness inside his mask. The blinds quivered. The windows rattled in their frames.

"Moi?" Mammon flattened a palm coquettishly over her heart. The slatted light exposed the raised tendons and darkened veins of an aging hand at odds with the rest of her appearance. His brain registered the discrepancy even as he brushed it aside.

"*You told me to take the call. You knew!*"

"I knew about the shipment to San Pablo. I knew you were depending on it to make your last quarter payment. I could also tell you recognized the number. Finally, I know American businesses lose more money to cargo theft than any other crime. I track those statistics. Suggest anything else and you'll be talking to my lawyers."

"*Nobody in their right mind steals hand sanitizer!*" The rafters above them groaned. Plaster dust floated from a dozen new cracks in the popcorn ceiling.

"Wrong," Mammon drawled, uncowed. "Computers and high-end electronics bring more per item, but low value cargo is easier to unload. Everybody wants hand sanitizer these days and they aren't particular about its source. By tomorrow all your precious, organic, one hundred percent recycled bottles will be stocking shelves from here to L.A."

"*My people could have been hurt!*"

The desk phone rang. He shook his head like a bull beset by a fly. Then he remembered. *Ari!* He grabbed the receiver, his anger doused with hope.

"Denny, it's a quake," Pia said. "There could be aftershocks. We should close. Ms. Ulmaker will understand. Ernes is based in San Francisco."

Dionysus took a deep breath and willed his pulse to slow. "It's not a quake. It's the building settling. That's why we got it cheap," he lied. "But if you and the maenads are worried, go. I'll lock up."

"Thanks, but I don't think anybody's going anyplace until the traffic lights start working."

He could only hope. Lowering the receiver to its cradle, he beamed good thoughts about stalled refrigerator trucks and traffic cams to whatever powers might be willing to receive them.

"You're a fine one to talk about hurting people," Mammon sneered. "That little tantrum of yours could have brought the building down. *Your people* would have been crushed."

She was right. The thought gave him chills. If Pia hadn't called… "No, they're old California hands. They know what to do in a quake."

"Undoubtedly, but that wasn't a quake. It was sonic disruption caused by the voice of a god. Standing in a door frame or trying to rescue their meal ticket could have gotten them killed. If you really cared about them, you'd tell them who you are and what you're capable of instead of passing yourself off as some chump named—"She flipped his nameplate so the letters faced up." —Dennis Leiber."

He'd been thinking something similar only minutes before. That made it unforgiveable. "Do you tell your employees they're working for a debased imitation of Ploutos, condemned to be reborn as a human generation after generation?"

If murderous glares could actually kill, he would have found himself instantly and permanently dead. Her voice sizzled with hate: "At least I don't pretend to be their friend."

"Touche." Reminding Mammon of her diminished condition was a low blow. Dionysus sank into his chair and winced at its squeal. Some good-time god he was. Even the furniture was mad at him. "Look, sniping isn't doing us any good. Let's cut to the chase. For some crazy reason, you, the apotheosis of profit, want to buy an operation that teeters on the edge of bankruptcy in a good year. I'm not going to sell. We're done. Let me know if you'd like some wine. You can have whatever's in stock, on the house."

"Oh, we're far from done, Dionysus Twice-born. If you don't sell to me now, *before* you default on your loan at five-oh-one, Liberami Wine and Spirits and all its attached assets will belong to Goldhen Trust. There will be no extension on your debt. The land, the buildings, the equipment, the product in off-site storage, even the lease on this building, will be sold to Maxwell Ernes at ten cents on the dollar."

"You know I won't let that happen."

Mammon chuckled. "'Let it happen?' It's done. Your truck and everything riding on it is gone."

"I knew it. You organized the hijacking."

"Ah ah ah! Remember my lawyers, *Denny*." She twisted the name like she wanted to break it. "They aren't just sharks, they're megalodons."

"I don't care what they are. If anything happens to my people…"

"Please, your people are fine. Today's highwaymen won't go near a truck if they see anyone around."

Assuming they know there's anyone around, he thought grimly. At least she hadn't noticed his slipped tense.

"I can't say the same for Ernes," she said.

He blinked. "What's Ernes got to do with it?"

"With the hijacking? Nothing at all. With the future of your precious human pets? Let's just say employees never fare well in a fire sale. There are lay-offs and salary cuts. Whoever's left gets reassigned and encouraged to take an early-out. Soon there's no one left to remember how things used to be. But they'll all remember how your bad decisions ruined their lives. I'll see to it personally. And you know what happens to a god who betrays their worshipers."

She drew her thumb across her throat.

He grimaced under his mask. This was why he avoided Mammon. Extend an olive branch and what do you get? Threats—empty ones at that. "So I'm torn apart a few decades ahead of schedule. It's happened before. I reincarnate and start over."

"*If* you die on your terroir. If you don't… The last time this nation went dry humanity suffered Pestilence, Famine, and War. This time, they'll collect the whole set."

She wouldn't.

She would. Mammon's black pupils lay flat across her golden eyes. She was serious.

She was seriously plotting a manmade apocalypse in one of the most geologically active places on the planet the same year Mother Earth decided humans needed schooling. Plague—check. Locust swarms—check. Coked-up feral hogs—check. Worst wildfires in forever—check, check, check! But that wasn't enough for Mammon. Oh no! She had to do it enthroned in vines wrenched from one of Earth's hallowed hills.

Thin crimson whorls eddied over the gnarled frame of her chair. *Not good.* Mother Earth stirred in the darkly polished wood. He'd seen it before, first in the Aegean on his way to Crete and three hundred years ago off the coast of Newfoundland. Only this time he wasn't bound to a pirate ship's mast. The humans working in the building were innocents, and the future of countless more hung on his missing truck.

Mammon's goat eyes flashed as he cursed in Egyptian and ancient Greek. She thought she'd won, when he was *this close* to upending his desk, hauling her off the chair, and pounding her head against the carpet until all the stupid ran out her ears. But he couldn't. He was the intercessor between Earth and humanity. He had to *fix this*—without thundering the place to rubble. It was his job.

Swearing harder, he reached for Mammon's papers.

* * *

The truck exited Route Twelve and zigzagged north over progressively smaller and bumpier roads. A final turn sent it juddering over gravel. Missy texted Gini: *Almost there.*

The message hung in the window. She tapped the arrow again. Still nothing. *Shit.* No signal. The truck lurched to a halt. Her skull smacked against the wall. *Shitshitshitshitshit.*

Rubbing her head, she slipped the phone into her fanny pack, grasped the flashlight, and unfolded herself from the toolbox. Time to abandon ship and find some bars. If Gini lost her signal, there wouldn't be any cavalry riding to Liberami's rescue or hers. But her insides were Jell-O. *Stop it! What would Wonder Woman do?* She wouldn't give up. Missy braced her shoulder against the boxes and ordered the rest of her to get with the program.

The hatch whined. She shut her eyes against the dazzle of late morning light. Sharp smoky air strafed her nose and throat. She adjusted her mask and clenched her teeth. She couldn't cough. Her only advantage was surprise. She risked a squint. In the glare beyond the almost open door, two men peered into the truck. But shadow still covered half the floor. They couldn't see her. *Yet.*

"That don't look like wine," the taller of the two men complained in a reedy voice. He cupped his hands around his eyes.

"I told you. Verdeante doesn't do wine." The shorter guy's growl was rougher than parched grass. "Let's see what we got."

He whipped a box knife from the pocket of his jeans and flicked the catch. Inside her, a switch Missy didn't know she had flipped.

"No!" The next thing she knew she was standing at the edge of the hatch waving the flashlight in their faces. It wasn't much of a club, but the sight shocked them stupid.

Now what? Tall guy was a raw-boned, unmasked teenager still waiting for his muscles and beard to fill in. The likewise unmasked box knife dude looked about forty. Despite a top-heavy wrestler's build, he balanced lightly on his feet. To her left she glimpsed the peeling boards and graying door of an old horse barn. Dirty sky, sagging fences, and overgrown fields stretched behind the two men. Whiffs of old hay and manure underlay the smoke. She didn't see any livestock or people. That didn't mean they weren't around. She had seconds—at most—to make her move.

"Stop!" she ordered. "You're under arrest!"

"Who the hell are you?" box knife dude demanded.

Good question. She squeezed the flashlight. *Not Wonder Woman: Dana Scully!* "FBI. Drop the knife. Put your hands behind your heads and step away from the truck."

Tall guy raised his hands and obeyed. "FBI? Shit, Trav, Mom's gonna kill me!"

"Shut up! She ain't FBI. Not dressed like that."

Summoning the quelling glare perfected over eighteen months of substitute teaching, Missy replied, "I'm undercover."

"Yeah, right." Trav jerked the knife for punctuation. "Where's your badge? I'm not doing nothing 'til I see your badge."

Without lowering her gaze or the flashlight, she groped left-handed in her fanny pack. For a giggle, she kept her *Agents of S.H.I.E.L.D.* fan badge in the wallet with her commercial vehicle license. She never dreamed it might save her life. But as her fingers brushed the wallet, her phone erupted in Gini's ringtone, "The Ride of the Valkyries."

Trav yelled, "Bogus! She's a fake! Rush her!"

"Me?" Tall guy bleated. "I'm not going down for assault."

"You're already up for grand theft auto!"

Tall guy shook his head and backed away.

"Then get your cousins. She can't fight all of us."

Missy grew up Air Force. She knew down and dirty self-defense. But she'd have to get close and Trav had a knife. She couldn't run either. That left slamming the flashlight on his head hard. People died that way. For the briefest instant, she hesitated.

Trav jabbed at her left leg. She hopped back. He cut right. Her body recoiled. She stumbled against the boxes. If the flashlight hadn't caught in the netting she would have landed on her ass.

Trav vaulted into the cargo compartment.

* * *

The temperature in Dionysus's office had climbed ten degrees since the power died. But that wasn't why his cheeks itched from perspiration and his shirt was soaked. Mammon's proposal left him stymied and alarmed in ways threats never could. He scanned the key provisions a third time and tossed the documents onto his desk.

"I don't understand. The money's good. I control production and you can't touch the terroir. Plus, I get final say on the use of the I.P. This isn't a takeover; it's a gift. What's the catch?"

She straightened. "Immortality. I keep you out of receivership. You make me immortal."

"You're a god. You're immortal by definition."

"My body isn't. None of them are. I'm born with no memory of what I am. I'm dumped on shitty parents or shitty foster parents or no parents at all. The world tries to break me, but I won't let it. I never let it. I claw my way to the top, recover my identity, and what happens? I'm one foot into my next grave. I get tuberculosis, cancer, pox. I'll probably get Covid. I'm hit by a truck or felled by a stroke and wind up rotting in my own filth." Her hands tightened over the chair, arms quivering with the effort of containing her anger. Her voice throbbed with it, but her eyes were haunted by pasts a thousand times worse than those she described.

"I'm sorry." He was. He ached for the pain and bitterness rising with her ire like the poisonous smoke from the Glass Fire. "But I can't help you. I die, too, and it's violent every time."

"And get reborn with your identity intact, cherished and cossetted by Earth herself. The spirit of commerce is your mentor. And if that wasn't enough…" Her nails dug into the wooden armrest. "You—a god so weak and insignificant you can survive on spilled beer—*you* hand out immortality like a party favor."

A ruby port stain radiated outward from her hands. The color widened the redness he'd noticed earlier, changing "not good" into "actively bad." "It's not that simple."

"It is!" She let go of the chair only to hit it with her fist. More red exploded under the finish. Mother Earth was transitioning from irritated to annoyed. "I've watched it happen for millennia. Your nannies survive centuries. Your attendants, no matter what stupid name you call them, never sicken. You even save the women who died giving you birth. You carry them from hell to Olympus and make them goddesses."

He lifted his palms in placation. "No. I don't. Their story makes them immortal, not me."

"Oh? Then what keeps Ariadne young?" Mammon hissed. "She hasn't aged a day since you picked her off the side of the road. She's ninety years old. She looks thirty! You're eighty-seven. You're a boozer and a glutton and people think you're fifty, while I look like this."

She ripped away her mask. After her build-up, he expected horror, a catastrophic injury or cosmetic procedure gone hideously wrong. Instead, he saw a perfectly good face. Based on her hands and the pheromones registering on his deific senses, her body was in its late sixties. Skillful plastic surgery allowed her to pass for younger, but an equally deific sense of self-preservation kept that observation silent.

She loomed over his desk. "Well?"

"What do you want me to say? I can't stop you from dying. I can't grant you eternal youth either. It's not mine to give. What you see in my wife and the people around us is a function of our roles serving Mother Earth. My wife retains her youth because she expresses Earth's fruitfulness. I embody its strength. But nobody's strong by themselves. When I'm a child, I require care. As an adult, I need help."

Help.

Was that what this was about? Was all the drama with the loans and the banks and the hijacked truck some kind of crazy, messed-up cry for help? Mammon was born from want, but damage made them a monster. He was Dionysus Liber—the Liberator, the god who released people from their suffering and the shackles of their minds.

"Mother Earth helps those who help me. She could help you, too." He extended his hand across the desk. "Join us."

She retreated to her chair, eyes wide and mouth slitted in a moue of distaste. "You want me to join your hippie commune picking grapes and handing out fliers wearing an elephant patch tutu?" She sounded utterly aghast.

He grinned under his mask. "No. I want you to use your brilliant moneymaking brain to get richer helping Mother Earth. Be the entrepreneur who makes trillions bankrolling technologies that reverse climate change and restore the ecological balance. I'm not asking you to work for me. I'll sign your agreement as it stands. The contract plus intent will make you part of the team. You'll get all the benefits. No tutus required."

"Benefits," she echoed in a hollow voice.

"Benefits," he repeated. "Perfect health, extended life, the happiness that comes from doing good for yourself and others."

He almost had her. Her features softened. Possibilities swam in her gaze. Then something snapped. He practically heard it crack.

"No."

"No?"

"You're as bad as the humans. You're a user. You want my money and my brains, but what do I get in return? Crumbs. Well, I've had it with users. You know my terms: immortality or Liberami."

"I can't give you immortality." Honestly, he didn't want to. An unchecked, undying Mammon was too horrible to contemplate. But he did want to help. Ploutos used to work with Mother Earth to benefit humanity. Maybe they could again.

Her mouth flattened. "Then get ready to lose everything."

Tiny nubs budded on the finials rising above her shoulders.

* * *

Trav rose unhurriedly, menacingly, to his feet. His shoulders blocked out the sky, and he still held the knife.

This time Missy didn't hesitate. She brought her heel down hard on his boot, then slammed her knee into his groin.

He dropped the knife to cradle his balls. Breath squealed through his teeth. He staggered, teetering on the edge of the hatch. She kicked him in the sternum. Arms pinwheeling, he disappeared over the edge. He landed with a hoarse "Oof" and a thud.

She nerved herself to check the damage. Trav huddled on his side, wheezing and cuddling his crotch. She didn't see any blood. That was good, but she needed to restrain him—her cords would work—find the truck key and leave before Tall Guy's cousins arrived. Only her knees had gone maximum noodle. There was something warm dripping down her inside right calf. Damn, the asshole cut her good leggings. He cut her leg, too, but it wasn't deep. The first aid kit was in the cab. But instead of retrieving it, she slumped on the edge of the hatch. She needed a minute. Wonder Woman wouldn't need a minute. But Dana Scully might.

A green pick-up barreled up the drive. It swerved to a sideways stop in a spray of gravel. The passenger door flew open and Gini leapt from the cab. Medusa curls the color of good pinot noir flared behind her like a flag. She charged over the rocks—*in her brand new kitten heels!*—and yanked Trav's head up by the hair. This was doubly impressive since Gini was all of five-foot-three, small despite her curves, and there wasn't a hair more than half an inch long anywhere on Trav's head. But that was nothing compared to the things Gini promised to do to him at the top of her not inconsiderable lungs. Missy never realized her mentor was such an artist in profanity. Her Air Force father would have been awed.

The area in front of the barn filled with cars, including a green Prius with the Verdeante Bottling logo pasted to its door. Belatedly she realized the pick-up had one, too. People swarmed from the vehicles. Two of them dragged Trav to the side, pushed him onto his stomach and duct taped his wrists while he sobbed, "Thank you. Thank you!" A man and a woman she remembered from the bottling plant raced toward the open door of the barn. Others jogged past the truck in the direction she'd last seen Tall Guy.

A nice baritone asked, "How many bad guys we got?"

The voice's owner, a black-haired, masked man in a vivid cerulean t-shirt and beige cargo shorts, stood about six feet from the truck. He held a bottled water in one tanned hand and small first aid kit in the other. He placed them on the truck bed and stepped back.

"You okay?" he said.

"Just a little dazed. I only saw two. Other guy's a tall skinny kid with a patchy beard. Trav told him to get his cousins, but he was scared. He could've run away. Anyway, there couldn't be too many, or somebody would've met the truck. Bad guys have phones, too." She was babbling. Grabbing the water, she turned away, ostensibly to drink but really to hide her embarrassment. "Sorry. Still shaky."

"You're entitled. You did great. You got us here. You took out the hijackers. You even got a name."

"The kid mentioned it. Trav was *pissed*." She glanced at the newcomer. It's not like he could see her cheeks burning through her mask, and if she was perspiring, well, the temperature out here had to be ninety.

"I'm Ken. From the bottling plant." He started to extend his hand, then remembered himself and did the elbow hoist. "Anyway, I'm Ken."

"Missy," she replied with a matching elbow lift. He had good eyes, with the beginnings of smile lines at the corners. She wondered what the rest of his face looked like. She peeked lower. A nice set of shoulders stretched the promo image for Balticon 2020 across his chest.

"Wow," she said, "You went to a con this year? I thought they were all cancelled."

"They were. Balticon went virtual. First time I could attend in years. You into SFF?"

"Big time."

His gaze took in her fox ears and tutu.

Missy laughed and fluffed her skirt. "This is my day gig. Maenads embody the Liberami brand—like the Cruxshadows Fairies. Ever hear of them?"

Ken nodded enthusiastically. This one might be a keeper.

Gini kicked Trav again and straightened her fitted black jacket. "Branding shmanding. The day Denny makes me dress like an escapee from the funny farm is the day I quit."

"Too on the nose?" Missy asked.

Gini's eyes glinted dangerously. "Gab later. We're on a deadline here." She flipped the key fob. "And I'm driving."

Now Missy was really afraid.

* * *

Missy's text ended: "Gini's driving. :'(" Smiling, Dionysus lifted his face to the vent. The power was still off. His office could've doubled as a sauna. But he didn't care. The women were safe. Liberami was safe. All he had to worry about was Ari. *And Mammon.*

"Bad news?" her voice dripped fake concern.

"The best. You're wrong, you know. It's not the strength of the god or the faith they inspire that matters. It's their people—their hearts, their minds. Their integrity. Gods exist to serve, not the other way around."

She snatched the documents off his desk and stuffed them roughly into the gray envelope case. "This isn't over."

"Yes, it is. Remember what happens to people who hold me for ransom."

"Those idiot pirates you scared off their ship?" She sniffed. "Pretending to be a leopard won't work on me. I'm as much a god as you."

"The pirates who drowned were the lucky ones. The ship ate the rest, and before it did, the deck looked just like that." He pointed at her chair. The wood had darkened to the tarry purple of bull's blood wine. Tiny buds furred its polished limbs. Pale shoots wreathed the finials on either side of her head.

"I don't believe this! You're still trying to sell that fairy tale about Mother Earth growing grapes from their blood. News flash, *Denny*," she spat. "Mommy isn't here."

An impossible breeze kissed his forehead. The scent of spring rain banished the fug of perspiration and over-priced perfume. His sweat turned to ice. He bolted around the desk and grabbed her hand. "Don't argue! Go!"

"No!" She threw her weight backward into the chair. "I've decided I like it here. It's all going to belong to me anyway—your vineyards, your neighbors' vineyards and all the little adjoining vineyards. Then I'll show you what real industrial production looks like. By the time I'm done, you'll beg to make me immortal." A cord-like stem flicked across her wrist and whipped around the armrest. "*Ow!*"

"Shit!" He ripped the growth off her arm. "Run!"

Her goat eyes widened. She started to rise. A vine as big as his thumb shot across her waist. She shrieked. He grabbed the vine and heaved. Despite his bull-like strength, despite her desperate efforts to wriggle free, the vine didn't budge.

"What's happening?" she cried. Fresh shoots burst from the wood.

"Mother Earth is in your chair. Apologize! Tell her you won't attack the land. It's your only hope."

She nodded, gold eyes graying. "I'm sorry. I take it back. I won't touch your terroir!"

Panic made her shrill, but she sounded sincere. It didn't help. Branches surged from both sides of the chair. They crashed together, forming a living cage. He wrenched the tangle off her chest. "Mother, enough! You won. Your land is safe. Call off your vines."

"Call them off and I'll do better," Mammon said. "I'll make Liberami profitable. I'll make all the vineyards profitable."

The chair growled. New stems erupted from still oozing stumps. The wiry tendrils sliced his frantic hands and raised welts on his calves. "Listen to her, Gaia. I'm begging you. She can help us. You don't need to do this." *You don't need to kill.*

The green seethed. "*Need?*"

"I will! I promise. Just let me go!"

Ligneous fingers ruffled Mammon's hair and fluttered against her face. Their rustling became a mocking papery whisper. "*I've decided I like it here. It's all going to belong to me anyway…Then I'll show you what real industrial production looks like.*"

"I only said that to scare him!" Mammon screamed. "I didn't mean it. I swear—"

Butterfly leaves swarmed over her mouth. Another recognizable echo of Mammon's voice vibrated through the branches. "*The development will overlook Blue Oak. The previous owners were forced to sell. The fires, you know.*"

He froze. Was that why she rejected his earlier offer? Webbed spider-tight to the chair, she tried to shake her head. Tears leaked from her human blue eyes. Fresh tendrils wormed across her cheeks and licked them dry. Clustered white flowers peeked through the leaves. Lemon, lavender, and vanilla flooded his senses, leaving no room for sulfur, bloody coin or mortal terror.

Bile burned up his throat. It didn't matter what she'd done. No one deserved to die like this. No one!

He tore into the leaves and flowers shrouding Mammon's face. The green mass convulsed, shoving him back. The branches closed against him. Blossoms fruited. Green berries turned red. Summer's heady perfume surrendered to the winy scent of sun-warmed grapes and dying leaves.

"*No!*" he roared. The bank shook from roof to foundation.

Neither leaf nor stem so much as quivered. He sank to his knees.

Eventually the vines covering Mammon receded. All that remained of the woman she used to be was a desiccated, eyeless corpse. Her fine clothes were rags. Her folio case and its contents had disappeared. But diamond studs the size of peas still winked in her mummified ears.

He wanted to puke.

"Denny?" Pia's voice cracked.

His assistant hugged the metal doorframe. Sour sweat glazed her forehead. Her heart drummed, but she appeared unharmed. His vision swam with relief as he rose, stiff and aching, from the floor.

Pia cringed, then caught herself with a jerk. Glaring defiantly, she straightened. Her hands fisted at her sides. "What's going on here? I heard screaming."

He could make this go away. He could make her believe whatever he wished. Madness and ecstasy were his to command. But Mammon got one thing right. He owed it to his followers to trust them as they trusted him. *As long as I don't end up dissected in some government lab.*

But Pia wasn't a puppy or a pirate or a Man in Black. She was a colleague, a friend, and twenty-year Army veteran who knew what it meant to serve.

He removed his mask and the small glamour hiding the crescent horns of his godhead. She was already familiar with the rest: the light brown skin and heavy jaw inherited from his father Amun, whose last name was *not* "Leiber," and the nose and hazel eyes of his mother Samara, whose name it was.

"Gods still walk the earth. I'm Dionysus. Emily Ulmaker was the current incarnation of Mammon. She was planning to destroy Liberami. Mother Earth destroyed her first."

Pia gulped. Her gaze darted to the riot of grapes dangling from every scrap of wood in the office. But she refused to quail. "Mother Earth or you?"

"I couldn't do this." *On any level.* "Is everybody all right?"

"You got the corpse from *Psycho* sitting at your desk, grapes are hanging from the ceiling, and you're worried about the staff?"

"Yes."

"They're fine. But what are we going to do about *that*?" Her voice only shook a little. She was holding it together better than he had any right to hope. But her question sounded like a test. "Turn everything into sanitizer," she prodded, confirming it.

The weak, purple-gowned godling tied to a pirate's mast would have agreed in an instant. But this Dionysus had left that boy and his leopard skin far behind. He pitied Ploutos and the Mammon they'd become. On a more self-serving note, it wouldn't be healthy for his kind to let humans smear their hands with a deceased god.

"Find something to cover her. She wouldn't want anyone to see her like this. Get the shears from the truck and all the garbage bags you can find. I'll drive to Shasta tonight and bury her there. It's a holy place. It might help…next time."

Pia's eyebrows rose. He foresaw *a lot of 'splaining* in his future. But she didn't argue. Or quit. Wrestling his laptop from the grapey profusion of his inbox, he called it a win.

His wife's ringtone sang through the foliage. He dropped the computer and seized his phone. His chest expanded with his first free breath in hours, filling him with light.

"What's going on up there, Dee? I can smell the fried ozone from here."

Chuckling, he wiped eyes that were dry a minute before. "Ari, my treasure. Where's here?"

Doc Saturday's Midnight Medicine Show

Mike Marcus

Reggie stopped outside the beat-up Winnebago behind the red and white striped circus tent, watching the crew move equipment ahead of tonight's show. He'd do anything for Doc, but damn he hated his boss's camper. There was just something about it that sent a chill straight down his spine. In the midday sun, it was just another camper with fading paint and peeling bumper stickers. But at twilight, it gave him the heebie-jeebies; the windows vacant eye sockets in a vehicle-size skull, the bent bumper a twisted, toothless grin. The hair rose on Reggie's neck as he stood there finishing his cigarette, putting off climbing inside to wake Doc for the show. He took a final puff and dropped the butt to the ground, grinding it into the dirt with one worn loafer. The camper's heater pumped a thin stream of steam out the vent pipe on the roof. It was 65 degrees outside, but inside Doc had the heater running full tilt.

"Doc! Hey, Doc. Time to get up," Reggie said, holding the aluminum door open behind his lanky frame as he stepped into the dark Winnebago and raised a window blind. "It's an hour till showtime. Looks like we got a big crowd tonight." The heat inside hung like a wet, heavy blanket and smacked Reggie in the face as soon as he opened the door. If he let the door close behind him, the camper transformed into a sauna. Doc said the heat reminded him of home, though he never mentioned where that might be. Reggie assumed it was somewhere in Louisiana from the Cajun patois that peppered his speech.

"Close that door, if it do ya', Reverend," muttered a deep voice from the bed in the far corner of the room. The mattress and box spring stacked on the floor consumed much of the space that doubled as living room and bedroom. A thin sheet covered the large black man from the waist down and one thick, tattoo-covered arm was thrown across his eyes. "You know that cold doesn't agree with me."

Reggie took a deep breath of fresh air and closed the camper door. He peered out the small dirty window at the former circus tent that housed Doc Saturday's Midnight Medicine Show. The sound of the show band's brass horns slipped into the camper over the hum of the heater. Most of the show team were already in the tent, but a few were still puttering around the mishmash of cars, trucks, and campers haphazardly scattered around the grass lot. A full moon was just starting its ascent above the tree line. Full moon shows were a bit unpredictable, but wasn't that always a risk with Doc?

"You should know, we had to run off a townie earlier today," Reggie said. "He was looking for his wife. Said she came to last night's show with a girlfriend and never came home."

Doc chortled and pulled back the sheet from the other side of the bed, revealing a shapely bare female back, her face hidden by a tangle of red curls. "She wouldn't happen to be a real redhead named Lizzie, would she?"

"Shit Doc, is she dead?" Reggie said, immediately thinking of the incident outside Lansing when he discovered a healthy-looking 43-year-old woman dead in Doc's bed while he was in the shower. Only later Reggie learned she had a heart defect that finally gave out on her, though he was confident her exertions with Doc played a part in her demise. The fear of finding another corpse in Doc's bed still wormed its way into Reggie's head from time to time.

The woman's deep snore answered Reggie's question.

"Oh, she alive." Doc rubbed one large, calloused hand over his shaved head. "She just plain worn out. I tried to tell her to bring her friend with her last night. She said no. Said she wanted me all to herself. Well, she got all of me, alright. Hand me my bottle, Rev."

Reggie handed his boss a half-empty bottle of dark rum from the counter. "I don't know how you do it. Traveling from town to town, a show every night we aren't traveling, then at least one woman in your bed half the day. When do you sleep? Keep going at this pace and you're going to find yourself in an early grave."

"Nothing more comfortable than a well-dug grave. Better than a featherbed." Doc took a long pull from the bottle. "Sleep is overrated. There's time to sleep when you're dead."

Doc gently shook the snoring woman, whispering in her ear. She rolled over onto her back, one thin arm flung across her eyes. The sweaty sheet bunched around her waist, revealing her pale, freckled breasts. The sunset painted her skin a golden tan far different than its natural alabaster. A plain gold cross on a cheap chain stuck to her sweat-slicked breast just above the faint outline of a love bite. If she was careful, her husband wouldn't see the mark until it faded into an indistinguishable bruise. It would eventually disappear and be forgotten, as all bruises are, but the night with Doc wouldn't. It was branded on her soul. Regardless what she tried—her husband, other men, women, alcohol, drugs—she would never again experience the unadulterated, orgasmic exhilaration she did with Doc in that rundown Winnebago. None of the women who shared Doc's bed ever did.

Doc gently brushed the red curls from her sweaty face and smiled at the exhausted woman as her eyes fluttered open, the light from the window glinting on his gold front tooth. "Ma petite, it is time for you to wake. I have to go to work and you need to go home. Your husband came looking for you this morning, ma chérie. Be careful when you go home. I wouldn't want to see you hurt." Doc turned to Reggie. The gentleness he showed the woman in his bed disappeared, replaced with a steely hardness. "Was it just the husband? No others?"

"Just the husband, but he wasn't happy when Big Hank sent him on his way. I expect he'll be back." Reggie handed Doc a cigar and a wooden match from the box on the counter. "Maybe it's time we moved on. The season's just about over. Why don't we just pack up after tonight's show?"

His boss left the question hanging in the air unanswered. Doc's eyes never left Reggie's face as he tucked the cigar between his teeth and lit the old-style match with his fingernail. The flickering orange flame danced around the end of the cigar until the cherry glowed red and a small cloud of sweet tobacco smoke wafted to the trailer ceiling.

Doc puffed twice, finished the bottle, and tossed it back to Reggie.

"How long we been together now, Reverend?" Doc asked, the cigar clenched between his teeth. The cherry glowed hot in the dark bedroom, flickering orange with each puff.

"A long time, Doc. Can't say I right remember exactly how long."

"Yes. And in all that time, have we ever closed down before the feast of All Soul's Day?"

"No, sir. Not that I can recall."

"And we never will. Fat Tuesday to All Soul's Day. That's my travel time and we be sticking to it, no matter the angry husbands. You just focus on the show. Don't worry about 'dem coming back. After tonight we got one more town and then we be done for the season."

Doc yanked the sheet from the half-awake woman's body and playfully smacked his hand down onto her bare thigh. She jumped up onto her knees on the bed and clutched the sheet to her breasts, suddenly aware of her very exposed nakedness. Doc leaned in close and gently stroking her flushed cheek. "I'm sorry, ma chérie. I wish I could let you sleep but I cannot. I'm sure you understand."

She started to protest, grasping his large hand and kissing his palm. "No, ma petite," he whispered, pressing one thick finger to her lips. Crimson lipstick was smeared across her face, black rivers of mascara lined her cheeks. "We had our time together, but now we must part. I belong to only one woman, though I love you all. Now I have work to do and you must go."

She nodded silently and released his hand as he stood and turned away from her. "I want her gone before I get out of the shower," Doc growled at Reggie before heading into the small bathroom, the sweet white cigar smoke trailing behind him.

* * *

Reggie was sipping a cold Coke on a steamy night at the Fulton County Fair the first time he saw Doc Saturday perform a miracle.

Reggie never missed a carnival passing near his little town. The Reverend Reginald Hoskins was the god-fearing minister of the First Baptist Church of Pine Bluff, but as a boy he grew up on stories of carnivals and traveling shows. Every Christmas he looked forward to visits from Uncle Bill.

Bill Hoskins was a war hero with a cigar box full of medals, but it was his stories from the road that captured young Reggie's imagination. Uncle Bill was known on the carnival circuit as Hercules Hannigan, resident strongman for C&K Traveling Sideshows. Between youth groups, Sunday School, and bible study, Reggie spent every free moment of his youth dreaming of joining a carnival, chasing the summer from town to town, and returning home for the winter only to wait for the weather to warm and do it all over again. Even as an adult, that itch for the carnie life seemed to return whenever posters showed up in businesses along

Main Street and under the windshield wipers of cars in the Piggly Wiggly parking lot.

That hot August night, Doc Saturday was one of a dozen ragtag conmen and hucksters along the back of the carnival, away from the crowds that packed the midway. These men were the last threads tying the modern carnival to the old traveling shows, a forgotten bit of carnie history that was going the way of fortune tellers, the freak show, and the hoochie coochie girls with their suggestive dances.

The further the Reverend wandered along the shadowy carnival perimeter, the deeper he slipped into the past, into the old carnivals that filled Uncle Bill's stories. While the midway was brightly lit and filled with laughter and the carousel's tinny calliope, the back row was lined with snake-oil salesman hocking their wares. The sugary-fried aroma of fresh funnel cake that wafted through the midway air was replaced by the stink of manure and desperation.

At the far end of the lane, a crowd gathered around a low stage in front of a cheap purple tent. The Reverend pulled up short of the stage, stopping next to a grizzled carnie leaning against a light post, his tam pulled down low over his eyes. They watched in silence as Doc Saturday sat on an upturned apple crate, plucking a blues rhythm on a well-worn acoustic guitar. He was oblivious to the crowd as he played, singing in a low, gravelly voice. Behind him, a tattered red banner hung on the tent reading:

Doctor Saturday
Fortuneteller
Purveyor of Charms and Amulets
Healer

The Reverend watched the man on stage for a moment, finished his Coke, and dropped the glass bottle into the nearby trashcan. "What's going on?"

"See that little girl down in front, with the blond pigtails?" the man said, gesturing toward the front of the crowd with a misshapen hand. The Reverend could just make out the girl standing with an equally blond woman he assumed was her mother. "Born blind. Parents took her to every doctor, but they can't do anything. Doc is gonna help her."

The Reverend watched for a few moments as the crowd grew antsy and Doc Saturday continued to play his guitar, his eyes downcast. "Seems kind of cruel to play on their hopes with a little girl that young," Reggie criticized. "I understand it's part of his schtick, but it just doesn't seem right. I hope he isn't taking them for too much."

The carnie turned his head and for the first time the Reverend could see his eyes. One was large and bloodshot, the other appeared to be glass and looked just slightly askew. "I've been with this show for a few years. Ain't nobody like Doc. Some of these guys are scammers, but he's the real deal. He doesn't let them pay, though everyone knows he's fond of his cigars and rum."

The carnie turned his mismatched eyes back to the stage. Doc Saturday was still playing, though he slowed for a moment when the mother placed a bottle and cigar box at his feet. Doc smiled kindly at the girl, nodding his head in beat with the music, the muscles in his large, tattoo-covered arms shifting and writhing beneath his dark skin like snakes. The Reverend found himself tapping his foot in time to the music. His living room radio set was on the local Christian station, but there was something about the way the man played the guitar that pulled at him.

Without flourish Doc finished the song and lay the guitar in its case. Elevated above the crowd on the small stage, he was a mountain of a man in simple black pants and a white tank top undershirt. After a moment, he nodded to the girl and her mother and reached down, helping them onto the stage. The restless crowd went silent as a grave.

Doc whispered briefly into the girl's ear, then did the same with her mother. The little girl giggled at the man's whisper but her mother blushed like an early autumn apple, the color rising in her cheeks as Doc's lips fluttered close to her ear. Doc set the girl on his wooden crate and had the mother stand behind with her hands on the girl's shoulders. From a trunk at the back of the stage, Doc withdrew a bottle of rum and a battered black top hat, the sides slightly dented and the brim bent in places. He turned to face the crowd and placed the hat on his head, carefully adjusting its tilt until he was satisfied. He pulled the cork from the bottle with his teeth and spit it into the dirt behind the stage before drinking deeply. Doc took a short, thick, dark cigar from his pocket, tucked it between his teeth, and lit a match with his fingernail. The last of the carnival noise faded and melted into the background and the crowd gathered around the low stage held their breath as the man puffed at the cigar a few times until the cherry glowed red.

"Open your eyes, ma chérie, and keep them open for me," the man cooed quietly to the girl. The cataracts that covered her eyes glowed thick and white in the lights scattered around the stage. She chewed her lower lip and her tiny hands fidgeted in her lap. Doc puffed the cigar three more times, blowing the white smoke into her open eyes. After the last cloud of cigar smoke faded, he gently closed her eyes with his thick fingers and covered them with one large hand that nearly enveloped half of her face. His lips moved silently as though he were praying. Finally, he leaned forward and kissed the girl on her forehead. As his lips made contact with her sweaty skin, two electric lights overhead blew out in sharp flashes and sparks and the crowd broke its silence. Reggie felt like he'd just stared into a camera flash and, as his eyes adjusted, he saw Doc's broad, dark face turn to that of a smiling skull grinning down at the girl. Reggie rubbed his eyes and the image of the skull was gone.

Doc sat back on the chest from which he'd withdrawn his top hat and gestured to the bottle of rum the woman had put on the edge of the stage. A carnie at the edge of the crowd tossed him the bottle and the healer drank deeply before wiping his mouth with the back of his hand. At her mother's urging, the girl opened her eyes and squealed. The plaques were gone, and her blue eyes searched the crowd before she looked over at Doc Saturday's smiling face.

* * *

"Ladies and gentlemen," bellowed Reggie into the handheld microphone, his voice rolling like thunder through the big top tent as he strolled across the stage, "welcome to Doc Saturday's Midnight Medicine Show. I am Reverend Reggie Hoskins and I will be your guide this evening." Reggie looked the part of a New Age reverend in black dress pants with a razor-sharp crease and a snow-white dress shirt open at the throat, the sleeves rolled halfway up his wiry, muscled forearms.

In these moments, alone on stage in front of the crowd, Reggie thought of his old church, though his congregation could never rival the size of Doc's audience in even the smallest towns. Years ago, he would pace around the pulpit every Sunday morning, reading from scripture and slowly ramping up the intensity of his preaching until the sleepy congregation rose to a rolling boil. Then, watching the clock mounted high on the wall above the church door, he'd time his sermon to bring them back down again just in time to pass the collection plate, their brows sweaty and voices hoarse as they reached into their wallets and gave more than they intended. He had been the star of the show in Pine Bluff, but he'd accepted long ago that under Doc Saturday's tent he wasn't the main act or even second fiddle. He didn't necessarily feel like a pastor anymore, but Doc insisted he continue to be called Reverend.

The wooden bleachers surrounding the stage were filled. The show didn't really advertise, but a few of the crew hung posters around town the day they rolled in and set up. Somehow, they always filled the seats. Most would say they were drawn to see Doc Saturday, though they didn't really know why they were there. They just knew they had to be in attendance. And as usual, there were far more women than men. From college coeds to grandmothers, the bleachers were always disproportionally filled with women.

"Welcome to the stage the man leading the band, Mr. Bobby Johnson," Reggie said, gesturing toward the risers where a dozen musicians sat with their instruments. Bobby Johnson waved to the crowd before ripping a lightning-fast blues riff on the cherry red Fender guitar in his hands. He looked like a blues man from another era in his black suit and matching Fedora, a ruby red band around the crown of the hat.

"And now, ladies and gentlemen, I have a question for you," Reggie purred into the microphone, squinting against the hot spotlight. He paced the stage, feeling the audience settle back into their seats. "Are you ready to be healed? Are you ready to have the healing waters wash over you and relieve you of your suffering, of your aches, of your grief and sorrow? We all ail in some way and that's why we are here tonight. Something brought you here tonight to see the Doctor, to ask him to help you."

Reggie kept his pace and volume even and low, playing with the audience's anticipation while Bobby picked up the pace of the low bass line, adding in more musicians until the audience began stomping their feet in rhythm with the band. Reggie glanced up and a shiver ran down his spine; the full moon had risen into view through the opening in the tent. Full moon shows always brought a special energy and tonight was no different. "That is why we're here tonight, to soak in the healing waters of the blues and walk away just a little bit better than how we arrived. Without further ado, I give you Doc Saturday's Midnight Medicine Show!"

Colored spotlights mounted high on the tent poles circled and spun in a dizzying array of color and movement, dancing over the crowd before all at once dropping the tent into complete darkness. The band continued a steady blues beat. Doc's humming, broadcast by the speakers, filled the tent like a distant roll of thunder. A thin plume of white smoke rose from the center of the spotlight, growing bigger, morphing into a column that rose up sixty feet and escaped through the tent's opening, rising into the night sky like an offering to the moon.

Doc's humming grew louder as the band and others joined until the wordless song rocked the tent. Some in the crowd stood and found the rhythm, swaying to the beat, their hands raised skyward. They didn't know the tune, but it didn't matter. In the darkness the music brought them together until it filled the tent like a tornado of sound, the audience chanting, clapping, stomping to a song as familiar as their own heartbeat.

Doc's voice cut through the roar of the crowd. "Thank you, ladies and gentlemen. Thank you very much. I'm Doc Saturday and we're here tonight to heal all your ills."

At the last syllable the tent lights flashed on, revealing Doc's imposing figure sitting on his familiar upturned apple crate, a seafoam green electric guitar in his hands. The last remnant of the smoke thinned and rose around him as the crowd settled back into their seats and Doc started his first song. Reggie knew all the tricks and effects the man incorporated into the show, but Doc never revealed how he appeared in the column of smoke. The stage didn't have a trap door.

Nearly an hour later, after a dozen delta and Chicago blues classics full of back and forth between Doc and Bobby, the healer nodded his thanks to the cheering crowd. Reggie stood at his usual spot just off stage, only stepping on to entertain the audience when Doc or the band needed a moment to reset before the next tune. Doc smiled over at him and set his guitar down, pulling a thick cigar from inside the apple crate.

Throughout the show, the smoke from Doc's cigar wafted throughout the large circus tent, winding its way around the crowd like a glowing serpent, slipping through the rows. They may not have realized it, but that tiny bit of mystical smoke was Doc's gift to his audience, in addition to the music. It wasn't going to cure cancer, but everyone left feeling a bit better, just a little happier and healthier than they were when they entered.

As the second set was ending, the clock passed midnight and the moon hung high above the tent, a crewmember crackled into Reggie's earpiece that Doc's special guest had arrived. Occasionally, Doc invited someone to the show from his carnie days, though they were usually already in their seat when the show began. Reggie stepped off the stage and frowned as Big Hank appeared at the tent entrance with a dark-haired boy in a wheelchair, followed closely by a woman Reggie recognized.

Three days ago, the crew caught Evie McGovern wandering around the camp while the crew was setting up the large tent. She insisted on speaking with Doc, finally explaining to Reggie that a few years back she'd seen him heal a girl who suffered seizures. Her boy broke his back three years ago and she was hoping Doc could help him. They'd turned her away, but somehow Doc must have heard and decided to heal the boy. He seemed to always know what happened in the camp.

The boy couldn't have been more than eight years old, and his thin legs were wrapped in metal braces attached to heavy, thick-soled shoes.

He looked frightened, his eyes scanning the tent until they settled on Doc. As the last notes of a big, brassy Chicago blues number quieted, Doc gestured for two stagehands to bring the boy on stage and they wheeled him up just shy of where Doc sat.

Doc continued to play the guitar quietly, his microphone on the ground next to him. Reggie could hear Doc singing to himself, the rumble of his voice rolling across the stage in the quiet tent as everyone watched with bated breath. Reggie knew Doc was in the trance-like focus that always came near the end of the show, particularly when he was channeling his energy. Reggie grabbed a microphone and stepped onstage.

"Ladies and gentleman, our evening is coming to a close and we would like to thank each and every one of you for coming out this evening. Before we go, we'd like to introduce a special guest," Reggie said, recalling what Evie McGovern had told him outside Doc's camper three days ago. "This is Donnie McGovern. Those of you who live nearby probably know Donnie and his mother, Evie. Donnie was thrown from a horse about three years ago and severely injured. While we all will be leaving the show a little better tonight, Doc has agreed to help Donnie in particular."

Doc glanced up at Reggie and nodded slightly while continuing to play. The bit of extra mojo from the full moon show along with tonight's crowd fed him an energy that seemed to fill and revitalize him. He'd looked tired earlier today, but at that moment, the man on stage looked years younger, his eyes glowing with the energy coursing through his veins. Reggie almost felt bad for whichever woman would be going to Doc's camper with him after the show tonight—she was certain to experience Doc's full appetite and, for some, it was too much to handle.

Doc set his guitar aside and began the ritual Reggie had seen countless times since he'd joined the show so many years ago. The battered top hat. The lighting of a new cigar. The low chanting. The blowing of smoke into the child's face and then Doc sitting back onto the apple crate, drinking his rum until he regained his senses.

Moments later, young Donnie McGovern took his first unassisted steps in three years. Evie laid a new box of cigars and an expensive-looking bottle of rum at Doc's feet before turning and walking off stage with her boy, the wheelchair left behind.

As the last of the audience departed and the tent flaps closed behind them, Doc rose from his apple crate, placed his guitar back into its case, and wandered back to his camper, the bottle of rum in his hand and the faint whisp of cigar smoke trailing behind him.

* * *

A shotgun blast shattered the quiet that blanketed the camp in the early morning hours after the show. Reggie stumbled barefoot out into the darkness, hoping it was just a truck backfiring or one of the crew playing with fireworks. The shouts that filled the air ended that hope as the crew ran toward Doc's Winnebago. The last Reggie saw of him, Doc had been grinning from ear to ear, climbing into his camper with a busty woman with long, dark braids.

Four men with shotguns faced the camper, the headlights of their trucks glaring on its side. Most of the crew formed a wall between them and Doc's camper, though the crew hadn't a weapon among them. Reggie pushed his way forward and, at the front of the group, recognized the husband they'd chased off the day before. His wife lay half-conscious at his feet, his large fist wrapped in her hair.

Bruises tinged her eyes and her nose had shifted grotesquely to the left with a smear of blood. She still wore the blue flowered dress Reggie saw her leave in the day before, but now it was ripped and she clutched it to her chest with one hand to keep it from falling.

"Where is the bastard who did this to my wife? He's in there, isn't he?" the man shouted, brandishing his shotgun. The crew didn't budge.

Reggie stepped forward, raising his open hands. He could taste the adrenaline flowing through his veins. "Let's just take a moment and calm down a little. Doc Saturday did not do that to her and we all know it. Why don't we put down the guns and talk about this? There's no reason for anyone else to get hurt. We've got a nurse on staff. Can she help your wife? From the looks of it, she could use some medical attention."

The man stepped forward, pushing her face down onto the dry scrub grass. "There ain't nothing to talk about. But your boss better git out here and do it pretty damn quick. It's going to be a lot worse for him if we have to go in after him."

The camper door swung open and a hot breeze swept across the field. Doc stood silently in the doorway. The tattoos covering his arms glowed in the moonlight. He clenched an unlit cigar in his teeth and held the remnants of Evie McGovern's bottle of rum. The crew parted as he stepped down from the camper and stood next to Reggie.

"What's going on here, Rev?" Doc asked as though he didn't see the men backlit by the headlights. "I was just getting to know my new friend when all this noise out here disturbed me, and you know I don't like to be disturbed."

"These men want to have a word with you, Doc," Reggie said, turning to look up into the face of the taller man next to him. Doc always towered over Reggie, but tonight he seemed even bigger, his arms thicker. "He believes you did this to his wife. She was at last night's show."

Doc's gaze dropped from the men to the woman on the ground behind them. His jaw tightened as he took in her tears, her bruises, her blood.

Doc looked up at the husband, his eyes were wide and wild, the whites glowing in the headlights. "I've never hurt a woman and I never will. It is not my way. This is your one chance to leave. Never come back or I will show you what happens to men who hurt women."

As Doc stared at the man, the breeze turned to a steady wind. Sandy grit and dry grass whipped through the maze of vehicles and blew the ball cap from the head of one of the gunmen, who turned to watch it tumble and roll off into the darkness. Reggie glanced up at Doc and noticed the top hat perched on his head, though he'd swear Doc hadn't been wearing it when he came down out of the camper. Despite the rising wind, the hat never shifted on Doc's head.

The husband shrugged off one of his friends who tried to pull him back toward the trucks. Without a word, he stepped toward Doc, leveled the shotgun, and fired both barrels.

Reggie's ears rung and the world spun. He was still standing, but he wasn't sure who was more surprised—him or the husband, still holding the smoking shotgun aimed at him and his boss. Reggie ran his hands over his chest and stomach, checking for blood. Maybe he was in shock from being shot and his body hadn't reacted yet. He'd felt the shot punch him in the chest and burst out his back, but there was no blood. No injury, except to the Winnebago behind him. One flat tire and two shattered windows. Light from inside the camper streamed out through the broken windows; the ripped shades fluttered in the rising wind.

Doc snatched the shotgun from the husband and flung it into the darkness. "You stupid, stupid boy. You hurt her and then blame me. You don't know who you're messin' with. You don't deserve the breath that fills your lungs. You have no honor." Doc's voice rose over the wind. A rumble of thunder rolled across the field, though there wasn't a cloud in the sky. Doc pulled a match from his pocket and flicked it with his fingernail, the fire sputtering for a moment. "I know who you are, Billy Watkins. I've seen the tarot cards and I've rolled the bones. Your Hanged Man card has turned up. You done nothing with your life but cause pain. Pain for your momma and pain for your wife. You haven't earned your days in this world, maybe you can earn them in the next."

The truck headlights exploded in bursts of sparks and shattered glass, plunging the field into darkness. Doc's voice roared out like a tornado. "You don't know me, but I know each of you and I've seen your headstones. I am the grave digger. I am the loa of the cemetery. I am the bearer of the dead." As the wind rose to a fever pitch, his words rang out. "I am Baron Samedi and I say your living days are done on this world, but you will have no rest." In the glare of the match, Reggie again saw the skull-like face he'd seen at the carnival the first time he laid eyes on his boss. As Doc lowered the match, the skull grew brighter, like the white glow of a lightning strike. Doc laughed a deep, rolling boom that shook the leaves on the trees.

Someone pushed Reggie to the ground and he scrambled to the Winnebago as the show crew fell upon the intruders. Shotguns fired blindly and by the muzzle flashes, Reggie saw the men fall one by one. They were ravaged by ghouls and wraiths, spirits and ghosts that bore a resemblance to the people he knew. The locals had no idea what happened and, in just a few minutes, all that remained were their bloodied, broken bodies lying in the dirt.

Baron Samedi never moved, a broad, toothy smile still creasing his skull-like face as he watched his minions slaughter the men. Finally, he stepped forward as the ghoul that was Big Hank held the kneeling Billy Watkins by the throat. He was bloodied, but still alive. Baron Samedi took him by the hair and stared into his eyes. "I have no patience for men who hurt women. You will suffer more than the rest. You led them to their death and their blood is on your hands, but they were stupid to follow you. Now you belong to me."

Samedi pulled deep on his cigar and blew a large cloud of glowing white smoke into Billy's face. Hank dropped him to the ground, but as the body fell, in its place was the ghostly, glowing image of the man. Billy's ghost stared wide-eyed at his corpse in the dirt, his spirit frozen in place by the sight of his own death. "Big Hank, see to the clean-up," Samedi said before turning back toward his camper. He stopped just outside the door. "Reverend, come inside. We need to talk."

Reggie cowered by the blown-out camper tire. He should be dead. Billy hadn't missed. Somehow, he didn't have a scratch. And then the people he'd known for years turned into monsters and tore the men limb from limb. Now they were back to their familiar human forms, cleaning up the site of the slaughter like it was nothing. Like they were simply cleaning up after a show. Off to the side, Big Hank was talking to Billy Watkins' ghostly form. Over just a few minutes, the glow had faded from his spirit until he looked as corporeal as the others. Lenore and Sally, the camp nurses, gathered the unconscious woman and carried her back to their trailer. Others were digging graves where the bodies of the dead men lay, their blood soaking into the dry ground. Finally, Reggie climbed to his feet and opened the Winnebago door.

Doc stood just inside with the woman who'd accompanied him to the trailer after the show. The skull face of Baron Samedi was gone, replaced by the face Reggie knew so well. Her clothes were askew and tears ran down over her cheeks. "I'm sorry, ma chérie, but I have some business to attend to." He gently guided her out the door. She walked across the lot as though in a trance, passing the crew without notice, climbed into her car and left as calmly as if she were driving to the grocery store.

Doc turned and sat on a rickety wooden chair at the small table in the corner, a glass of rum in front of him, the top hat still perched on his head. He kicked the other chair out and gestured for Reggie to sit.

"I know you have questions, my friend," Doc said, sliding the glass of rum over to Reggie. "I will answer them, but first you drink. You been with me a long time, but there's much you don't know. Don't remember. It's time you did."

Reggie gulped down the tumbler of rum as Doc blew a cloud of glowing white smoke into his face. Reggie blinked and tears ran from his eyes as the memories he didn't know he'd lost came flooding back.

He'd first seen Doc Saturday at the carnival when he returned the girl's eyesight. He met Doris that same summer at a church revival in Memphis in 1946, got married a year later. Their son, James, was born two years after. There were sermons and holidays. Births, baptisms, deaths. But then there was the sickness. Taking James to doctor after doctor. Cursing God when he accepted that his boy was going to die. Then the carnival poster in the Piggly Wiggly window and, at the bottom, Doctor Saturday's name. Reggie visited the carnival twice that weekend before bringing James, each time delivering cigars and rum and pleading his case to the healer until finally he agreed to see his boy. Lying to Doris when they went out that night so she wouldn't come along. Doc Saturday told him not to bring her. There was a price to be paid and it was his debt, not hers.

"You healed my boy," Reggie said. "The doctors said it was a miracle. He shouldn't have gotten better, but he did. He went to college. He got married. I held my grandson. Doris died in the hospital. Cancer."

Doc Samedi nodded and sipped his rum. "And then?"

"A car accident and darkness. I woke up here, in this camper, with you."

"And you have served me ever since. We been together now almost fifty years, traveling and healing, playing the blues and having a hell of a time."

"I don't understand…"

"I told you there was a price. You were a preacher and you put all your trust in the Jesus-man. I taunted you. I asked why your God didn't heal your son if he was so powerful. Don't feel bad. You aren't the first to abandon him when you don't get a response. You won't be the last. So, we struck a bargain, you and I. I healed your son and you came to work for me. I was impressed. You didn't hesitate and we drank the rum to seal the deal."

Reggie ran a hand through his thin hair. "Why could I remember some things, but not others? I remembered my church and seeing you that first time at the carnival, but I couldn't remember my wife and son."

"I allowed you the memories you needed to run the crew," Samedi said. "Others I wiped away because they would have just gotten in the way of what I needed from you."

Reggie sat, staring at the glass on the table in front of him, a trace of rum in the bottom. He remembered it all now, the years of traveling with Doc, of serving him during their travels, then the darkness at the end of the travel season, only to be reawakened when Doc decided it was time again.

"Everyone on the crew made some kind of bargain with you."

Samedi refilled the glass in front of Reggie. "They all have a debt to pay. Some made a deal. Others had no honor and don't deserve to rest in the grave. I keep them in my pocket and put them to use. You a good man, Reverend. You're here because you loved your son. And tonight, you tried to save me, even if there was no way they could have hurt me or you. But you didn't know that, now did you? Now, we make a new deal. I can release your spirit to the grave and you can rest forever, your debt paid in full. Or you can travel with me and have a hell of a good time."

Reggie took the bottle of rum and refilled his glass. He looked around the beat-up Winnebago and sipped the liquor. "This damn camper always scared me and I never knew why. There was just something about it that made me uncomfortable. It's because this is where you keep us, right? When we aren't traveling, you keep us all penned up in here, in the dark. The entire crew. You keep us in here while you rest or whatever. It's our prison."

Samedi blew a ring of smoke toward the ceiling, leaned back, and smiled that broad, toothy grin he used with the women he brought back to the camper. "Everyone has their own prison. I'm giving you a choice. Make up your mind. What's it going to be?"

Reggie hesitated, looking into the eyes of the voodoo god sitting across from him. "I should be angry with you. I should be livid that I've been working for you for so long with no idea that I'm dead and without any memory of my family. I was a good Christian. I tried to live a righteous life. I don't know if you're a god or a demon or something completely different, but I don't know if it matters. You gave me time with my son that I wouldn't have had otherwise. Despite what my faith tells me, you can't be all bad. For all of your faults, you help people who need it."

Reggie smiled at the man sitting across from him. He knew a lot about Doc Saturday from the years on the road and he could never turn down a good bargain. "I have a counteroffer. I'll be your assistant, but I keep my memories. When we aren't traveling, I want my freedom. I'll always return as soon as you call for me, but I want to be able to enjoy the life I have now. Someday I may ask you to let me go. But right now, I want to help people and you're my only way to do that. I want to help you heal the living and redeem the dead."

Doc took the glass from Reggie and finished the rum, stubbing out his cigar in a small metal ashtray before reaching out one large hand to shake and seal the agreement.

* * *

Reggie looked over the old paper map spread out on the hood of his truck. They were headed south into Louisiana for one more set of shows before the end of the season. A wad of folded cash was heavy in his pocket, the first time he could remember collecting pay. After the final show, he was headed to New Orleans until Doc called for him again.

"Hey, mister. I'm new and Big Hank said I should ride with you. My name is Billy." The man walking up to the truck looked a little ghostly, but Reggie knew his form would grow more solid until most couldn't tell the difference between him and the living who came to the shows.

Reggie folded the map and shook his outstretched hand. "Good to meet you, Billy. Hop in. It's about time for us to get on the road. We've got places to go, people to heal, and I believe you have a debt to pay."

Grandmother

A.L. Tompkins

There was something intensely satisfying about the scrape of a broom's bristles against the threshold. Dirt swept away, slate wiped clean, order from chaos. Just a few rhythmic passes and everything was set right again. The kids from the cellphone place next door always offered to do a pass with their shop vac when they were closing up for the night, but she turned them down every time. Told them she was old; she was allowed her idiosyncrasies. Good kids, though. Their mothers must be proud.

Maybe that's all it was, an old woman's stubbornness keeping her going. Certainly, there was no one left who could make her do it. Still, she continued. Each night after the last of her guests headed home, full of good food and warm comfort, she'd sweep the tracked-in dirt back out the door and into the street. Sometimes it clung harder than others, but she always got her way in the end. Good riddance.

The sign above the door had been off for nearly an hour, but she used the light of the ever-burning lamp beside the door to pack and light her pipe. Her last ritual of the day, breathing out a lungful of smoke into the crisp air and reading the wisps and curls for hints of what tomorrow might bring.

She was frowning at a particularly twisted bit when two young women made their way past the restaurant, the heels of their boots scuffing against the sidewalk.

"—and he says he needs more space. Like, we've only seen each other three times this month, how much space can he need?" The young woman tucked her chin into the collar of her coat to escape the night air, but it did nothing to muffle the bitterness in her voice as she complained to her friend. "I'm just so sick of the mixed messages."

The huff of laughter escaped before she could think to hold it back. Both women glanced back at her, startled in the way of people who expected a conversation on the street, however loud, to remain private. Not promising, but she'd take a crack at it. It was in her blood to meddle.

"There's nothing 'mixed' about it. You just don't like the message he's sending you." She puffed on her pipe, releasing a thin ribbon of smoke. "How do the kids say it? 'He's just not that into you.'"

She met the young woman's gaze squarely, letting compassion smooth away humor. "Don't you deserve better than that?"

Expression caught somewhere between embarrassment and offense, the woman turned away, muttering with her friend as they hurried up the street.

She shrugged, hooking her pipe over her teeth. She'd tried.

"Kids never change," she groused to the crisp night air. "Think they know everything."

The night, for once, kept its opinions to itself.

* * *

Nothing in this world lasted for long; no one knew that better than she did. Things changed over the years, sometimes drastically, but one of the most comforting constants was food. Sure, the flavors might transform, or the method of preparation, but everyone had to eat. Young or old, rich or poor, all everyone wanted was something tasty to fill their bellies. And everyone who came to Grandmother's got it in spades.

She slid the last golden-crisp potato pancake onto a plate and tucked a ramekin of her homemade sour cream next to the stack. Beside her, Marianne ladled up some beetroot stew. Marianne gave the rim of the bowl a careful wipe with a towel before putting it up on the stainless-steel counter for Kristie or Helena to whisk away to the dining room. The familiar scents of garlic, paprika, and frying bacon wrapped around them all like a downy soft blanket.

She slipped her apron off to hang beside the door and left the kitchen in her assistant's capable hands. Marianne had turned up at her door one night years ago with a haunted look in her eyes and hands that trembled so hard she could barely hold a spoon. After watching her polish off two bowls of pelmeni and broth, she'd offered the other woman a place to stay and a job, no questions asked, and had never been given a reason to regret it.

Especially since it freed her up to leave the kitchen from time to time and check on her guests. No one who frequented Grandmother's would ever drink to excess, or be rowdy, or rude to her teenage servers, but it still didn't hurt to remind them just whose house they were receiving hospitality in.

She checked on a few tables, to make sure everyone was enjoying their dinner, and was met with smiles and enthusiasm. Candles and contentment kept everything warm and golden, with the muted clink of glasses and silverware providing a comforting background.

Halfway across her little thirty-table dining space, she paused beside a booth holding two young men.

"Nicholas," she said, after polite greetings were exchanged. "How is your mother doing?"

Nicholas hastily wiped his face with a napkin, sitting up straight. "So much better. That tea you sent her was really something. Thank you, Grandmother Yaga."

She patted his shoulder and didn't point out the crumbs he'd missed on his cheek. Nicholas was always well-mannered, and he'd been smart enough to ask her advice when his mother's doctors had been frustratingly vague. Such a good boy.

His companion spoke up for the first time. "Yaga? Like the witch?" There was laughter in his tone, like he was waiting to be let in on some joke.

"Something like that," she said, mildly.

Once they'd hailed her as a goddess and sacrificed whole oxen to her in hopes of gaining her wisdom or to appease her wrath. Then the world had turned and they'd branded her a witch, whispering about how she'd steal unattended children for her stew pot.

It was funny, in a way. No matter the stories they told, they never seemed to veer far from her fondness for fresh meat.

Even in the worst times, when they saw her as little more than a beast in the woods, they still called her "Grandmother" and spoke her name with hushed respect.

"Hey, knock it off." Nicholas reached across the table to smack the other man's shoulder.

"What? I'm just asking."

Nicholas shot him a look. "Do you really want to risk insulting the person who makes your favorite blini?"

Mouth hanging open, the young man shot a half-panicked look up at her and hunched forward over his plate defensively, as if he really thought she'd snatch away the little buckwheat cakes.

She laughed, waving them both off. "Don't worry. No offense taken."

It took almost an hour for her to complete her rounds, touching a shoulder here, exchanging a greeting there, to make sure all her guests were seen to. By then it was time to return to the kitchen, and she did so greatly satisfied. Full bellies and full hearts under her roof, and the cold wind stayed firmly outside.

* * *

It was past closing and she'd long since shooed her workers off home. The floors were gleaming, the kitchen put to rights, and the lights off. All that remained was to sweep the threshold and have her last smoke of the evening.

She'd gathered up her broom and her pipe both and headed for the door when the light outside dimmed. Clouds scuttled over the face of the moon, casting the world in patterns of shadow. The night was uneasy about something.

Well, nothing to do but go and check.

Just beside her door, pressed up against the brickwork, a figure huddled. Two figures, she realized when she examined the lumpy form a little more closely. A woman carrying a child had flattened herself against the wall as though she was trying to merge herself with it. She rocked ever so slightly, a soothing, repetitive motion, but controlled, trying not to draw attention.

Something had driven them out onto the streets to huddle on a stranger's doorstep in the middle of the night. Nothing good in the air, there. Desperation floated on the breeze, stinking like spoiled milk.

Carefully, now. They wouldn't be the first wounded birds she'd lured into her hand.

"Hello?" She let a little bit of the rust of age into her voice, bending forward as if struggling to see. "Is someone out there?"

Just a frail old lady, nothing to be frightened of. No danger here, little ones. Old women were never a threat, until they were a convenient target.

Still the woman hesitated for a breath, until the little one in her arms gave a tiny sound of distress. Then she stepped forward, but stuck to the places the lamp didn't quite reach.

She probably thought it would hide the bruises better.

"Hello. I'm so sorry to bother you, but..." The young woman paused to swallow, running her hand over her child's back in a soothing gesture. "I'm sorry. I was told I could get some help here."

Always. That was the promise she and her sisters had made, when the world was young and golden-green with potential. All they ever had to do was *ask*.

But all she said out loud was, "Why don't you come inside?"

In short order she had them both sequestered in the booth in the back corner of the restaurant, away from the windows. Not that the night would let anyone peep into her house, but she could hardly explain that without seeming like a dotty old lady.

The young woman, who belatedly introduced herself as Heather, wrapped her hands around the offered cup of coffee but didn't seem interested in actually drinking it.

The little boy, Ryan, didn't have any hesitation tucking into the hot cocoa and cinnamon cookies she put in front of him, but children were often practical about such things.

Heather kept fidgeting, clutching her drink one moment, reaching out for Ryan the next, as if to reassure herself that her son was still there.

She watched them quietly as the tension built between them, each reacting to the other's anxiety. Embarrassment and fear sharpened the lines beside Heather's mouth and she knew if she didn't intervene they would disappear back out her door without ever telling her why they'd come. When Heather bit down on her lower lip, making the split there reopen, she stood.

Both of their heads swiveled in her direction. She handed Heather a napkin, nodding towards the bead of blood at her mouth. "Wait here a moment."

She bet herself there was better than half odds they'd still be there when she got back, then gave herself a mental five dollar win when she returned from the kitchen to see they hadn't moved.

The tub made a small thump when she placed it on the table and she offered Heather a peeler. The young woman took it with a confused look.

"How are you at peeling beets?"

Heather blinked at her, but then obediently lifted one of the lumpy vegetables out of the tub and set to work.

Busy hands could settle the mind, true, but it was more than that. You could tell a lot about someone by the way they went about things. Especially little things. Heather's fingers were slow and fumbling to start, but then her hands steadied out. A little frown appeared between her brows as she concentrated on removing the skin without sacrificing too much of the beet.

She was shaken, but determined. A woman used to doing things that must be done.

That was promising.

Eventually, she started talking.

"He's never been like this before," Heather said in a hushed voice, even now afraid of being overheard. "I mean, he's always had a temper. And sometimes he was mean. But he was always sorry."

"He's never been violent before?"

Heather tucked her chin, never taking her eyes off of the beet in her hands. "Well, he sometimes had fits. He'd just get so angry, he'd break things, but it wasn't his fault. He can't control it."

It was an effort not to set loose the derisive sound lurking at the back of her throat. Instead, she concentrated on her own beet. Long, even strips of peel fell into the tub. "Tell me. When he has these fits of temper, does he ever break his own things? Or only yours and your son's?"

Heather froze, a string of peel dangling. Watching emotions flash over the young woman's face made even her old heart twinge. She kept her expression clear of pity as Heather looked up fully for the first time that night, eyes glassy with tears.

Besides the split lip and the purple bruise dusting her jaw, she didn't have any other visible wounds, but that didn't say much. There might be more under her clothes, or worse, under her skin. *Sometimes he's mean*, she'd said. People of this age had finally started to realize how words could cut worse than knives, how being treated like you were worthless could grind your bones to dust and collapse your soul.

The beet in her hands thudded back into the tub as Heather reached up to bury her fingers in her hair, tugging at the roots. "God, I'm so stupid. I can't believe I just let him…and then running into the night to cry to a stranger—"

She reached across the table to poke the younger woman in the forehead and Heather stared at her, surprised into silence. Ryan gave a tiny breath of a giggle at the look on his mother's face.

Satisfied, she went back to her own peeling. "Don't kick someone when they're already down. Not even if that someone is you."

Heather's mouth finally closed and she blinked, looking abashed.

"Stupid would be not asking for help when you need it. There is no shame in needing help. No shame in asking for it. It's brave." She kept her eyes on her work, giving the younger woman the illusion of privacy as she dabbed at her eyes with her napkin.

When Heather placed the crumpled cloth back on the table so she could run a comforting hand over her son's hair, the bloodstain from her lip gleamed ruby in the dim light.

Blood and tears. She tore her gaze away, forced her lips into a kindly smile. "Come on. There's a place for you to stay upstairs." The apartment had been empty for more than a year; Marianne had long since found her own place, but she kept it clean and well-aired. You never knew when it would be needed. "Get some sleep and we'll sort things out tomorrow. No one will trouble you, and the morning is always wiser than the evening."

She got her charges settled before returning to the dining room to gather up cups and plates. The crumpled napkin was tucked into the pocket of her cardigan.

They'd eaten her food. They'd shed blood and tears in her house. They'd accepted her hospitality and her protection. That gave her the right to act.

When everything was tidied, she stepped out, locking the door behind her.

Then she placed her palm against the warm brick of the restaurant wall.

"Watch over them."

The building shivered under her hand, like a great bird settling its feathers.

She turned and walked into the night.

* * *

Heather had a lovely home. A neat little bungalow with fresh white paint and edging done in a cheerful blue. The gardens were full of flowers, all wrapped around with a short wooden fence. It was almost idyllic. Pity about the misery clinging to the eaves like tarred spiderwebs.

The door opened under her hand when she asked it to and she stepped inside.

It was just as neat and tidy inside, almost artificially so, but there were still touches that felt homey to her. Small acts of defiance eked out between the cracks like flowers pushing up through asphalt.

She passed through the living room and paused to examine the framed photograph half-hidden behind a potted plant. In the picture, Heather had her arms around a woman a couple of years her junior with similar features. A sister, perhaps.

Julia, the night sighed outside the window.

She nodded her thanks and put the photo back in its place.

The kitchen was the heart of any household and this one was no different. There were more signs of personality here, with the dairy cow salt and pepper shakers and the toy cars on the table. A 'World's Best Mom' mug sat in the sink. Hairline cracks running over its surface told her it had been glued back together, possibly more than once. She clicked her tongue reproachfully before setting it back down.

There was a shuffle from above, then heavy footsteps clomping down the stairs. The scent of stale beer and aftershave wafted through the doorway at her back as she perused Heather's spice cupboard with approval.

Silence behind her, the calm before the storm.

The linen napkin in her pocket warmed. Blood and tears, hospitality and protection.

"Where the hell have you been?" The man's low, furious tone made it a demand, not a question.

She didn't bother to turn, squinting down at the bright yellow package she'd unearthed in the cupboard. Mrs. Dash. Interesting. "I went for a walk." She lifted the packet to her nose, no longer straight as a blade but Heather's gentle upturn, and gave an approving hum at the rich savory aroma that she could smell even through the paper.

"Are you stupid? Where's my son?"

His son. A possession. Interesting. "I—I took him to Julia's," she said in Heather's tremulous voice.

A kitchen chair scraped across the floor, a large, angry sound. "Why the fuck would you do that?"

She was careful to keep her back turned. It wouldn't do for him to see the gleam in her eyes, not yet. "He was upset. I—"

"Upset?" The mocking tone landed like a slap. "You're turning that kid into a pussy. I don't want him near that little bitch." The heavy footsteps came closer. "She's got a big mouth, and never knows when to shut it. I don't want you talking to her anymore."

"No." She kept Heather's voice soft, but firm.

His stomped closer, until she could feel the hot wash of his breath against the back of her head. "What the hell did you just say to me?"

She rested her hands on the marble countertop, fingers spread against the swirling pattern of white and gray. It looked like smoke. "Julia is my family. I'm not going to stop talking to her just because you don't like her."

The tension in the room yanked tight as a noose and she waited to see which way it would snap.

There was an order to things, after all. Some rules were old, even older than her, though it was hard to believe at times. She was the oldest, the Crone. She was wisdom, the repository of knowledge hard-earned, the end of all things.

The young must be taught. If they would not listen to a grandmother's gentle instruction, well, there were other faces, other aspects to invoke.

"You listen to me, you stupid bitch—" His hand clamped down on her shoulder, fingers digging in. Another person would have bruised.

Her lips pursed in displeasure. She'd always disliked rude children.

"—I'm your goddamn *husband*." He yanked her around to face him, ignoring how she didn't stumble into his much larger frame. "I'll teach you to—"

She raised her head and smiled.

He blanched when he caught sight of her iron teeth.

"Oh please, do continue, 'husband,'" she purred in the voice of deepest winter, when the snow piles up to the rafters and everything but hope is extinguished. The night pressed eagerly against the window by the sink, shadows spilling over the counter, down to the floor and up to the ceiling. A cloak of icy darkness curled itself around her shoulders.

"What will you teach *me*?"

* * *

Another busy day gone by and she lowered herself down onto her freshly swept stairs for a well-deserved smoke. Earlier, before the restaurant had opened, she'd seen young Ryan and his mother safely to her sister's. They'd contacted the police to escort Heather home so she could gather their necessities. Her husband hadn't been present, fortunately enough. The police assured her that he was probably just trying to escape the consequences coming his way, but that they'd make sure he didn't bother them.

Incidentally, the new lamp outside the restaurant was working out well. There were days she missed being able to post skulls with glowing eyes around her territory and be done with it, but it would raise too many questions in this age. And she'd relaxed a little as the years went by.

She drew on her pipe and exhaled in a steady stream, watching the smoke unfurl in smooth ribbons up into the sky. A tiny spark jumped, blazing bright in the bowl of her pipe. Her eyes crossed staring down at it. Iron gray brows drew down until they almost touched above her nose.

Well. That was interesting.

"My brother says you're a witch."

She turned towards the cellphone store, where a girl no older than thirteen stood, arms crossed and chin raised in challenge.

She hooked the pipe over her teeth, watching the girl silently as she shifted from foot to foot. Not so unaffected then. It wouldn't do to smile, she reminded herself.

"And what do you think?"

The girl scowled. "There's no such thing as witches."

The words were tossed at her like a dueling glove. She fought back a chuckle, knowing it wouldn't be appreciated, and took another lazy puff.

The girl bristled, indignant. "Well?"

"Well, what?"

One leg jerked, like the girl wanted to stomp her foot like a toddler but resisted at the last second. "Are you a witch or not?"

The corner of her eyes crinkled. No matter the century, one of the greatest joys of old age was riling up the young. "How can I be a witch if they don't exist?"

She expected outrage, or for the girl to make a dismissive comment as she turned away.

Instead, dark eyes fixed on her with an almost calculating air.

"If you're a witch, can you show me how?"

She released a gust of smoke in surprise. Almost against her will, curiosity unfurled its golden petals. When you reached a certain age, the unexpected was the most wonderful gift you could receive. Normally one this young wouldn't fall under her purview. And yet…and yet.

She considered, tapping her pipe against her lip.

It had been a long time since a woman had come to her door with eyes like a moonless night and a gnawing hunger in her soul.

A smile crossed her face. It had far too many teeth to be considered polite. The girl, not taken aback in the slightest, straightened up like a hound spotting prey.

It was promising.

"How are you at peeling beets?"

Age Is Just a Number

Daryl Marcus

Dead private detectives are a dime a dozen.

I've met vampire detectives, zombie detectives, ghost detectives, and more than my share of living detectives marching down their own paths to death by alcoholism or by violent proxy. It's enough to make me wish I'd decided on a different career when I was still young enough to reap the benefits of it.

As far as I know, I'm the only demon detective in the city. My name is Thoth. My history is long and the details muddied with time and interpretation. Suffice it to say, I've been around for a very long time. I've tried to put those years to good use since I started this endeavor.

This particular job came to me like all my jobs do: I was recommended by the friend of a friend who knew a guy who thought he should get in touch with me to see if I was interested. Leaving that story for a tale of its own, I found myself staring through a pair of binoculars at an illegal party in the middle of a plague-ridden Denver. The partygoers were spread throughout a penthouse apartment, moving in and out to the patio and the pool, wearing a mixture of heavy sweaters, bikinis, and nothing.

They were all young people, beautiful people with their lives ahead of them and no cares in the world. All told, there were about three hundred gathered on the roof of the building. Somewhere, in all that press of flesh, I had to find one person and get them out of there before the plague brought them low.

Under normal circumstances I could slip in and out of crowded places without anyone even being aware. The host of this party, however, seemed determined to maintain the privacy of the guests and the exclusivity of access. The whole building was warded against surreptitious entrance.

Admission into the building was supervised by a standard security triumvirate: three guards made up of a wizard, a brute, and a psychic who were working together to scan the surface of the guests' minds. Anyone who tried getting in with a forged invitation, no invitation, or the false pretense of being an invited guest's plus one was kicked to the curb with professional politeness and stern warnings to never return. This was one of the most effective ways to ensure only the right guests entered the building and it was one of the hardest to circumvent.

Magic in the modern era had become way more security conscious than in my youth. I chalked it up to money. Magic used to be a thing of beauty and wonder, like the results of an amazing painting or sculpture. People would flock from miles around to see a true wizard work. Now, if the product of the magic couldn't produce money, it was used to protect money. No one cared about the beauty or the simple art of it anymore, which made anyone using magic strictly for practical purposes as easily mesmerized by spectacle as those without the gift for wielding it.

This was where I could use my strengths to my advantage.

I approached the entrance like any other passerby. It was still early enough in the evening, about 11:00 PM, so that my slow, meandering walk wasn't out of the ordinary. People were still walking the streets, out on dates, enjoying the nightlife. Even in a city besieged by plague, no one seemed to want to admit the better course was staying home and avoiding others as much as possible. The difference between magic and magical thinking was vast.

The wizard of the triumvirate, a short, plump man wearing tortoiseshell glasses and a suit tailored to make him look as good as it possibly could, saw me, looked me up and down, and dismissed me. Of course, what he saw was an unassuming young man in a slightly rumpled and ill-fitting brown suit with windblown hair and a distracted look on his face.

The psychic barely looked in my direction. He, too, wore a well-tailored black suit that streamlined his wiry frame into something more stylish and attractive than he would have been under normal lighting. His mirrored sunglasses never left the river of people flowing along the sidewalk before him. I felt his gaze and his mind flow over my psyche as he evaluated the surface of my mind, seeking my intentions for entry into his building. He found a mind too preoccupied to do anything more than hurry past and be on his way.

His gaze swung over me, past me, paused, then jumped back to me and over me once more. He snapped his fingers and pointed at the couple in front of me trying to make their way to the front entrance.

The brute, a hulking man wearing a brown suit that didn't fit well over his muscles or the sidearm in the shoulder holster, bullied his way to the couple and barred their path with his bulk.

As the confrontation ensued, I finished my illusion. I'd plucked the real invitation from the forefront of his mind using misdirection against the psychic. I couldn't literally take his invitation, but I could make the psychic believe the real one belonged to me and the young man's intentions were the false ones. It took little effort but was worth it when the illusion continued and the lovely young woman slipped away from his side and found her way onto my arm.

Together we walked into the building, both of us looking back like we were interested in the commotion, but not interested enough to delay our entry into revelry.

The wizard didn't glance at me a second time and I sent the young woman up to the party alone on the excuse that I needed the men's room. I could hide from the minds of men, but cameras were a different matter. I didn't want to be seen in an elevator with her once her boyfriend sorted himself out of the mess I'd put him in.

Instead of riding, I climbed. Thirty stories up the stairs, taking my time and walking easy. It wouldn't do to appear winded right before I entered combat or a magic show. I didn't know how the night was going to play out, but being prepared and looking like it are often confused by the unwary.

I paused at the twenty-first-floor landing to take stock of myself. I always wore an off-the-shelf dark suit covered by a nice wool overcoat that hung down to my knees. Even though summers in Denver can get pretty hot, the combination of clothing gave me plenty of pockets for my various magical accoutrements, not to mention it allowed me to look snazzy and fit into almost any gathering outside of a nudist camp.

After brushing a few fibers off the lapels and ensuring the lines were straight, I was satisfied I wouldn't look too out of place in the party. I exited the stairwell and found my way to the elevators. It was the only way a guest could access the penthouse.

The elevator doors opened onto a large foyer. I paused a moment, taking a breath and letting my eyes and senses flow from the elevator into the penthouse. My magic met no resistance and I sensed no additional magical security in place. I didn't even sense the natural ward of threshold that came from entering a home uninvited. Even with my stolen invitation, the house should know whether I was a welcome guest. But not here. Instead, I was welcomed as a guest like any other public place. Despite the setting, this was no one's home. Interesting.

A tall woman in another well-tailored suit examined me and gave me the cursory nod of a bodyguard who didn't expect trouble. I'd made it past the triumvirate, so I had to be cool. She offered to take my coat, but I refused. The top of a building in Denver still has chill winds blowing a bit, even in summer.

Smiling, I let her see my admiration for her dashing figure and stepped past her before she could get offended.

Inside, the mass of people in such close proximity made me shiver. I was thankful for my own breed of immunity against this plague; otherwise, I'd have jumped off the building to avoid dying of it. In every corner of the apartment—every room and on every seating surface; in the pool and against the railing on the outdoor patio—people were in each other's space, talking, laughing, touching, kissing, groping, and many were getting ready to do more. It was an orgy of decadence and denial. Somewhere in all of this I had to find a young woman who shouldn't be here.

But no one belonged here and that was the problem. I couldn't use magic to find my target. There was just too much energy being directed and redirected and redirected again as people sent their bodies and minds about the party in search of pleasure and escape. I wouldn't be able to concentrate enough to get a bead on a single psyche. In addition to all the natural chaos, there was something else going on that I couldn't put my finger on. I could feel the penthouse as if it were a living, breathing thing. It was pulsing with the heartbeat of the guests, and under that was a steady, inaudible hum of power permeating everything, as if the apartment were feeding on the vibes of the party.

Without magic, I would have to use my natural senses. I pulled the photograph of the young woman from my coat pocket, cupped it in my hand, and kept checking it against the faces I could see as I made my circuit through the house. Not subtle, but old-school effective.

As I moved around the apartment, I found myself unconsciously following the flow of bodies in a wide circle that shrunk with each round. The people were pushing me in a spiral, inexorably driving me to a central point at the heart of the party. Without meaning to, I had become another heartbeat in the pulse of the place and the intention of the penthouse seemed to be drawing me toward its center along with the rest of its guests.

I let the press of bodies drive me along, no longer checking the photograph every two steps. They carried me to what would have been the largest bedroom if this were a normal apartment. Instead, the room I was swept into was devoid of furniture, the carpet had been removed, and the bare concrete floor revealed. The central point of the floor had been meticulously cleaned of all glue and debris. Laid into the floor was a golden circle perhaps six feet in diameter. It fairly glowed in the light of candles mounted in short holders.

We moved like a conga line without the rhythm, no music, no smoothness to our motions. We walked along the edges of the room, in one side of the door, around the perimeter, and out the other. It was as if we were touring every inch of the walls while evaluating our desire to purchase the place.

For a moment, I was caught up in the simple beauty of the magic at play here. There was power like I'd rarely seen, and none of the guests even knew it was happening. They smiled. They drank. They danced to tunes no one could hear.

The backbeat of the music faded for me as I entered that room and stepped out of the line of people. I stared at the woman kneeling in the center of the circle. She was beautiful, but her youth had long since been left behind. She was slim, with all the assets of a woman her age. She wore a dress cut to accentuate her figure. It fit in with the crowd and the intention of the party. The glamour she'd cast over herself to hide her own appearance was a good one. In passing I wouldn't have seen it, but with her being the central focus of the penthouse, and obviously the reason this party was taking place, I could see through everything.

She was the young woman I'd come here to find, but she hadn't been young in a long time.

I studied the ring and the music and the ebb and flow of bodies around her and finally understood. The party, the penthouse, even the building itself, was a vortex, drawing the energies of youth and exuberance and excess into this one spot. Even as I watched I saw her skin shift slightly, a year fading from her face, her gnarled hands shrinking and smoothing over her knuckles.

She was siphoning life energy into herself as the people mingled and enjoyed themselves. Everything in this penthouse was designed to create the mood and the situations where people would let go of inhibitions and revel in the exhilaration of simply enjoying themselves. The energy one could collect from such a gathering of people was immense and terrifying. It was also theft of the worst kind. Each year younger she looked was months of life taken from someone in the apartment. With so many people around her, and their ages so close together, none would notice the drain. They were having sex, they were flirting, they were being pumped to give their energies by the music, the food, the drink, and the magic driving them to visit this room and quickly leave. They'd never notice what had been taken from them, never notice the drain, and even if they did, they would chalk it up to the fantastic orgasm or three they'd had with that totally hot complete stranger. They'd had a good time and moved on.

But how much shorter would their lives be for the experience? These people were too young to care. They already believed they were immortal. What's the harm in taking a little life from those who don't know how to appreciate it?

These thoughts went through my head, but I knew they weren't mine. I'd moved closer to the circle to stand directly in front of the woman. Her eyes were open, and her lips were moving in the rhythm of the incantations required to keep the vortex focused and centered on her, but her gaze told me she knew I was there and what I was doing. She wanted me to understand her plight, her quest for eternity and eternal youth and life beyond what she was allotted by the natural order of things.

There is something to be said for silent communication. Direct mind-to-mind contact was as intimate an encounter as could be had. It conveyed so much more than words were capable of. Emotions, sensations, desires, hopes, and dreams all came through clear as an epiphany. You not only know what the other felt, you knew how it felt to them personally. It surpassed sympathy, was deeper and more powerful than empathy, and revealed something deep inside that you could never shake. It was also something rarely done by those of my kind simply for the vulnerability of it all. We don't like to be seen as weak or known for who and what we truly are. We've taken great pains to hide in plain sight. That she revealed herself to me this way proved just how desperate she was.

But she was human, or had been a long time ago. Even as I watched, more years slipped out of her body and she grew younger. The process was moving faster, and with each passing breath she would get younger, look prettier, and be more dangerous.

I looked at the picture in my hand and realized I'd been sent here to stop this, but I didn't know by whom. My job had only been to find her, take her out of this party, and drop her off with her father, yet I knew now she had no living father. The man who'd hired me was what?

A rival? A Watcher? I'm not sure I'd ever know. He'd paid up front, so the job would be done. That was my oath to him and my oath to myself. Once a job was paid for, the job got completed. I couldn't leave her here to do her dirty work, and I couldn't not finish the job. My professional integrity demanded it.

She was thirty now, rapidly approaching her twenties.

Closing my eyes, I let myself feel the magic, feel the options for disrupting this. Depending on the spell she was weaving, I could stop her now and everything would freeze in the current state: she'd be younger, the life force stolen would be hers forever. Or, I could destroy the magic and send everything in the vortex spinning out of control to explode in my face. Rather than saving the partygoers, I could end up killing them all.

"No." The simple denial told me volumes.

Hearing the word jolted me out of my meditation, then the force of the intent behind it sent me stumbling backwards.

She was on her feet, her arms spread, feet planted apart, ready for a fight. She hadn't left the circle, but that didn't matter. She was surrounded by power, filled with it, and she already had it all under her control. I was the intruder here, my invitation stolen from the mind of a guest, and she knew it. The rule of threshold didn't work on me, and this place had never been a home. I wasn't powerless, but I was unprepared.

The vortex of power picked up speed, growing in intensity until I could feel it spinning around me. I lost my balance and stumbled into the crowd of people behind me. They grabbed my shoulders and kept me from falling, then they gripped me harder and held me tight. Their hands found my wrists, ankles, shins, forearms, waist, neck, and hips. The whole crowd was suddenly a prison, keeping me in place as my captor stared daggers at me from the circle.

Would she step out and break her hold on the vortex, or would she merely instruct her new minions to kill me? Did it matter? She didn't feel like the type who would kill on a whim, but I'd been wrong on such counts before.

"I'm not here to hurt you," I said. "I only want to take you someplace safe."

She frowned and the wind died a little. "Someplace safe? I am safe. Who are you? Why are you here?"

In the grip of the partygoers, my hands loosened and the photo of this woman in her youth fluttered to the floor. A young man picked it up and walked it to her. He held up the photograph so she could see it without either of them crossing the circle.

Her eyes widened and fury aged her, stole some of her stolen beauty back. She waved a hand and the young man went crashing into the pile of bodies against the walls. "Who gave you this? Who are you working for?"

These were questions I didn't like giving answers to even if I had them. Anonymity of my clients is something I take pride over. No one gets to my clients through me, ever.

"End this. Come with me and you'll meet them."

She shook her head again, this time denying me. "No. I will not go back. This world is where I belong." She took a deep breath, closed her eyes, and gathered her strength.

In a vortex like this, with this much power already swirling around her and under her control, I didn't have time to make a plan.

I gathered my own strength and reached out with my magic, touching only the minds of those touching me. I wanted them to suddenly feel heat and fire coming from my clothes. They felt what I wanted and their grips loosened just enough.

Yanking myself free, I stumbled deeper into the room, away from the grasping hands. In my pockets I always keep a couple plastic bags of those "snap 'n' pop" firecrackers you find in flea markets by the hundreds. I tossed them with all my might at the floor, at the walls, at the patrons at large.

With a little push of my mind, the small and annoying pops became roars and explosions. Soon the people were yelling, stumbling back from the circle, and trying to exit the room as fast as they could. Someone shouted, "Fire!" Then there was a stampede trying to get away from the witch in the circle and me.

She lost control of the guests when I gave them something else to be witless about. The vortex that had driven them to her and had them dancing around her, giving her their strength and their youth and their exuberance, shifted on her and twisted out of her grasp. The control she'd wielded only a moment before was gone and the magic broke around us.

When a magic spell isn't carried out to completion, things can get unpredictable. That's one of the things that gives magic its power and makes it so dangerous. In a movie or a sitcom, this sudden turn of events would allow the villain to fall and all that she had stolen would be returned to those she'd taken it from without anyone being the wiser. A suddenly twenty-nine-year-old woman would be eighteen again. An old man would return to his middle age status. Any number of people suddenly dying of their genetic diseases would have their youth back and chalk this whole evening up to a night of debauchery and they would be back to their old lives and habits in a day or two.

But this wasn't a movie. This was a world where magic had stepped out of fantasy and into reality. And like anything wild and natural but tamed, it had a nasty streak in it that it liked to use to remind us all that it was incredibly powerful and could do as much damage as it could good.

She shouted her denial one last time, this time at herself and the loss of control I'd caused. The vortex didn't reverse as one might expect. Instead, it burst like a water pipe. Everything she'd pulled into herself escaped the broken circle in all directions. One side of her released a lot more than the other, as magical pressure points, drawn in her tense mental grip, broke and spilled what they contained.

A young man to her left suddenly doubled over like he'd been punched in the gut. Before his knees touched the floor, he was drowning in his suit as the youth of others flooded into him and he was too young to see a PG-13 movie.

In the space of seconds another woman, this one middle-aged but still pretty, regained twenty youthful years as what exploded from the circle held her against the wall and pummeled into her, raising her cheekbones and plumping her lips.

Still another woman, this one too old to have been here in the first place and who might have died tonight had I not entered the building, simply flew apart as the magic that entered her proved too much for her form to gather and hold tight. Beside her, a young man, now covered in her blood, screamed in shock and surprise.

His voice lent more energy to the chaos and the bodies began to writhe and push against each other in an intense need to escape.

I don't know exactly what hit me. It could have been the force of magic alone as it sought places to go and expend itself. It could have been a few decades I didn't want forcing themselves down my throat. It could have simply been her hatred for everything that I stood for. In any case, I found myself unable to move from the floor where I'd been knocked down. Everyone ran around me. Several times I saw high heels and spit-shined shoes fly over my eyes, yet somehow nothing and no one touched me.

It seemed to take hours and probably was only seconds, but when I could think again the world was silent. The wind had died down and I could control myself. I sat up, staring around at the scattered viscera on the floor and walls. Clothes were strewn about the room as if people had simply stepped out of them or were Raptured into oblivion. People had exploded here. People had died here. And in the center of the circle, still surrounded by the youth and magic and time she'd sought to steal for herself, was a crumpled old woman, her body on its side, curled in on itself.

A wave of cold air rolled out of the circle and over me, the last of her magic as the vortex took from her what it had originally given. Somehow, she was still alive and she reached out after the wave, beseeching it to return.

I forced myself to stand up, looked out over the penthouse at the mess the exploding spell had created, and realized there were people still alive in there. Some were younger than when they'd entered. Some were visibly older. One or two were dead, either from the magic, the aftermath, or the stampede of scared people running from something they didn't understand.

I'd caused that. My simple firecracker distraction had been too much, too intense for this place and this night. I was sure this would come back to haunt me one day, but not yet. I had business to finish first.

Turning back to the witch in the circle, I approached. I knelt beside her shrinking form, watched her watch me. I could still feel power boiling beneath the surface of her old, shriveled face.

"Don't get too close," said a woman's voice from behind me. "That one likes to bite."

It was the bodyguard who'd ushered me into the penthouse. Her suit was still clean and stylish, fitting nicely despite the weapons I saw bulging in conspicuous places.

"Why did you allow this to happen?" I asked.

She looked at me, raised an eyebrow as if wondering who the hell I was to ask such questions. "My place isn't to allow or prevent anything. I was instructed to ensure you entered unimpeded. Everything else that happened was between you and her."

I returned my gaze to the witch. Her gaze faltered, fell, to my knees, my feet, and with one final breath, everything she had left flowed out of her in a thin, white mist. I watched her last breath of magic flow down and dissipate like so much vapor on a cold night. The witch folded in on herself and died, fading into the dust of ages long since passed.

"Who are you?" I asked.

"Wrong question, detective. I thought you were better at this."

She was right. The correct question was on my tongue, but it was one I usually didn't want to know. My line of work precluded the relevancy of such knowledge. I couldn't help but ask.

"Who hired me?"

She smiled, as if I were a child guessing the right answer but not knowing why it was right.

"You used to be a god," she said. "You know the end is always around the corner. Death is the inexorable onslaught of the inevitable. It cannot be avoided forever. It stalks. It follows. No matter how far or how fast you run, it will always find you."

I took one last look at the dust on the floor. It had once been alive, vibrant even. And now it was so much flotsam to be blown away. I knew one who would appreciate just such an outcome.

"Osiris," I said, more to myself than her. "He's my employer for this. She must have been very naughty for a very long time."

She nodded, approached the circle, broached it, and scooped up a handful of dust. In ritualistic fashion, she blew the dust off her hand. Together we watched the mist swirl and caper and vanish into the night.

Standing, we looked at each other once more, sizing each other up, deciding not to engage.

"What about them?" I asked, gesturing toward the apartment in general and the individuals still reeling from the effects.

She shrugged. "If they're not dead yet, they're lucky. We'll come for them when the time is right."

"And if they put up a fight?"

She smiled at me, stepped forward and patted my cheek with her dusty hand. "Who cares? Death calls us all, and in the end, we answer it."

She walked past me toward the elevator. I followed more slowly, taking the time to examine a few people and try to help. I could hear the sirens of fire trucks and ambulances and police arriving down below.

"What—" I turned back, the question dying in my throat as I realized I was alone. The bodyguard, a pyschopomp really, was gone. She'd claimed her soul and had moved on to the next job.

As if on cue, my phone vibrated inside my coat pocket. A quick glance at the screen told me I had to make myself scarce. The authorities approaching would not appreciate my presence.

I wrapped my overcoat tighter around me against a sudden chill I was sure only I felt. The witch was dead. Osiris had revealed his hand in the world. And I had a new job to do.

The One About Gone to Flowers

Alma Alexander

"What do you think you are doing?"

The tone was modulated, pleasant, the woman's voice just deep enough to be sexy, but also imperially aggrieved, and Eddie sighed as he turned to face her. In the crowd of protesters he had felt safely anonymous, alone, but of course she had found him without any trouble at all.

She had not been there a moment before, but this was a Goddess and she did what she pleased. She had stepped out from a fold in the air, from a twilight shadow in the waning light between streetlights just beginning to flicker on, to stand there beside him. On the face of it, she didn't really "fit" the moment, the context, or the people who surrounded her on the street. Her narrow feet were upholstered in an expensive pair of heeled leather pumps, an above-the-knee dove-gray pencil skirt showed off long lean legs, and there was a matching tailored jacket over that which nipped in her waist and silhouetted (in a thoroughly professional manner) a delicate full-bosomed but slender figure. The golden torc of the Brisingamen encircled her neck, and earrings that appeared to be falcon feathers dangled from her ears. The ash-blonde hair was scraped back and coiled neatly into a French twist at the back of her head; above a gray cloth mask that color-matched her suit, her eyes, a disturbing shade of deep green like moss under water, glared regally at Eddie. She was his height, maybe even a tiny bit shorter, but she still managed to give the impression of looking down at him.

"Hello, Freyja," he said. "So which one ratted me out? Hugin or Munin?"

Freyja snorted elegantly. "Odin's ravens have better things to do than go flitting back to him tattling on his disobedient children. Did you think he would not know that you were gone?"

Eddie shrugged, then gestured around him, by way of an answer. "This is important."

"A gathering ground for Odin's halls?" Freyja asked, raising her eyebrow.

Eddie's lips thinned. "Whom would he call? The 'warriors' yonder dressed in their armor and bearing their cannons?"

"Not necessarily," Freyja said, her voice oddly gentle. "But I ask, again. What do you think you are doing?"

"There will be someone," Eddie said. "There will be someone, here. I know it, I can feel it."

"Someone? Someone here? What are you talking about?"

"Someone for Val Hall," Eddie said, looking away from her to rake the crowd with his gaze. "There is a superhero waiting in this crowd. Somewhere. I could hear the voice calling me."

"Who?"

"I don't know yet. I'm here to…"

Freyja tapped him on the shoulder and he glanced back at her. She was holding out a folded piece of paper and he took it reflexively.

"What's that?" he asked, holding the paper in an awkward finger-and-thumb pincer grip that made it look as though he had picked up something slimy like a garden slug.

"I didn't know what name you'd be using, so the ink's still wet," Freyja said briskly, "but if that is what it takes… That is your subpoena. I am become a lawyer, here, in this world you love so much. Here's my card." She handed that over, too, as she spoke. The name on it said Vanadis Hörn; Eddie's mouth curled into a grin. She was using all of her names. All of her powers.

"My subpoena?"

"Your father wishes you to return to Valhalla," Freyja said, all business. "As in, right now."

"But this…" Eddie gestured again, with the hand holding the paper, and the subpoena from Valhalla fluttered at the crowd around him like butterfly wings. Above his own mask, hand-made from a cotton swatch which showed Star Wars characters wielding red and blue light sabers, his eyes sparked with passion, with defiance.

"Just what is it that you think you can accomplish here?" Freyja demanded, a shade truculently. "Really, Odin sent me after you—but do you think I have nothing better to do than chase down an ungrateful bastard son whose mortal blood suddenly sings too loud in his veins? When Odin called you to Valhalla, he honored you. He gave you more than some get, than some deserve—"

"Freyja," Eddie interrupted, "peace. I would have returned. But I need to..."

"*You don't understand*," Freyja said implacably. "Your obedience is required. Not your rationalizations."

"The things I've heard about," Eddie said. "The things I've seen. The people I've already spoken to, right here, tonight, any of them could be..."

He noticed someone being led to the front of the crowd, a black man wearing a patch over one eye, the other swollen almost shut and dark with bruises—it was clear that his vision was so compromised that he required assistance to move without doing damage to himself. Eddie pointed to the impaired man.

"That one," Eddie said. "I just spoke to that one, maybe an hour ago. Those eyes? He lost his right eye. Direct hit from a rubber bullet. He should probably still be in a hospital bed, truth be told. But he's not—he's here. I don't know what hit him on the other side; all he can make out right now is light and shadow." Tiny crow's-feet lines wrinkled around his eyes, showing that beneath the mask he had smiled. "Offhand... remind you of anyone?"

"You're not calling him Odin just because he has an eyepatch," Freyja said, with a touch of asperity.

"No, but when he spoke to me...he said...he might be the one. He told me he would ask them to take him to the front line. Because he thought...he thought he could... *Look*, Freyja! Look!"

Freyja was about to smack him down again but his sharpening tone made her turn to look in the direction he was urgently pointing in. At first it was just a glance, an annoyed sideways flicker of a look cast under duress, but then she paid closer attention, those moss-green eyes narrowing.

The line of black-armored police standing implacably before the blind man facing them stirred, rippled. People gasped as they saw what was happening: officers dropping batons which were losing their stiffness and falling down in blossoming honeysuckle vines, guns which suddenly sprouted leaves from the stocks and white flowers from the barrels, shields which turned into falling water and then pooled formlessly at their feet, zipties and handcuffs hanging from the officers' waists uncoiling into long hanks of marsh grass or seaweed which wrapped around their thighs in damp embrace, helmets which turned into wreaths of leaves and flowers. Behind them, one half of an armored car which had been in what would have been direct line of sight of the blind man melted into the bulbous orange shape of a gigantic pumpkin, its rear wheels vanishing into a mess of leaf, stem, and vine. A handful of the National Guard troops stationed behind the first line of the city police, wearing camo, suddenly found themselves furiously brushing off rustic and unraveling straw hats, vestments made of woven plants, soft animal skins draped at angles which offered no protection whatsoever, and streaks of dried mud which crackled and fell off their naked limbs as they backed frantically away from the transformation zone.

"Did you say you were just talking to that guy?" Freyja asked, taken sufficiently off guard to allow herself to show her astonishment. "What were you talking about? Tannhäuser?"

"Not…specifically," Eddie said. "We *did* touch on the matter of forgiveness of sins."

"Did he get the idea that he was the one who was supposed to forgive them?" Freyja asked.

Before them, the lines of the protesters and the police were wavering. The police phalanx which had found itself armed with honeysuckle and water had scrambled to retreat; there had been an attempt at reinforcement but the moment anyone armed with anything resembling lethal force came into the line of sight of the man half-blinded by violence, the same thing happened to them as had happened to the officers they were replacing.

Eddie jumped as the unmistakable sound of a flash bang grenade came from somewhere beyond the faltering barricade. From a sheltered place where clearly the flower power magic didn't hold sway, someone shot a canister of tear gas at the feet of the crowd. There were screams from the protesters, a recoil, but then they stopped—the cloud of gas rising towards them was now in line-of-sight, and what reached the crowd, scrambling to deploy the open umbrellas they carried to protect themselves as best they could from tear gas and pepper spray, was a mist shading from a bilious poisonous shade of yellow to a hint of lavender and smelling faintly of lilac.

Someone in the crowd laughed, suddenly, and people began to dance.

Eddie was smiling so broadly that his face threatened to split in two.

"Not tonight, ValFreyja, Lady of the Slain," he said. "For once, not tonight, not here. Not for your field of Fólkvangr, not for my father's halls. Tonight, no blood. No dead. No maimed bodies dragged off the battlefield." His hand curled into a fist, crumpling Odin's subpoena.

"I did not think there was a war here," Freyja said slowly, thoughtfully, her eyes narrowed at the still writhing greenery which the police officers were frantically trying to scrape off themselves. One or two of the braver—or more foolhardy—protesters had even crossed the divide, grinning broadly, and began to offer assistance in removing the strangling vines.

Eddie barked out a short, sharp, mirthless laugh. "Of course there is. This one is just better concealed than others. I fought in wars, Freyja. In what you would call 'real' wars. I wallowed in the mud of the Great War trenches. I marched in the 'other' world war, the one that followed the War to End All Wars. You think that you and my father split the dead heroes between you, half to him in Valhalla, half to your own broad field of glory—but that's been going on for centuries, for thousands of years… Did you stop to watch the world change? Even Odin acknowledges heroism in other guises now. Does anyone ever stop to wonder why they occasionally see children in Valhalla, or women who should not have been fighting in any 'war' of the kind you are thinking of?" He gestured again, at the crowd around him, the crowd that appeared to be completely oblivious to the two of them and their exchange. "Freyja… *Freyja*…they're fighting invisible wars every day, out there. Some of them have been fighting for a long time. Some have just begun. There are times—like this, right now—when it bubbles over—and it gets noticed, across the Bridge, in the Halls of the Gods—but most of the time you forget to listen to the voices crying out from here below."

"We hear it," Freyja whispered. "But your voices haven't been crying to us, not for centuries now. Sometimes other gods hear the prayers. Sometimes there are ripples in the continuum and things cancel each other out and nothing really gets heard at all and really it's just easier to let things…coast…"

"Because there isn't, even, you know, a *war* on. Not really, right? I mean, you look down on the world, and mostly it just gets on with getting on. But really—they're never at peace, there's something they're fighting, some of the time, most of the time. Sometimes there are actual soldiers on the ground somewhere and you look and you see the things you recognize and understand—live ammo, explosions, fire, ruins, blood. And you know there are people on the way, to you, to Odin, as always, even if some of them don't know that's where they're going. But the rest of the time…you see a single mom trying to raise a kid or three while battling poverty and often disease that she doesn't have the resources to fight…you see a young man walking the street with his hoodie up around his face and somebody decides he looks dangerous and shoots first and doesn't wait to ask questions…you see inequality, with very similar infractions bringing very different consequences to different people of different circumstance…when I was down here, living down here, that is what I saw—up close, personal. Those are the people who scrape bottom and then find the strength to rise with wings of fire, with gifts you never expected, never understood, could barely believe."

"Your people," Freyja murmured. "Your Superheroes. Third Class."

"Yes. The humans. The human beings who stand, who cry enough, whose power can no longer be contained. I am a son of Odin. If he can have a hall for heroes…so can I, Freyja. So can I. And I have a responsibility to it."

"He wants you home," Freyja said. "At home, with him. He is Odin. He is the First of us. He is your father. When he demands…"

"I was there," Eddie interrupted. "When he called, I came. And I would have gone back. I would, Freyja. But this—here—I needed to be…" He paused, and glanced back at the man who still stood before the fracturing police barricade, which was getting overgrown with flowers now—at the man who could see none of it with his physical sight, but in whose mind this was all born, the one who saw it first, the one who had the strength to superimpose that vision on the very real dangers that had been facing him.

"He will probably get a handle, that one," Eddie said. "It's inevitable. Too many people saw this; a name will follow. You and I called him Tannhäuser, just because you saw a staff burst into flower like the legend says—but that may not be what he will call himself, in the end. But he earned his place in Val Hall, *my* Val Hall, tonight. And I need to go and tell him. I need to let him know that there is a place that is waiting for him, for when he needs it. I can't just…"

Freyja reached out and plucked the crumpled subpoena from Eddie's hand. He stopped talking, tilting his head at her quizzically.

She reached up and took off her mask, and the expression that blazed on her face took Eddie's breath away.

"They call me the Lady of the Slain, but they came to me, first, talking about love," she said. "And what I brought to Odin and his tribe…was seiðr, the magic that tells the future, and shapes it. Now I choose to use that magic."

She closed her fist and the paper that was the subpoena disappeared, disintegrating into the twilight.

"I did not find you tonight," she said firmly. "But I know you will be back at Odin's side by morning. I know that you will leave again, as you need to, when you need to. I know that I will cast shadow to follow in your wake, so that you remain hidden from prying eyes to do what you must. Go, build Val Hall. I understand."

She reached up to her earrings, the fingers of both hands brushing the feathers that dangled from her ear lobes, and in the blink of an eye the elegant professional lawyer, the goddess of the Vanir, was gone. In her place, a falcon arrowed upward, circled once above Eddie, and vanished into the darkening sky.

Eddie smiled, lifting his hand in a gesture of thanks and farewell even though she could no longer see it.

Then he turned and stepped back into the clamor of the world, picking his way between people who were still dancing all around him, to music only they could hear—but he heard melodies tumbling in his own mind, songs from all the wars that had come before, that he had fought in, lived through, watched people he cared for die in. *Waltzing Matilda, Roses of Picardy, Over There, Lily Marlene, After the War Is Over, We'll Meet Again.*

And other songs, from other times. *This Land Is Your Land. We Shall Overcome.*

Random lines swam through his head—*love one another, right now.*

And then, inevitably, watching the soldiers battling blossoms in their ranks, the questions about where all the soldiers had gone.

Gone to flowers, every one.

"When will they ever learn?" Eddie half-murmured, half-sang, as he walked slowly towards a tangle of honeysuckle and the man in whose mind the world had burst into bloom...to tell him that there was a place to call home.

Oak, Broom and Meadowsweet

Kari Sperring

"You don't remember me. Why should you? My story is not only old, it is mostly discarded. What you know of me, if you know anything at all, came down to you through the words and necessities of men.

"I had a husband who fell under a spell. I had a father-in-law who thought himself clever. I traveled the borders of my world, and yet you have forgotten me. But ask yourself this, while Pryderi fought or sought magics, while Manawyddan wandered and worked magics, who kept their homes and wove their garments, tended the gardens and cooked their food, bound their wounds and set the delicate stitching in the shoes and saddles, painted the fine tracery on the shields? I am the woman who served, the woman who waited, the woman who shouldered the burden of male worry and fret.

"Humankind do not like their goddesses too domestic. That kind of work is more assumed that recognized, and valued only in its absence. Men take it for granted. Where they seek goddesses at all, it is for vindication of their manhood. And women… Just as men have written female divinity as the seductive—and female power as insanity—men have lessoned human women to seek the goals they approve. Virtuous, patient wives and mothers who seek neither praise nor validation for their service; or else, wrapped up in talk of feminine power, goddesses in male trapping, conquering, owning, destroying. As men have written gods, so certain gods continue to write and manipulate men. But we remain, even so, some of us old ones, and we do not forget.

"Know, then: my name is Kigfa. I was there, in the beginning, and I am here beside you now, long after Pryderi and Manawyddan passed into the haze of story. I am Kigfa, and my other name is Fortitude."

* * *

The girl blew in one dank November night, a skinny smudge of a thing, all eyes and elbows in dirty leggings and a hoodie. A skirl of leaves followed up into the porch, oak and ash and blackthorn all mingled in with crisp packets and gum wrappers. PC Williams hovered behind her, ready to snatch at a sleeve or a wrist should the girl try to run. She looked at me ruefully over the girl's head, a blush heating her broad face, and said, "I know you're full, but this one… We found her under a bench just up past the Muds, and, well…"

"And she doesn't have a home?" I sounded hard, I knew it. But the refuge was full and we could have filled it twice again.

"None she'd tell us. And anyway…" Williams hesitated. "Show her, *cariad*. You can trust Keeley. She's here to help girls like you."

The girl glanced up at her, once. Then she fixed her eyes on me and slowly rolled up one sleeve. Her arm underneath was rail-thin and marred with line after curving line of cuts and burns. Her fingers curled back into their palms, protectively.

A lot of the women I see self-harm. But this…this was something more. Something familiar. Something deadly. Williams went on, "She won't say who did this, neither, nor let me take her up to the surgery to be examined. I thought maybe you…"

"Williams. You know I have to follow regulations."

"I know, I know. But…there's no place to put her at the station apart from one of the cells, and the Social are done for the day, so there's no chance of a temporary foster. And since they closed the Children's Home…"

The girl rolled her sleeve back up and her shoulders slumped. I knew that posture all too well. She was fourteen, maybe fifteen and she had already given up. I sighed, and fixed Williams with my best hard glare. "All right, but just this once."

Williams grinned all across her face. "Thanks, Kee. You're a star."

Not a star, no. Not me. A hearth-fire, maybe, or one of the strong strands of yarn that hold cloth together, but not, and never, anything to which men looked up to.

I watched Williams make her way back down our drive and buzzed her out through the stout iron gates before holding out a hand to the girl. She ignored it. "Come on then, you'd best come in."

A silence, a long hesitation. Slow to trust, this one, and all the safer for it. She eyed me, scanning me from head to toe, doubtless finding me wanting. I waited, letting her stare as long as she needed. She hovered on the step, glanced back once over her shoulder as the gate clanked shut behind Williams, then nodded. "*Diolch.*" Her voice was rough; too many nights out in the cold, maybe. The accent, though…not a local girl. Down here on the coast, they're mostly English-speaking, vowel sounds inflected with traces of Liverpool or Stoke passed on by parents. This one came of older stock; that one word held generations of slate and mountain grass.

The refuge was full and more than full. We'd had two families come in this last weekend, on top of the twelve women and their children already here and the three further families in the overflow shelter down the coast. Gwen had managed to find a flat for the biggest family, and a room-share for two of the younger women, but even with them gone, all the pull-out beds and folding cots were in use and some of the smaller children were sharing beds with their mothers or older siblings. The only space left for this girl was the futon sofa in the warden's flat.

We really weren't supposed to let the residents sleep there. But this girl…the marks on her arms said everything I needed to know. This girl was different. This girl needed more than shelter; she needed me and Gwen.

I switched to Welsh, and said, "Come on up, then. You hungry?"

She nodded, face still suspicious. I pretended not to see and kept talking as we climbed the stairs to the top of the house. "I can do you some pasta. That all right?" She nodded again. "I'm the warden here, by the way. You can call me Keeley. Want to tell me your name?"

She eyed me as I opened the door to my flat. I don't bother to lock it. There's nothing in there I value much, and the women who stay here have more needs than me. I've lost some stuff, over the years—underthings, mostly, and warm sweaters—but less than you might think. They're poor, these women, and desperate and frightened, but they're not evil. When they steal, it's from need, not greed. She hesitated in the doorway before following me inside, gaze darting this way and that. I know that look, too. The look that expects danger and seeks escape routes. I let her study my rooms and me as I kicked off my trainers and headed to the kitchenette. Pasta from the jar on the shelf; a tin of corn; a couple of tablespoons of sour cream. "You eat meat?" Another nod. I chopped a couple of slices of ham and added them. By that time, she'd ventured from the doorway to stand by the counter. She'd left the door ajar behind her; I pretended not to notice.

Food is the leveler. A person might not trust you—they might never trust you—but hunger has its own compulsions and the body takes over. She watched me as I cooked, tracking the time it took for her meal to be prepared. When I set a plate in front of her, though, she waited until I joined her before taking a bite. To be honest, I ate only to reassure her; I'd had my main meal earlier, at lunch with some of the women in the shelter. She ate neatly; someone, somewhere, had taught her formal manners. When her plate was clean, she set her fork down neatly across it and said, "Thank you. That was good."

"There's a little more, if you like."

She shook her head. Then she said, "Fflur. That's my name. You asked me, earlier." I'd set a glass of water out for her, too. She took a sip from it.

"Nice to meet you, Fflur."

I stacked the dishes on the side to wash later and picked up my sewing. There's always mending needing doing in a place like this, and not all of our residents had mothers or guardians to teach them. Fflur watched me in silence for a while, sipping her water.

Most people think you're concentrating, when you sew. They see downcast eyes and busy hands and assume you don't pay much attention. A woman sewing is invisible in their eyes. They forget we have ears and minds. Fflur finished her water and resumed her study of me and the flat, turning her head this way and that. Then she rose and went to look more closely at the bookcase that stood under the dormer. I don't have a TV up here. I've never felt the need. I see enough drama in my everyday life. Fflur rubbed at her arms as she browsed. The cuts on her arms were probably sore. She'd be better for a bath and some attention to those. But I wasn't sure she was ready, yet, to let herself relax that far. Trust can't be forced. So I kept stitching and let her explore. When she yawned, I put my work down. "You'll be sleeping on the sofa. It pulls out. I'll get you some sheets and some night things." I always have spare clothing on hand, donations, mostly. The charity shops on the High Street pass on things they can't sell. Shabby and worn, most of it, but, like I said, I sew. Fflur tugged at the sleeves of her hoodie and I pretended not to notice. "Bathroom's through there. There are towels under the sink and a spare toothbrush in the drawer. Plenty of hot water if you want to shower. I'll leave the night things outside the door for you."

I wanted a closer look at those cuts. I would not, however, force it. We'd a fair way to go before she was likely to open up and I could wait. I've enough practice at it. I made up the bed, found a pair of leggings and a long-sleeved soft gray top, and left biscuits and milk out on the counter. Then I took myself off to my own bedroom and closed the door. I sat tailor-fashion on my bed and resumed my stitching. Leaves and flowers, valerian and lavender and lemon balm. Their sweet scents rose up around me, drifting under the door into the room beyond. I sewed and waited and listened until the girl's taut breathing loosened into sleep.

She looked younger now, the alarm smoothed from her face. I revised her age down: fourteen at most, and more likely thirteen. Even in sleep, her fingers curled into her sleeves. As I gently rolled the blanket backwards, I saw why. Their tips poked through the fabric, more talon than nail. The top was a little big for her. Part of one shoulder showed, and it too was marked in curving lines, like leaves, like feathers. I pulled the blanket back up to cover her, and whispered a blessing over her name. Her body was her business, whatever men might believe. And her arms had told me enough to know my suspicions were right.

* * *

You see, I've seen that pattern, those marks before. Too many times before. The long sweeping curve of the spine with its pendant fronds. A veined structure that might once have been leaves, tightened and constrained into the discipline of feathers. We think them soft, when birds come to rest nearby and we see the downiness of neck and breast. But they are horn and nail, at their heart, formed from rigidity. They resist the disruption of wind and the easy dance of leaves. The last time I had seen this was maybe thirty years ago, back inland over to Wrecsam. Before that, Yr Wyddgrug, Aberhonddu, Caerloyw, Rhosan yr Wy, down the border and then a wide sweep inland, to Abertyleri and Merthyr and Llanbedr Pont Steffan. The procession alters course, but it never stops, criss-crossing the old kingdoms again and again and again. And every time, we have been one step behind, always playing catch-up. He leaves us bodies, over and over, to taunt us with what he sees as our lack of power. He has always thought us powerless, because we lack the privilege of arms and armor and the right of control over our fellows. He considers us weak.

Perhaps we are weak, as the world counts such things. We are weak, at least, in the ways that men consider strong. Yet we have tracked him and watched and waited over many, many long years. Some of the girls he marked and tormented survived, and we cared for them, though their minds wandered. And as we waited and cared, we learned. I told you, did I not, that one of my names is Fortitude. I was made to endure, to wait and to learn.

You wonder, of course, who he is. The identities of men are significant, after all. Their names are what the monks recorded in their annals of times past, what we use to describe and define the passing eras. Their deeds are monumental, every step accounted a marvel. If I do not tell you his name, you will hunch with impatience and mutter at the inconsequence of women. His identity matters to you, where the names of all those lost girls do not.

Thus, then, if you must have it. He is the lie that spins power out of cruelty. He is the hand over your mouth, about your neck, the knife at your throat, the poison that makes you always lesser. He is the glorious bard welcome at every feast, honored for his golden tongue and his skill with spear and sword. He is your hero, who breaks lives with every breath.

You know him. He has many names. But to me and my sisters, he is Gwydion.

I watched the girl breathe a little longer, setting intentions of security and calm around her. And then I slipped out into the night.

Gwen waited where she always did, leaning on the chipped wall of the old lido. Her eyes narrowed as she took in my form, and her shoulders grew tense. After all, I usually walk to our meetings. As I shook myself free of feathers, she said, "You have trouble," and her tone held no question.

"The police brought it to me. Her. We have another one, and she still has her self."

"She's strong."

"I hope so. But she's hiding her hands from me." Gwen considered this. I went on, "I haven't looked closely. She doesn't trust me yet."

She nodded. "Where was she found?"

"Out near the Muds."

Gwen huffed a short laugh. "Of course. Where the flotsam comes to rest. He's fallen a long way."

"Not far enough."

"He will," Gwen said. And then, "He'll look for her, of course."

"Yes. I'm taking steps to cloud his path."

She nodded. "Good. And meanwhile I will hunt his spoor, and then… Well, we shall see."

* * *

Story is a precious gift, and more—a precious responsibility. She who holds the tale shapes what others understand. But there is never only one tale. Two sides, the men say, but the truth is there are many, many more. All those passers-by, those unnamed servitors and soldiers, artisans and farm workers and factory hands; each of them has their own version, with themselves at its heart. We are taught as women to feel afraid at this centering: we are trammeled to be mere bit-players in our lives. But that is not the whole of us, nor yet the right. It is just one form of the story, and one told by men.

Told by Gwydion, who took to himself the title greatest of bards and offered no chance for another to challenge him. He told you that male desire is a reason to trick and maim and kill; that women lie; that children are the property of men. Century upon century, his words held sway. But stories change with time. People change. Little by little, syllable by syllable, other voices wore away at his tale. He laughed, at first, certain of the range and depth of his power. But then the laughter grew thin and forced, and he fell silent. And in that silence, his rage grew. Each of those curving cuts on Fflur's arms spoke of that rage. Each of them were steps on the ladder he sought to build to regain his old mastery of the narrative. Each of those preceding girls were footholds he carved to hang on to his status. His wounds in their flesh rewrote the stories that belonged to them into mere footnotes to his own.

The wise reader pays attention to the footnotes.

* * *

A day and a night, and another. The weather took a turn to the wet. Rain kept the children indoors and at night wind clawed at the windows. But no cold-handed huntsman came to the door, though Williams dropped by, and brought boxes of doughnuts and pastries. "Fruit is healthier," I told her, but the truth is her sweets were probably more welcome. Fflur ventured out of my flat after her night's sleep, at first huddling in corners, wary-eyed. By noon, she had got as far as one of the harder chairs, listening to some of the women talk while the younger children played on the rug. Iris, the oldest of my residents, was feeding her biscuits and occasionally smiling her way. Most of the women come from east of here, towards Liverpool, and only speak English. A few are from elsewhere in Wales, and learnt Welsh in school (if they went). A couple are reasonably fluent, including Iris. By the afternoon of the second day Fflur was on the rug with the toddlers, teaching them their numbers in Welsh.

The women take turns with cleaning the shared areas of the house, and sometimes with the cooking, if a group decides to eat together.

I'm one of them, as far as these tasks are concerned. So through those waiting days, I cooked and swept and washed and dusted, answered phone calls and letters, fretted over the accounts and talked with any resident seeking my assistance. If I swept a little more often, paying attention to the path round the house as well as the inside, or spent a little longer polishing the glass of the windows, no one commented. I'd provided Fflur with new—or new-to-her—clothing from our stock, and taken care to wash her original garments three times each, with salt and juniper, and to mend them with particular attention. From the hidden drawer under my bed, I took skeins of hand-dyed wool in cream and green and yellow, to embroider the cuffs and necklines and hems. And as I mended and washed and cleaned, I sang the words I had from my mother, and she from hers and so back to the beginnings of my people.

Gwen comes by on Wednesday nights, after her solicitor's practice is closed for the day. She helps those women who need restraining orders against husbands or boyfriends or fathers, assists with applications for child benefits and allowances, and, if time allows, listens to their stories. Most weeks, she brings takeout—Indian or Chinese—from one of the restaurants in town, or else fish and chips from the best of the vans that trawl the housing estates. This week, it was Chinese, and all the residents gathered in the big sitting room, balancing plates and babies on their knees. Gwen and I ate with them, and I took notes while she talked to the women needing legal assistance. It was well past midnight when the last problem was discussed and the last dish cleared away. Gwen and I sat in the kitchen with cups of tea finishing up the last of the regular business. As Gwen slid the last folder back into her bag, she nodded towards the windows. "He's hunting."

"Yes."

She pulled a notebook out of the bag and flipped through the pages. "Your defenses are holding."

"For now."

"For long enough." Finding the page she wanted, she turned the book round. "I did some digging. He's good at disguises but he isn't as clever as he thinks he is when it comes to what people do with their technology these days. And he forgot that teenagers know far more about it than him. She's from a community home over to Caernarfon. In care since she was six. She ran off a month ago, according to the key worker."

"A boy?" That was his usual lure, even after all these years.

Gwen shook her head. "Apparently not. She was a quiet one, it seems, not the kind they associate with trouble. She didn't come home after school one evening and they didn't realize until a couple of days later. There was trouble with some of the other kids, and they were distracted."

Fflur had volunteered nothing about how she came to the Muds, how she came to be patterned. I rather suspected her memories were clouded. It would be like him. He muddies everything.

"As for him—" and Gwen retrieved the book and turned over a few more pages. "—he was living up towards Bethesda, in an old farmhouse. The owner can't remember renting it out, or why, but his bank noticed when a large transfer of funds into his account just vanished from the records at the end of the month. Since then, there's a hotel that had a check disappear, and an elderly man near Bodelwyddan with a lodger he can't recall."

"And then here." Small stages east, away from where Caernarfon brooded over the straits. "And she was with him?"

"Not that anyone remembers, but…"

"She got away from him somehow."

"He's weakening. Time was, he'd have needed a week at most." She hesitated. "He'll have an eye on his recent tracks. But," and she smiled, "he's near the end of his season and the moon will be full by Friday. And then…well, we shall see."

Thursday dawned gray; the sky hung low and rain pounded the roof. Condensation steamed up the windows and puddled on the sills. A motley collection of bowls gathered on the landing, where the skylight over the stairs let slow dribbles of water through. I would need to get a ladder up there sometime soon and try and fix the insulation yet again. The lights had been flickering since early morning and the boiler clunked and complained, straining to provide warmth. Just after lunch had been cleared, it gave one final painful groan and fell silent. There was a brief pause, then a bang and all the lights went out. "Fuse has blown," someone said. Someone else grabbed a torch from a drawer and went to peer at the box in the under-stair cupboard. Another went to grab a quilt to wrap around the fridge. They're practical, these women. They have to be, the lives they've had. The power remained stubbornly off, though lights shone from the houses all around us. That evening we cooked over an ancient camping stove and ate by candlelight, wrapped in blankets.

We woke to windows coated inside and out with ice and a thundering at the door. A knot of angry men gathered on the path outside, calling names and making threats. Husbands, boyfriends, fathers. I knew them all. Oh, not necessarily by name, but those faces—those screaming, hate-filled faces—I had seen over and over through all my years. My women gathered in the lounge, some huddling with their children, some pacing, some swearing. Children shrieked or clung or asked questions. Fear takes people in different ways. I used the last dregs of my phone battery calling the police, only to be told that no officers were available. They'd all been diverted to an incident down the coast. Gwydion was always thorough. I sent a message to Gwen, though at this hour she'd be working.

Fflur shadowed me, never close enough to touch but never far either. When the first stone smacked into a window, she jumped and caught at my arm, clawed fingers digging through the cotton of my sleeve. I put my hand over hers. "It's all right. They can't get in. The doors are reinforced and all the ground floor windows have bars."

"What if they change?" Her voice trembled.

"They can't. They're just ordinary men." I wondered again what she had seen, trapped by Gwydion. But, even though we were speaking Welsh, I hesitated to ask her.

"I've had enough of this!" Iris jumped to her feet. "Haven't these bastards caused us enough trouble already? I'm not taking any more." She marched out the door, returning a few moments later with the nappy pail from one of the bathrooms. "Let's show 'em, girls."

A couple of the other women stood. One stared at the pail. "Can we do that? Is it allowed?"

"Self-defense," Iris said, stoutly, and opened a window. There was a sucking, squelching sound as she up-ended the bucket, then a cry of shock from outside. "See?" Iris turned round and grinned.

Someone grabbed the nearest ash tray; others ran to fetch the bins from the kitchen and other bathrooms. A cascade of vegetable peelings and cigarette butts, used tissues and sticky sweet wrappers, cooking oil and cold tea and a catering tin of baked beans rained down on the heads of the men outside. There were a series of baritone yelps and squeals as the men tried to retreat.

There's a reason I let the brambles and briars of our small front garden grow long. Two or three leapt sidewise and got tangled in the loops of thorn. The rest made towards the gate. Iris stuck her head out of the window and catcalled. The gatewards tide bunched up and stuttered to a halt as a long-handled spade swung through the opening, catching the leader in the midriff. He stumbled back and dropped to his knees.

"*Llwfrgwn*!" Old Mr Gronow, who lives in the bungalow to our left, stood in the gateway, brandishing the spade like a boar spear. His elderly dog, a reddish-black beast, stood beside him, mouth open. "*Cachwyr!*" The handful of women who understood Welsh spluttered into giggles. One of the men took a tentative step forward and Mr Gronow thrust the spade towards him. "Bunch of cowards, the lot of you, going after women like that! I've a mind to set Griff here on you!" He nodded towards the dog. More of the women began to laugh. Griff may be the size of a Shetland pony, but he's about as vicious as an ice cream cone. Sensing his master's attention, he pressed forward, drooling in excitement. "Get out of it, the lot of you! I've called the police on you! And my niece. You won't mess with her! She's twice the man any of you are." As he spoke, Mr Gronow turned slightly, leaving enough space for one man at a time to squeeze past him. Not one said a word as they passed. Any that even looked like he might linger earned a blow across the back from the handle of the spade.

He's lived next door as long as I've run the refuge, Old Mr Gronow. He could be sixty or a hundred. In all the years, he's never changed, a big man with rugby shoulders and a wind-worn face. He yells at the kids when they kick balls over his fence, and grumbles if the women have their music on too loud. In winter, he leaves boxes of carrots and potatoes on our step; in spring and summer, beans and tomatoes.

And his niece? She's the leader of the local council and few people cross her. Gwen does a lot of work for her.

Several of the women blew kisses. Mr Gronow met my eyes through the window and glared. "I always said this place would bring trouble." Then he stomped back towards his bungalow, banging the gate behind him.

"Right," Iris said, closing the window. "That's the garbage collected. Time to scrub away their traces, ladies."

"Leave that to me," I said. "You get yourselves sorted with overnight bags. Gwen'll be finding somewhere safe to take you." Fflur's eyes widened at that, and she grabbed for my arm again. "You're with me," I told her. "It'll be all right."

Most of the women scattered to their rooms, while Iris heated water on the camp stove and I fetched salt and the juice of bitter sloes and vinegar. I gave Fflur the oak-handled broom and set her to sweeping, while I scrubbed the steps and the path and Iris wiped down the doors and lower windows, all the while singing under our breaths. As we were finishing, a bus drew up, and Gwen jumped out. "Councillor Gronow's arranged for the old hotel up by Caerfanas to take everyone for a night or two. Meals included, and the police know."

It took little more than fifteen minutes to get the bulk of our residents loaded onto the bus. Iris wanted to stay—her two kids are both in their teens and would be fine by themselves overnight. I hesitated. Gwen said, briskly, "Another pair of hands always helps."

"It does," Iris said, "and my gran taught me a thing or two." She slid an arm about Fflur. "We'll keep this one safe."

* * *

Gwen had brought spare canisters for the camp stove, tall wide candles, and, best of all, three great thermos flasks filled with hot water. Back in the house, I took up my sewing again while Gwen set her clever wards and Iris saw to an evening meal. I kept Fflur with me, showing her how to set small stitches to make a hem. When the garment was finished, I shook it out, and led Fflur to the bathroom. Gwen had filled the bath with hot water, adding to it the tinctures of her memory. Together, we helped Fflur undress, and step into the tub. Usually, I insist my women have privacy to wash, but this was different. Fflur gave a little gasp as she slid into the heat, and the curving cuts all down her arms and spine flushed a deep, unhappy red. They had begun to swell, hard lines of cartilage forming under the skin. I washed them one by one, using undyed linen soaked in another of Gwen's potions.

My gifts are those of house and hearth; Gwen's run to more public things. She sees into the hearts of others and beyond. Once, kings petitioned for one hour of her time, to seek her teaching. What she had stirred into these waters seeped into the plots of men. Gwydion had sought to harm her, once, and she was wise to his ways. Now, while Fflur bathed, she walked the bounds of the house, inside and out, and set her wards. Downstairs in the kitchen, Iris sang as she cooked, and her lilting contralto voice wove in and out of the candlelight.

Women's magic takes its time, bound as we are to the rhythms of nature. Let Gwydion come, now. We were ready for him, house thrice cleansed and warded, and marks of protection woven into every threshold, every room, every garment.

Fflur rose from her bath, and the marks on her flesh shimmered in the dancing light. They were softer now, the curves more rounded. She lifted her hands, and her nails were short and pink like those of a child. Her eyes rounded and I smiled at her. I handed her a linen towel on which to dry herself, then, one by one, gave her the garments I had prepared. The garments she had worn when Williams brought her to my door, mended, reworked and renewed. Each stitch, each new pattern set new lines of intent and memory. Self-colored, on her underwear, soft fronds to build the florets of meadowsweet. Around cuffs and waistband, the rounded shapes of oak flowers, in brown and beige. And along every outer seam of her jeans and hoodie, the bright blooms of broom. One by one, Gwen, Iris and I also changed, swapping jeans and t-shirts for home-dyed, hand-stitched gowns. Then we led Fflur downstairs to the hall, where Gwen had hung garlands of dried flowers and wreaths of woven straw and Iris had washed the floor with salt. Cold moonlight filtered through the fan light over the door and cast patterns over the tiles. Sitting on chairs brought in from the kitchen, we drank the soup Iris had made and waited for the fall of full night. Outside, the wind howled and branches scritch-scratched at walls and windows.

This house is not old, as my kind count such things. But in this town, it's old enough. As the light faded, the walls receded and the worn carpet turned to rushes and sweet herbs. Tallow-dipped rushlights burned in bronze sconces, fragranced with the flowers of Gwen's choosing. We sat, four women, in an arc, one for each season, each age. Men cast the turning of the year in terms of battle, the new king against the old, but time is not linear and women spin the wheel. We waited in greens and yellows, blues and gold, russet, amber and blazing white. Fflur looked down at herself and gasped. Her top had lengthened, out and down, into skirts brocaded with flowers. Fresh garlands ringed her wrists and waist. What had once been worn and old and utilitarian become the robes of a May queen.

As the first knocking came at the door, Fflur gave a small cry. I took her hand and squeezed it. "All will be well. This is my house, and our dominion, not his, and we are prepared for him."

A second knock. Iris rose, and on her brow a white jewel glowed, casting moonbeams. A third, and Gwen stood. Her crown was gold. She looked over her shoulder at me and nodded. I released Fflur's hand and, as the fourth knock came, stood also, completing the line between Fflur and the door.

At the fifth knock, the door flew open, on a great gust of wind bearing dry leaves and scraps of twigs. Outside, around the garden, stunted trees strained at the gate and hedges, reaching towards the house with jagged fingers: his army, with which he boasted he had overthrown even Blessed Bran himself.

A boast is a boast; truth often wears a different face. Gwydion's magic, men's magic, is rife with trickery and false coin. His trees are things of high beauty and brief vigor. My brambles and briars are low-lying and untidy, but they, like women, endure. Now, they choked the path, looped constrictive limbs about the trees, holding them back. Clouds scudded overhead, threw shadows across the face of the full moon. On the porch a single figure stood.

He was not impressive. The full moon denied him glory. He wore an old army greatcoat, at least two sizes too big for him. His boots were caked with estuary mud. On one shoulder crouched an elderly, tick-ridden hawk.

Fflur gasped.

Gwen raised her hands. "Master of Treacheries," she said, in our old tongue, "what do you want with us now?"

"What is mine," Gwydion's voice was as worn as his garments. "What you took from me."

"We took nothing," I said, stepping forward to stand beside Gwen.

"You have my property," Gwydion said.

"Nothing here belongs to any man," Iris said.

He looked at us, then, looked properly, as the light from our brows mingled, throwing rainbows in his path. "Goewin."

Gwen inclined her head. Goewin the queen, to whom all these lands owe dominion. Under Gwydion's feet, the path shuddered, denying his footing.

"Kigfa."

I nodded. Kigfa of the threshold, guardian of hearth and home. At Gwydion's side, the door frame grew thorns to deny him

"And Arianrhod."

Iris smiled, and the smile held steel. Arianrhod the goddess, the moon, ruler of seas and seasons and change. Over Gwydion's head, his clouds tore to rags, and clean moonlight enshrouded him.

He laughed, even so, and the hawk raised its head. "I've beaten all of you before now. You are weaker than I. Brambles and tremors and moonlight? Return the girl." He gestured with his right hand and tree roots erupted through the cement path.

"No," I said.

"Return the girl." He gestured with his left hand and great heavy branches clawed out across the yard.

"No."

"Return the girl." He gestured with both hands and the massy bole of an alder rose up before the porch.

I looked at Iris, then at Gwen, and nodded. We joined hands and began to speak. "May the trees you command bind your limbs and break them. May the hawk you trained pluck out your eyes and eat them. May the sword you bear cut out your heart and crush it. May the evil you plot fill your lungs and choke you." With each sentence, we took a step forward. With each sentence our wards awoke. My briars rose up, mighty serpents, ripping branches and choking boles. The ground shook, as Gwen bade it to throw off the claims of Gwydion. Scouring salt winds blew in from the coast, stripping leaf and bark from trees and garments from Gwydion. The hawk gave one despairing cry and flapped away towards the mountains.

Gwydion twisted, sought to curse. The winds snatched his words and tore them to rags. He gestured again and brambles clawed his arms, reshaping his intent. Feathers began to sprout from his wrists and shoulders. He stumbled backwards and tripped on the roots he had summoned.

The scent of broom and meadowsweet wafted from the hall behind me. We three women, three queens—Goewin, Kigfa, Arianrhod—stood aside as she came. Fflur, all her truth restored, the flower-maiden, clothed in summer light. Blooms sprung up where she stepped; garlands robed her in fragrance. She reached the threshold, and the great alder bowed down before her. She stepped into the garden, and all my brambles blossomed. The tree roots sank back down into the path, to be replaced with green fresh grass. She reached out to Gwydion and he cringed away. She smiled and her hands touched his. "Not your will, but mine." His fingers shrank, cramped into talons. Her hands passed up his arms and the feathers grew thick and brown. She looked into his eyes. "We are not your property, Master of Deceit."

We stepped forward, then, a circle of women, of seasons, surrounding this one heartless man. He crumpled, erupting into talon and feathers. At a word from Iris, the wind dropped and the moon shone down, clean and strong. And under its gaze, Gwydion spread owl wings and flew away into the night.

Surviving Time

A.J. Cunder

It had been so long since anyone had noticed me. I wandered the great cities of the world, relegated to the shadows, pushed to the edges of myth and legend, performing my duties unseen and un-thanked. So, when I heard a prayer offered to my name, I abandoned the homeless wishing their nights away and came to a small room filled with clocks of all shapes and sizes, some ticking, some frozen, some going backwards. A tattered couch propped up an old painting of a muscled god whose white beard nearly rivaled his wings. I stifled a chuckle.

A young woman stared at me and asked, "Is it really you?"

"Of course! Who else would I be?" I paused. "Who, exactly, do you think I am?"

"Kronos? Saturn? Father Time?"

"Ah. Those old names."

"So, it is you. I'm Gaia."

I quirked my head. "Named after the goddess?"

She shrugged. "I was named after my mother."

Her eyes seemed to shift from ocean blue to pine needles to soft, soil brown, but it might have just been the lighting. A sudden whiff of incense reminded me of the Romans and their extravagance, of the power I once wielded as worshipers begged for more time.

"Where's your scythe?" Gaia asked.

"You know about that?"

"It's in the legends."

"Well, Death stole it from me." I'd like to say I didn't pout, but I couldn't help the subtle, petulant curve of my lips. "I'm sure they leave that part out. I'm left with an hourglass." I opened my trench coat to show the ancient piece dangling from a thin chain, its dark brown wood carved from a branch of Methuselah when the tree was still young, the sands inside its cloudy glass quivering like quicksilver. "Which reminds me, I'll have to flip it soon."

"Or what?"

"Time will cease to flow and the world will end."

She didn't seem convinced. "You don't look like I imagined."

"I dropped the toga after the Roman Empire, and it was getting terribly hard to manage that beard down to my waist."

"I thought you'd be taller."

"Oh. Well. I'm as tall as I need to be." I crossed my arms.

A sudden pull like gravity drew me to the window. Though no one prayed to Kronos anymore, I still sensed those who needed more time, the morning commuters who missed their alarms and needed an extra minute to catch their bus, or the college students who crammed an entire paper into an all-nighter. A boy ran down the sidewalk, stuffing an essay into his backpack. Gaia stood beside me as I unhooked my hourglass and tossed him a few extra minutes. It was no guarantee that he'd pass English class, but at least he'd turn in his paper on time.

"How does it work?" Gaia asked.

"The exchange of time?"

She nodded.

"Can't say I have an explanation for you." I flipped my hourglass and set it back on its chain. Not that I even needed to take it out, but I had an audience today, so why not add some flare? "Even the greatest philosophers of the world could never agree on the nature of time. Some said it was an illusion, some called it the thread that knits together the fabric of space. I guess it's a bit like instinct, for me. Or thought, or consciousness. You can pare those down to synapses and neurons and electrical signals, but can that really explain opinion and emotion and feeling? I know who needs time and I give it to them. I can't create it, though, that much you can understand. Like matter, it must be brokered. Or stretched, or manipulated. Can't be created or destroyed."

"Where do you get it from?"

"You know all those times when you thought to yourself how *time flew*?"

"You stole my time?"

"Not just yours. And *stole* is such a strong word. I'm sure you've benefited, too. Remember all those moments you were *just in time*?"

"Yeah."

"You're welcome."

"How come I've never seen you before?"

"No one sees me anymore. Which makes me wonder, how *did* you summon me?"

She pointed to a thick book. If this were a fairy story, it might have been dusty, with a crumbling leather binding, its pages worm-eaten and filled with spells and sorcery. But it was just an ordinary encyclopedia, faintly tainted by library must, opened to a page with Roman gods and goddesses. I had to chuckle at Mercury and Vulcan. They weren't really so fiery and angry-looking, though don't get me wrong, if anyone insulted Vulcan's metal-working, he'd give them a lashing. I scowled at Pluto holding my scythe and considered asking Vulcan for another one. It wouldn't be the same, though, just a sad replica without any power.

"I read about Saturnalia," Gaia said. "How the Romans celebrated you with merrymaking and sacrifices."

"You couldn't look that up on your phone? Isn't that the hallmark of this generation? Why read a book when you can read a computer screen?"

"I like books. And for some reason, I never quite found what I needed online, like the pages kept changing. Nothing stays the same on the internet. You find something one day and it's gone the next. Not like a book. Once you have it in your hands, the words never leave the page. And besides, this was the only entry that mentioned anything about incense. I had to experiment to find the right combination of frankincense, myrrh, cardamom, juniper, laurel, and sandalwood. But here you are." She smiled.

"And now that I'm here, I accept your worship!" I tried to project my voice like I did for the Romans in their marble temples, but it didn't have the same clout. I coughed. "What is it you'd like to ask for?" I spread out my arms. "Blessings on your merrymaking? Victory over your enemies? An abundance of wealth?"

"I would like a day, please."

"Sorry?"

"I'd like a day."

I scratched my head—a decidedly human gesture, but it felt comfortable. "I can't just give you a day."

"I'll barter for it."

"Doesn't work like that, I'm afraid. I can't sell time."

"Of course you can. What about the expression *buying time*? Who else would sell it?"

I cursed the infernal idiom. "A few minutes, maybe. An entire day would forever offset your place in the timeline of this world. Why do you want it, anyway? Are you sure you don't just want an abundance of wealth? I can give you that, you know."

"I want a day to save for the future."

I almost laughed. "Impossible."

"You must store it somehow. Maybe your hourglass."

"That's a legendary object. Out of curiosity, what would you trade for a day?"

"Give me a day to save and I'll give you a day of mine."

I scoffed. "Why would I want a day of yours? I've got all the time in the world."

"No one celebrates you anymore. You wander this earth, practically a ghost. The Age of Reason erased you. Give me a day to save for later and I'll spend a day with you now."

I struggled to answer.

She pressed on. "When was the last time someone prayed to you? When's the last time you had a conversation with someone other than yourself?"

"I spoke to Bacchus just before the moon began its current phase. He mentioned a lovely new wine he's developing. And Apollo! There's a renewed interest in his healing abilities, he says, with that novel virus going around. He's not entirely convinced the Horsemen aren't to blame for it, but keep that between us."

A shadow flit across Gaia's face and she licked her lips, lost for a moment. But then she said, "I mean someone other than a deity."

"Well, I'm speaking to you now, aren't I?"

"Before me."

I rubbed my chin, distracted by the symphony of ticking clocks. "Might've been Newton. Or Aristotle. Leibniz! That's the one. The last two suggested that I don't really exist. Newton called me a container. Imagine that! Philosophers always make for good conversation." Except, they never really spoke *to* me, so much as *about* me. But Gaia didn't need to know that.

"You miss it, don't you?"

"What?"

"The attention. Everyone likes to be noticed."

I stared out the window at the world passing by. So many lives, so many minutes and hours tracked and spent, or wasted, or lost. I wasn't forgotten. Time was still worshipped, the commodity everyone wanted. More than wealth or fame or love, people needed *time*.

That's what I told myself, anyway. I remembered the weight of my scythe as I reaped the ages, until Death replaced me as the Reaper, as the god everyone knew and feared.

"I'll need something to put it in."

"Put what in?"

"Your day, if we make this exchange."

She held out a silver pocket watch. The back had been engraved, but time and the exchange of hands made the words illegible. "It was my grandmother's. I always wanted to hold it when I visited. So she gave it to me before she died. It doesn't work anymore, and I keep telling myself to fix it, but I'm afraid that if the broken piece inside is repaired or replaced, it won't be the same watch anymore, not the one that my grandfather gave to my grandmother who gave it to me. It's probably silly to think that, but I can't help it. And besides, I don't really use it to tell time anyway."

I held the piece and its history seeped into me. It began to tick and I tucked it into my pocket beside my hourglass.

"Hey!" Gaia said, stepping toward me. "Give that back!"

"When your payment is complete, I'll return it to you."

She wrung her hands for a moment, but then nodded. "The deal is done, then. What shall we do for the next twenty-four hours?"

"What I always do." The walls around us faded and we stood in a hospital corridor, a man rushing towards us.

"Maternity wing?" he panted at a nurse's station.

I took out my hourglass and tossed a few minutes in his direction.

"He would've been here sooner," I told Gaia, "but there were delays on the subway. He's about to miss the birth of his son."

"But not anymore?"

"I think he'll be just in time."

A sparkle glinted in Gaia's eyes. "I always wonder if I'll be a mom someday."

I bit my lip. I almost peeked into her future to find out, but divination really was best left to the oracles. They trained for that sort of thing. And it could be dangerous if I let something slip.

"Where did you get those minutes from?" Gaia asked.

"Not sure. I've got ages with me. Mostly from people sleeping."

"I guess that's why morning always comes so quickly."

The hospital vanished and we appeared in Paris. Who doesn't love the City of Lights? Besides, everyone tends to run behind schedule there.

We ate baguettes as I gave an extra minute to a girl pouting at her parents across the street. The girl whined from inside the curio shop, "When can we go home, you're taking forever!"

"Just another minute," her mother said, perusing a delicate china set.

I tossed her five more.

"What?" I said as Gaia looked at me. "That girl has no manners. Kids these days, they need to learn the value of patience. How do you like the food?"

"It's okay. Nothing can compare to my mother's cooking, though."

We sat in silence for some time and I tried not to stare. For so long, I had sat alone, watching couples laugh at tables around me, families spending time together. "Watch this," I told her. I held my hand over our wooden table and the paint suddenly began to fade, bleaching away, the knots and whorls becoming more pronounced. I smiled as her eyes widened.

"Is that like magic?" she asked.

"Yes," I lied. She raised an eyebrow and I shrugged. "Sort of. I nudged our table into its future." I lowered my hand and the table returned to its original state. "Best to do that only with inanimate objects. So don't ask me to make you older or younger. I tried that once and it didn't turn out the way either of us expected."

"What happened?"

"Ever hear of Benjamin Button?"

"Wasn't that a movie?"

"Yes. Imagine something like that, though."

She smiled and it was almost like the sparkle of snowfall across the tundra.

"Why do you want the day?" I asked.

Her smile vanished and she crossed her legs.

"I'm sorry. I shouldn't have asked." I waited, hoping my apology would prompt her to say something, but she just looked down and I suddenly knew what regret felt like.

We went to Japan next, mostly because I admired their punctuality. A businessman checked his watch and I tossed him twenty seconds. Gaia looked nervous here, though, where everyone wore masks. She didn't say anything, but kept close to me, away from the crowds. I wanted to ask about it, but decided on a joke instead. "Hey, what do you call a guy who never has a second to spare?"

"What?"

"Justin Thyme."

She cracked a smile. Not quite the laugh I was hoping for—I imagined it would sound like the peal of a glass bell—but better than nothing.

"I didn't know gods could make jokes."

"Have you never heard of Loki?" She edged closer to a laugh. "We're quite a riot once you get to know us. Except Zeus. He's always serious. I asked him once if I could borrow a thunderbolt and it nearly drove him into apoplexy." Someone near us coughed and Gaia flinched.

I took her back to America, the lampposts in Central Park just beginning to flicker on.

"Is it night here already?" Gaia asked.

"The passage of time can be fluid when you're with me. But don't worry, I'm keeping track of your obligation." I took out her pocket watch. "The hand will complete a full revolution when you've spent your day with me."

"That would only be twelve hours—"

"I can make a minute last a lifetime or compress eons into a moment. Trust me on this." The stars rolled overhead as the glow of the setting sun flashed from gold to purple before it leaked out of the sky entirely.

Gaia shivered and rubbed her arms. "Didn't think I'd need a jacket."

"I'll make this quick."

We walked along a path over hills, through a darkened tunnel, under Inscope Arch. There I found her, a woman huddled under blankets begging the cold night to pass, struggling to fall asleep, a coughing fit keeping her awake. I knelt beside her and put a hand on her shoulder.

Gaia stood in the shadows some way off, the collar of her sweater pulled up to cover her mouth and nose.

"Does the stench of human suffering revile you so greatly?" I asked. "Will you come and lay a hand on this woman to feel her pain as I do?"

"You don't understand," Gaia said, her eyes darkening. "I can't."

"Is the filth too much for you?"

She didn't answer, but took out a bottle of hand sanitizer and squeezed a generous dollop.

"Panicking like the rest of the world, I see."

She turned away.

And again, the itch to look into her future nagged me. Or perhaps I'd sneak a peek into her past.

The homeless woman's face brightened as she slipped into sleep and the light and warmth of dawn came rushing to greet her. I flipped my hourglass, its sands now a few hours heavier.

The arch began to melt around us, but Gaia said, "Wait!" She pulled off her sweater and quickly laid it over the woman, holding her breath and dashing away as if remaining too close to the homeless might somehow infect her.

I tried to read her face, to puzzle out the look that faltered between what I thought was disgust and compassion. Gaia rubbed her bare arms, clad now in only a t-shirt. "Wherever we go next, can it be warmer?"

"Where would you like to go? Is there any wonder of the world you've always wanted to see?"

"How about a beach?"

Paving stones gave way to sand and the dull roar of ocean waves crashed around us. The moon bathed the dark Ne Pali waters in rippling silver and a breeze brought moist air along with a taste of salty spray.

"An empty beach at night?" Gaia asked, taking off her shoes and digging her toes into the sand. "Who could need time here?"

"Do you know how old these waters are?"

She shrugged. "I never paid much attention in science class."

"Three-point-eight billion years. Almost as old as the earth itself. How much has changed since then? And yet the majesty of the sea remains, its relentless, unceasing churning. With all the power humans have gathered for themselves, they can never command the oceans, or tell the tide to stop coming."

"And with global warming, it may come sooner than we expect." She nudged my arm. "Maybe you can talk to Poseidon about that? See if he can help us out there?"

When she touched me, I couldn't stop myself. Like a present tied with a bow, left out in the open, begging to be unwrapped, her lifetime stretched before me and I looked. I saw a future with a hospital bed, a past marred by a childhood diagnosis, filled with daily therapies and medications and hand sanitizer, the smell of Clorox and Lysol overpowering the perfume she wore to her high school prom, the surgical masks stocked in the medicine cabinet for when a sibling had a cough, the lectures she missed in college when a viral outbreak overtook the campus.

"Kronos?"

"I understand, now, why you want the day."

"How?"

"I saw."

She thrust a finger at me. "Don't tell me anything."

"You don't want to know how much time you have left?"

"No!" she shouted. "I don't want to know." She buried her face in her hands and sunk to the sand. "I don't want that knowledge. I don't know what it would do to me. So please respect my wishes."

I sat beside her, running my fingers through the grains of rock eroded and battered through countless eons by wind and water and time.

"Why only a day?" I asked. "Why not a week, or a year, or a lifetime?"

She gazed at the horizon and said, "I read a story, once, about a world where everyone wears a watch that counts down to the moment of their death. They can't change it, they can't stop it, they can't take the watches off. But since everyone knows exactly when they're going to die, they never really live, ignoring precious moments because they know they'll have more time, they can fix a broken relationship the next day, or the next year. And then when their watches come close to the end, they realize they don't have enough time to do everything they wanted. And instead of living then, like they always told themselves they would, the fear of death consumes them. So no, I don't want to know how much time I have left, and I don't want more than a day. Living a year, or even a week on borrowed time, would be too much." She shivered. "Postponing the inevitable is never a good idea, like waiting to rip off a Band-Aid, but a day should be enough for me to say the goodbyes I need to say and to brace myself for what comes next."

Time stretched around us, filled with the crashing waves.

"Have any of your doctors given you a timeline?"

"Only statistics. Median age of survival for someone born in 1997 with Cystic Fibrosis is thirty-one. But it could be sooner or later. Impossible to tell, really, with so many factors playing into it."

I took out my hourglass and stared at its swirling sands. *Time*, the lifeblood of the universe, some called it. "You know, my timeline isn't entirely unlike yours."

"What do you mean?"

"In a way, Aristotle and Leibniz were right. I don't really exist, not in the same way that the earth and the oceans exist. I'm simply a way to quantify a rate of change, whether that be the time it takes for the planets to revolve around their stars or for an electron to spin around the nucleus of an atom. But the universe doesn't care about quantifying any of that, it's humans who care about that, who created this ancient system like they created mathematics, to better understand the language of the world. When humans disappear, so too does this thing you call *time*."

Gaia tapped a finger against my hourglass. "Is that why you have all this? To postpone the inevitable when your time comes?"

I watched the sands trickle down. "I've never really given it much thought. I just keep collecting time, telling myself it's what I do, my purpose. But I suppose you're right. Deep down, it's always been a way for me to postpone the inevitable. My own insurance policy for the end." The last few grains neared the channel.

"Shouldn't you flip it?" Gaia asked.

I waited.

"Kronos?"

The last grain passed through and the world around us quieted, the waves waiting to fall, the stars watching patiently, the wind listening, for once, instead of whispering.

"We can stay like this forever, Gaia. You and me. Neither of us have to die."

She smiled at me, then, like a mother watching a child who doesn't yet know that a lick of salt doesn't taste quite the same as a lick of sugar, no matter how similar they look. "You really should read that story." She put a hand on my arm. "Living forever in a frozen world might seem like immortality, but it's exactly the opposite. A life like that is no different than death. Actually, it's worse."

"But we'd have each other. And the rest of the gods. This won't affect them. We could be like Ariadne and Dionysus, or Psyche and Eros."

"To me, it would be a prison." She reached over and flipped my hourglass. "How much longer do I have left?"

It took me a moment to process her question. I checked her pocket watch. "A few minutes until your obligation is fulfilled. Is there anything else you'd like to see? The pyramids, perhaps? The great Sphinx of Egypt? Stonehenge?"

She leaned back in the sand and looked up at the moon. "This is nice. Peaceful. I'm enjoying this moment."

"Very well, then. We'll enjoy it together."

* * *

Back in her room of ticking clocks, I handed over the pocket watch. "When you want to use it, wind the hand one full revolution."

"Thank you."

I wasn't sure how to say goodbye. Perhaps because I've never needed to. I studied one of the clocks on the wall ticking backward. "How'd you make this happen?"

"Tinkered around with the mechanism inside. Just for fun."

"Brilliant. Well, don't tinker around inside that pocket watch too much. You might trigger something."

"Like what?"

"Oh, I'm not sure. I just figure it's best to warn you. Cover all the possibilities, you know." I shuffled toward the window. "I suppose I should go now."

"If you ever want someone to talk to, you can always come find me."

I knew she meant it earnestly. But I also knew that I couldn't be part of her future. Or, rather, she couldn't be part of mine.

I left her that day and watched from a distance as she returned to her life, to her dreams of motherhood. I saw the great pandemic pass over her, as she sheltered under its black cloud. She soon found a husband and they had a son, sooner than they expected, and I couldn't interfere with that. I always tossed them a few extra minutes, though, even when they didn't really need them. And whenever Gaia was just in time for an appointment or meeting, she'd laugh and give a quick nod. When she walked with her family along the Ne Pali sands for what seemed like hours, she'd smile, even though she couldn't see me. She'd tell them about me, about someone special watching over them. When she showed her son Kyle how to take apart a clock, she told him he'd never be late for anything, no matter how far behind he might be. She showed him her pocket watch, told him it was special but never said why, always saving it for the day that would inevitably come.

And I saw it coming. Each visit with her doctor brought discussions about treatment goals, and then, later, when she struggled to climb from bed each morning and her cough interrupted every other word, the doctor mentioned *end-of-life* planning. Kyle wondered why she no longer played with him, why she couldn't hold him the way she always used to. He asked his father why mommy moved to the hospital and when she'd be coming home. "Hopefully soon," Brian answered, looking over the lung-transplant paperwork.

I saw the day Death came. I saw the look on his face when Gaia told him to come back tomorrow and she used the day I had given her. She hugged Kyle in the hospital room until he squirmed and wriggled out of her grasp. She kissed Brian until he asked what was wrong, but she just shook her head and told him how much she loved him. "There's still hope," he said. "There's always hope. They're going to fast-track our transplant request." He squeezed her hand. "Promise me you're not giving up yet. We still have time. And your parents are coming in from California, they should be here tomorrow. You'll wait for them, right? I told them you'd wait."

"I'll try," she said as her day neared its end.

Just before her pocket watch gave its final tick, she handed it to her five-year-old son and reminded him that time always heals all wounds.

* * *

I stood with Gaia when Death returned and he huffed, "Ready now? Not going to say *come back again tomorrow*?"

"Pluto," I greeted.

He eyed me with a hint of distaste. "Kronos. I should have suspected you. Have anything else to give her, or may I do my job?" He fingered his scythe—my scythe—and I almost offered some witty remark.

Gaia's face had aged, her eyes still hopeful but shadowed.

"You fear what Pluto brings," I said.

"When this moment comes, faith has a way of fading. Your day helped, though. I said the goodbyes I needed to say. Have you made peace with your own future yet?"

"Why don't you ask Pluto about his future? He'll have his day of reckoning, too, though he hates to admit it. When nothing living is left to die, Death too shall pass away."

Pluto rolled his eyes. "You always remind me, ever since the legends gave me your scythe."

"Maybe I'll share a few years with you, if you return it."

"Enough banter. Gaia, come."

I almost gave her another day just to irritate Pluto, but she took his hand and I knew she was ready.

"Gaia," I said. "Thank you. For your day."

She smiled. "Try not to forget about me."

And then she was gone. I lingered with her family in the hospital waiting room as Kyle held the pocket watch. For a moment, I thought I saw something in his eyes—recognition, perhaps, as he looked in my direction. I put a hand on his shoulder, wondering if he could feel it, as commuters missed busses and students turned in papers late. I'd get back to them eventually, but for now I stayed with those who needed me, who needed time to heal.

Till Death Do Us Part

Irene Radford

Anshar folded together the ragged ends of his smoke existence, not liking the grayness of his color. He'd been away from his hidey-hole too long. This Babylonian baked-clay oil lamp in the storage rooms of an obscure museum in Los Angeles was one of his favorites. The lid had not broken and rested tightly against the rim so his smoke didn't drift out and he could rest easily.

Without interruption.

From his perspective, in his djinn form, the room inside the lamp was just large enough to appear cozy and comfortable. Outsiders saw a lump of pottery the size of an American football; if they ever ventured into the back shelves of the museum warehouse.

He wasn't sure why a flit over to his original home near the Persian Gulf left him so weak and tired. After all, he hadn't plumbed to the depths of the Atlantic Ocean to make sure no one was plundering the wreck of the *Titanic.* That was part of his duty as the ancestor of the Gods.

He refused to admit that perhaps age ate at his energy. Oh well, the *Rams* were playing the *Packers* in two minutes. He had just enough time to grab a beer from the mini fridge—that craft brewery up the coast a bit had re-created the beer that Hammurabi had codified with all the flavor and syrupy thickness without the need to filter it through cloth and drink with a small reed—and stretch out in his recliner when a vibration at the spout of his pot irritated every nerve ending in his body.

Tiamet, the StormMother, his sometimes-beloved wife, knocked on his door. How in the realm of Hades (in any of his representations) had she found him?

He sat there, frozen in place, remote control extended, his thumb poised over the power button.

Maybe, just maybe, if he remained perfectly still, not disturbing so much as a whisper of air, his lovely wife would give up and go away. He could miss the opening kickoff of the game just so long as she went elsewhere.

"Anshar! Anshar I know you are in there. Now let me in."

Long ago he had learned patience in avoiding her. As much as he loved her, she had a knack to disrupt anything that gave him pleasure, like sports, and he'd seen the best of them from before the very first Olympic Games to modern day televised teams.

"Oh, why must you hide out in your dusty old pots. You know I could decorate a lovely sea cave for us. You could have your own room to watch those filthy brawls you call sports." He felt her shudder in revulsion.

"You nearly drowned me last time I didn't do everything you thought I should, like trash my forty-two-inch flat screen," he muttered.

"So, you are here, dear." Tiamet fluttered into his room in a swirl of thunder clouds. Lightning outlined her voluptuous and luscious figure. About two thousand years ago she'd given up her lithe maiden look of abundant dark braids coiled around her head like a crown, clad in clinging draperies of seaweed adorned with coral and pearls. Now she chose the form of an elegant—and still lusciously shapely—matron in whatever the latest fashion was. This time her day dress of draped whisper wool in Mediterranean blue complimented her short, ash-blonde hair, threaded with gray. She could have stepped straight out of a Paris fashion magazine for matrons. As long as you didn't look at the leather sandals barely covering her webbed feet. Even after all these millennia she could still stir his lust.

"What do you want? You are interrupting my game." If she didn't leave soon, he'd miss the first quarter. Might be worth it if he could change her focus and engage in a little exercise with him.

"Anshar, have you even bothered to look in on Celia? The only descendant of ours with the wonderful potential of becoming a full Siren and you can't even be bothered to keep an eye on her."

"Celia and her sisters are managing very well on their own." He took a long quaff of beer, wishing it had the alcoholic potency of the original.

"No, Celia is not 'managing very well' and her sisters have no magical potential at all."

"What are they doing?" He sank into himself, resigned to at least pretending to listen to Tiamet's rant.

"Singing in sleazy bars in *Cleveland*! Cleveland of all the hideous places on Earth."

"Last I looked they were singing in a rather posh country club and doing quite well." He held the remote up again, prepared to watch even if his wife didn't leave.

"That was last month. The club decided to replace them with a woman who can't sing half as well but will wear costumes with less than half the amount of fabric Celia will consider." Tiamet waved her hand and produced a sea foam green with black trim recliner, a match for his in size and style, but in stark contrast to his vibrant deep-sea green.

"If I leave and go check on the girls—all three of them are our descendants even if Celia is the strongest singer—will you leave me alone to watch the game? The club will be closed tonight, it's Sunday, the day of rest for most humans. Next Friday night will be the best time to go."

"Oh, all right. But make sure you do." With a huff and a swirl of icy, rain-laden wind, the StormMother departed.

"She didn't even kiss me good-bye." He turned on the game, happy to discover that the cheerleaders dancing and waving their pompoms in glee meant that the *Rams* had made their first touchdown before the end of the first quarter.

* * *

True to his word, the next Friday Anshar stood outside *The Blue Moon* bar and grill near the lake in Cleveland, Ohio. He burst out laughing at the irony. Plenty of water to attract a Siren, but it was *fresh* water and thus repulsive to Tiamet, the StormMother, Goddess of Creation and Chaos. Celia's parents had chosen their home well; nurturing their instinctive need to swim in free water—not in a confined and highly chlorinated pool—and as far away from Tiamet's saltwater habitat as one could get.

Canned recordings of Dolly Parton and Kenny Rodgers spilled out of the tobacco-smoke-encrusted front windows.

Oops, Anshar's casual slacks and blazer, his usual nod to modern clothing, was definitely out of place. He blinked his eyes and spun in a circle. Jeans, plaid shirt, western boots, and a hat replaced his garments. He'd rather wear the linen kilt and sleeveless tunic of his origins, but Cleveland in early October required more clothing just to stay warm without using too much personal energy. He also trimmed his beard and hair to modern standards.

He opened the double swinging doors and stepped inside to face a wall of noise. He winced and made his way to a table near the tiny stage at the back of the room. With a gesture he ordered a beer. The waitress brought him a pint of something dark. He sipped carefully. Definitely not in the same class as his favored craft beer but it was almost thick enough to chew.

The noise in the room lessened and four young people pulled chairs up to his table and turned them to face the stage.

They all exchanged nods as a way of introduction. Acquaintance would go no further than sharing the music tonight. Four young professionals, white, black, Asian, and one of so many races mixing he could have been from anywhere and everywhere.

In the shadows, he smoothed out his own wrinkles and age lines that took his appearance from early fifties to almost forty. He left the wings of silver hair at his temples as this culture considered that an emblem of authority and wisdom, like a crown of olive or laurel leaves in ancient times.

A middle-aged woman in a too tight pseudo-cowgirl uniform of spangled plaid shirt, denim mini-skirt, snakeskin boots, and white Stetson bounced onto the stage, microphone in hand. She engaged in some humorous patter welcoming one and all to hear Cleveland's newest singing sensation, *The Fisher Triplets*!

At the mention of the name of the evening's entertainment, the crowd stopped talking and engaged in floor-shaking applause and stomping.

He became aware of another supernatural presence hovering in the shadows. Sure enough, Tiamet watched and simmered with rage.

He heard the sound of heavy rain against the skylights.

Three girls in their late teens trooped onstage, demanding all of his attention. They, too, wore variations of the hostess's uniform but with more sequins, and their boots looked more like tooled leather than reptile imitations. The pale blonde in the center he knew to be his multi-great granddaughter Celia Fisher. The other two were also blonde but darker and their skin more tanned. They all wore portable microphone headsets with battery packs carefully hidden in their clothes.

He remembered fondly the night those three had been conceived. Tiamet had thrown a stormy temper tantrum that sent everyone within a thousand miles into a mating frenzy. He hadn't been immune. He was just surprised Tiamet hadn't produced a new heir nine months later.

Celia stepped forward, nodded to the musician at the upright piano on the floor below her. He struck an opening chord. She belted out the first stanza of *Clementine*, a song that had traveled west with the first wagon trains.

Anshar's jaw dropped. Shivers tingled up his arms and settled in his nape. He knew the girls could sing. They were descended from Sirens after all. But Celia! Oh my, Celia was wasted on this miniscule audience.

Even Tiamet applauded.

His girls kept the audience enthralled for an hour and through six encores. Their repertoire expanded as the time ticked away, starting with Country Western standards and moving on to popular music. Nothing original, but they made each tune their own with intricate harmonies and Celia's magnificent soprano winding through the other voices, highlighting each in turn.

"You are definitely wasted in Cleveland," Anshar whispered. "I'm going to find you a better venue. Tomorrow. And it won't be where Tiamet thinks you should go." He waved toward the dim corner by the bar where he'd last sensed the StormMother.

* * *

Normally real estate deals didn't interest Anshar, too time-consuming and complex using volumes of corporate and legalistic double-speak. But this time his descendants needed him to *do* something.

The human lust for gold had driven societies for millennia. In his guise as Poseidon, Anshar had access to every shipwreck and lost cargo ever.

Spanish doubloons held more value now than they did during the European conquest of the Americas.

Anshar willed himself into the spirit realm where his essence turned to salty mist. He headed south, using the Mississippi as a guide; in moments he landed in the Gulf of Mexico where many a gold-laden Spanish galleon had met its watery fate. He took one of his ancient forms of a bearded man in his prime, dark hair with a crown of clam shells, a linen kilt that never got wet, and a trident. He dove deep and long out beyond sight of the shore, sniffing for sharks and eels. He followed them to their hidey holes among the rotting timbers of a fleet of ships.

"Shoo!" he shouted to the denizens of the shipwrecks. They couldn't harm him, even if they dared, recognizing his immortal divinity.

Too easy. He scooped up double handfuls of golden coins and placed them into a large leather pouch. As an afterthought he gathered six dozen perfect pearls. His girls could use them with the new costumes he designed for them in his head while he swam back to a remote cove in Texas.

Only drug dealers in their cigarette boats used this place anymore. The sandy track through tough saltwater grasses challenged all but the sturdiest military-grade vehicles.

Anshar swam ashore just as dawn glimmered on the eastern horizon, too much light for darkness-hugging drug runners, not enough light for the hardiest of swimmers and photographers.

Almost as an afterthought he churned up the sea bed to create a long, wide, and jagged reef just beneath the waves. Normally he didn't mess with the natural flow of tide and storm, but this bit of interference seemed necessary. The shallow keeled drug boats would ram onto it and rip out their hulls one hundred yards offshore. The shellfish might get a bit high for a few days, but the next storm would dissipate the drugs.

Tiamet would approve of this interference. Occasionally they did have similar objectives.

From there he decamped to his clay pot in Los Angeles for a rest and study of maps and show business magazines.

* * *

Anshar's next task began with bankers, antiquarians, and gold dealers.

Converting his plundered coins to cash without revealing his source or method of retrieval took over a week. While they fussed and fiddled and tried to cheat him for half the value, he did drop in to watch Celia and her sisters perform every chance he got. Tiamet was almost always there; twice she joined him at his table and shared a pitcher of beer.

Finally, when his patience wore thin and he was nearly ready to let the gold dealers jack up their premiums, they came through with a tidy sum that he figured would be enough. Then came the real estate agents.

He'd scoped out six clubs in Las Vegas. None of them offered all that he wanted for Celia and her sisters. A few hours of tending bar in each of them gave him a better idea of what needed to be done in order to make them venues that scouts and agents haunted in search of the "next big thing." Cleveland never attracted that kind of attention.

Las Vegas thrived on it.

He drove a hard bargain, getting the owner to pay for a new roof and paint inside and out. The family of the deceased owner wanted out from under running the place and gave up without much of a fight. He'd taught the art of bartering to the masters of the bazaars in Mesopotamia four thousand years ago. He knew how to make his opponents think they came out the winner.

He found another clay pot on display at the Luxor hotel and casino. Tiamet didn't know about this one. He could rest in comfort between getting the club, *his club* named the *Neptune Supper Club,* up and running. Then he had to find a way to hire Celia and her sisters, along with a live band. No canned music for his girls.

The girl's father was acting as their agent and manager from his computer in the family home in Cleveland.

Maybe it was time to set up a real office in a building, with an assistant to answer phones and deal with people.

But then he'd have to wear a suit.

Nope, wireless internet from a clay pot inside the Luxor—even if it did turn out to be a fake that smelled of natural gas fired kilns. Management listed it as authentic. Maybe he should have a word with them…

Eighteen days. Eighteen long days it took him to get everything set up and rehearsals under control. He had to hire kitchen, bar, and wait staff. Publicists swarmed him.

It was all too exhausting. He returned to the Luxor each dawn so tired the obnoxious smell of his pot didn't keep him awake. Tiamet had left him alone since the girls left Cleveland and rented a small, cheap apartment over a storefront within walking distance of the club.

But he got to watch Celia and her sisters while they learned new songs, invented new harmonies, got fitted for lovely gowns with lots and lots of glitter and sequins. And the pearls. Each of the girls wore a strand of twenty-four matched pearls.

If Tiamet watched as well, she disguised herself and her temper, though that winter Las Vegas endured more rain than usual.

He sighed in relief on opening night. His girls sang to an enthralled audience that included Tiamet gowned and jeweled as if she'd just walked off a fashion runway in Paris. She stayed all night, watching three shows separated by a ninety-minute interval.

Anshar didn't worry about tiring their voices or testing their stamina. They'd done the same routine in Cleveland.

Before Anshar left in the wee small hours of the morning, the restaurant portion of the club was booked solid for a month. The bar had to re-order multiple cases of…well, of everything. Talent agents and managers whispered among themselves, and Celia's name was on everyone's lips.

He returned to his digs at the Luxor, content. Celia and her sisters were safe.

He'd go home to Los Angeles tomorrow and let Tiamet find him.

* * *

The next day, he drew in a deep breath of sea-laden air, not as polluted as usual, and dove into the narrow spout of the lamp in LA. As soon as he crossed the threshold of his home, he regained more of his natural seafoam green color, reminiscent of his first home with sun sparkling on the waves of the Mediterranean Sea. He still needed rest in his abode before he regained true color and energy.

Many of the gods had given up and retreated to other realms. He still had descendants he cared about and wanted to protect.

He grabbed a dark, craft beer from his mini-fridge and leaned back in his recliner to watch his newest favorite channel on the big-screen TV that dominated his dwelling. For once he turned on the sound, needing to listen to life as well as watch it.

He'd just put up his feet, and admired how his striped socks matched his brightly flowered shirt and khaki cargo shorts, when the seal on his front door popped.

"Not now, Tiamat. I'm tired."

"You've been busy doing what?" The column of dark storm clouds hovered in front of the TV. The voice of his beloved wife of six millennia or more reached way above her usual thunderous tones into the screech akin to a metal ship grounding on treacherous rocks.

He loved her dearly, always had, always would, and couldn't imagine life without her. But when she was in a mood, he preferred their agreed-upon separations.

"What brings you here to my lair, Tiamat?" Anshar asked, letting an edge of annoyance into his voice. Normally she'd be sensitive to his mood shifts and retreat in a huff for a few decades.

"Don't you ever clean this place?" She picked up and discarded stray socks and underwear he'd left in a territorial trail across the living space. Now the trail was an untidy pile in a corner behind the TV—out of her sight, out of her mind.

"For a goddess who thrives on chaos, you seem unnaturally concerned with my housekeeping."

"Or lack thereof. You are just a lazy slob. Too lazy to help monitor the world and keep the humans from despoiling it." She ignored the television which he used to monitor the world as well as Celia and her sisters, and an occasional—okay weekly—football game.

Finally, she coalesced from smoke to solid form.

"Will you turn that thing off so I can talk to you?" she demanded as she gestured at the TV without looking at it.

Anshar muted it with the remote. He could still watch his great-granddaughters rehearse live at their new gig as lead act in a Las Vegas nightclub, he just couldn't hear their amazing harmonies. That was all right, he'd catch their performance live tonight and every night.

Tiamat continued to glare at him. He turned off the device so he could focus on her temper tantrum. As always.

"Our girls have taken a job in Las Vegas! Of all the worthless places in the world, Las Vegas!"

"They stand to make a lot of money there. It is becoming more of an entertainment center than either Hollywood or Broadway."

"That might be okay for Britney and Joycelyn, but not for our Celia. She has a greater destiny. She is a Siren born and bred. She needs to find her place at the sea…"

"She doesn't want to lure sailors to their deaths on rocky shoals. And she may be a born Siren, as is her mother, but her parents have raised her to respect human life. They live in Cleveland, about as far from salt water as they can get on this continent. They swim in Lake Erie, or chlorinated pools where you cannot follow them." He gulped the last of his beer and tossed the bottle at the wall, narrowly missing her.

She didn't duck or blanch, just stood in front of him, eyes burning red and the sound of wind and waves crashing against the outside of his home.

He waited her out, returning her glare-for-glare until she blinked and parked herself in the matching recliner to his right, closer to the exit spout. She had the power to smash the walls of his fired-clay pot if she wanted to. If he let her.

He was tired of mending walls and patching cracks. Maybe he should retire to the tiny pot in a Turkish museum. She hated visiting him there and quickly got claustrophobic, though he could make the interior seem as large as he wanted. She hated dodging the security spells and alarm systems even more than he did. That pot had been his original prison, and it still had the virtue of repelling his wife. She had her own bespelled prison. The spell magic surrounding both containers had broken down soon after the casting.

Arrogant magicians. They thought that forever meant their lifetimes. They hadn't considered that for the Ancestor of the Gods and the StormMother, one human lifespan plus seventy years was merely the time it took to yawn and nap briefly.

"If we are going to save this planet from pollution we need Celia's help," Tiamat huffed. "She should work her magic into her voice, not suppress it to entertain humans. She should be enticing them to their deaths. We'd all be better off with fewer sailors on our seas."

"The world will right itself eventually, it always does. We need to support Celia in her goals. You say she doesn't need a vocal coach, that she should let her instincts guide her songs. But look at how quickly she learned breath control after just a few lessons with her *high school* teacher. Think about how powerful she will be given the chance to study with a true operatic coach. For that she needs money, money she'll earn singing in that little club in Las Vegas." He couldn't help the swell of pride in his chest at his role in guiding his great-granddaughter along her chosen path. And buying that nightclub would irritate Tiamat like a lump of cement inside an oyster shell when she found out. Not if, *when*. He knew her too well to think he could keep any secret from her.

"I'd rather see our world end in a boiling pool of global warming than watch her throw away her talent," Tiamat pouted. She started to fade into smoke.

Bad sign. Knowing her as he did, she was contemplating conjuring a storm-to-end-all-storms that would come ashore in southern California and push all the way into the Nevada desert to destroy his little nightclub.

Anshar couldn't let that happen. He'd spent too much time and trouble acquiring it for Celia and her sisters.

"Tiamat, my darling, it has been a long time since we've been alone together." They spoke frequently via the wind as messenger, but rarely saw each other face-to-face. "Why waste this lovely, *quiet* interlude on arguing?" He reached his hand out to entwine their fingers.

The storm outside built to a brief crescendo and passed on, dissipating as it traveled.

"Why, Anshar, beloved, I didn't know you still cared." She grew younger, more vibrant with each word until her designer dress became taunting seaweed drifting in an unseen current to partially reveal and then conceal her bounty.

"Of course I still care, beloved." He brought her hand to his lips, lingered long enough to lick her fingernails, then turn her hand over to caress her palm.

She shivered in delight as he moved his mouth to the inside of her wrist and licked the vulnerable spot that made her lose control.

He shifted position so he could morph the twin recliners into a king-sized bed with pristine sheets and colorful pillows.

His hips pressed against the TV remote.

The TV that dominated one entire wall of his domicile blared to life with full sound.

Celia's magnificent soprano reached across the airwaves to caress his ears with the serenity of an ancient ballad.

"What!" Tiamat screeched.

"Umm…" Anshar tried to turn the blamed thing off, but only managed to change the channel to a broadcast trivia game show.

"Change it back!" Tiamat demanded. Her metal-crunching-on-rocks tones returned. She grabbed the remote from his fumbling hands and clicked the proper button to take the program back to the live rehearsal of Celia and her sisters.

They didn't really need accompaniment, but the solo piano in the background enhanced their notes rather than drowning them out. The musician had learned how to deal with a true Siren Song since Anshar had auditioned him and taught him all of Celia's signals for alterations to the original play list.

"Why do you have to spy on the family with your gadgets? It is easy to drop in on them unannounced." Tiamat gathered her anger like thunderheads piling together on the horizon. She touched another button on the remote, and images of herself and Anshar sprawled on the bed came into view.

"You switched to our channel, Beloved. Want to watch yourself make love to me? We can still make little water nymphs and mermen."

"Pervert." She turned off the TV by slamming her fingers onto every remote button at the same time. Confused by multiple commands, the TV simply went to sleep.

He'd have a terrible time rebooting the blamed thing and syncing the remote again.

"Are you jealous of my gadget, my dear? I'd think you'd want to watch every minute of the lives of our descendants, so you can interfere at will." All traces of lust dribbled away from him, like desert dust dissolving in a fine misty rain.

She threw the remote at him. "How? How do you watch them so easily? How did you place a camera where you have access to our girls? Even you do not have the power to just watch from so far away. It's not like Babylon of old when everyone lived on top of each other within walking distance from one landmark to another and eavesdropping was just a matter of separating the voices in your head. Tell me how you can *watch* from three hundred miles away."

"Two hundred ninety-seven point four miles. Why? You can do it, too. You just have to find a dwelling place to house your TV and take the step into modern technology. You might even have to get a smart phone." He fished his own mobile out of the thigh pocket of his shorts and held it up, the same scene playing on the screen as had been on the huge TV. Though he had to admit, he'd only acquired this newest model while conducting the multiple transactions necessary to buy, renovate, and open the *Neptune Supper Club*.

"I can understand how you got into the family house in Cleveland to place a camera. But the night club. How did you do it?"

"I bought and renovated the club. Celia needed me to do something to get her out of sleazy cowboy bars around the Great Lakes. She needed the boost to her confidence and her career."

"Traitor!" Tiamat yelled, louder than thunder, as she stood and paced toward the exit. "You will pay for this, Anshar. You know as well as I do that Celia is destined to be a true Siren, not a no-account *lounge* act. I will destroy you and all the sycophants clinging to Celia and her magical voice." She left in a wave of nearly black, impenetrable cloud.

"We'll see, beloved. We'll see. I can counter anything you throw at the world. After a nap. Buying that club with Spanish doubloons and managing to hire our girls as the lead act took a lot out of me. I'll deal with your temper tantrums after I've slept a while." He dozed off, oblivious to the thunderstorm of the millennium racing toward Las Vegas.

The End: not quite.

The story picks up in "Confessions of a Siren Singer" by Irene Radford from Book View Café.

Charon Taxi & Limo Corp.

N.R. Lambert

"Not all my passengers are dead." The cabbie takes a deep drag from his cigarillo, his fingers as thick and calloused as his New York accent.

"I mean, most of them aren't." He chuckles. "Can't make a living that way. But every now and then I get one like you." He points toward me with the cigarillo stub. "A 'special.'

"Not sure why specials pick me. I dunno. Maybe it's 'cause I helped that first guy and word got around? That's how the city is though, you know? A small town hiding behind a lotta big buildings."

He ashes out the window as we turn onto one of downtown's shadowy canyon streets, heading east. An old baseball game crackles over the radio. I don't say anything about the cigarillo; the smoke won't bother me.

"When one of yous hops in, I can tell right away. Wasn't always the case. But now I know like that." He snaps his fingers. "Sometimes even before you do! Some specials get a little bit lost, you know? Like confused? So I just give 'em time to catch up, try to be supportive. What else can you do?"

He stops to listen to the game for a moment—something from the '86 Mets, I think—and nods in approval before continuing.

"So yeah, some of you get all chatty while you're figuring it out, and some of you clam up. But usually, by the time we make it to the toll, even the ones who are lost start to get it. I got no idea what happens once you reach your 'destination,' so to speak." The cigarillo's ash quivers with his air quotes. "Only that it's my job to get you there."

The cabbie checks the mirror to see if I'm still listening. I smile at him. I always enjoy hearing their stories.

"Some of them catch on right away though. Like you, I assume you've figured it out, you're not all upset or confused like the ones who haven't." He shakes his head, sighs. "Ahh, but some of them just kill you. There's nothing you can do, but still...some of them just break your heart."

The meter clicks away rhythmically, but the numbers spin wildly and without order, like a slot machine. The cab he chose is an old one; they really don't make them like this anymore.

"Like that first guy." The cabbie runs his free hand under his Mets cap, pushing back his lanky gray hair. "Ha! I mean, I was probably no treat for him either. I had no idea what was going on at first."

With a few quick taps, he ashes into a stained paper coffee cup and for a moment I can barely make out the rumble of the sports announcers quibbling over stats.

"So. That first day. Normal day, normal shift, just your regular mix of fares. Then this guy gets in, nice suit, asks me to take him to the Trade Center. Now, at that point, they'd cleaned it up and stuff, but nothing was there. No construction, no museum, just a whole lotta zilch. All the bigwigs were busy fighting over who's gonna make the most money down there, and we all know how that goes." He rolls his eyes.

"Anyway, so the Trade Center's still this giant open wound in the ground and at first I think, maybe this guy has a screw loose in his noodle or something. But then I start thinking, maybe he just wants to pay his respects, or maybe he works for one of those bigwigs. I dunno. Not my business. But the way he asked, it's like he still expected 'em to be standing there. You know? I mean, *I wish*. We all do, right?"

He takes another long drag of the cigarillo and sighs.

"So, I turn down 7th and the kid starts muttering and I'm like, 'What? Speak up! I can't hear you!'" The cabbie cups his smoking hand to his ear.

"And I look back and this guy is crying, just bawling like a little kid. He's got his hand up by his ear—like he's on the phone—but his hand's empty. So I pull over and I get out and I open the door and I'm like 'Buddy, you okay? You want me to take you to the hospital or something?' But it's like he can't hear me! He's just staring out the windshield at where the towers should be.

"Finally, he turns to look at me and that's when I see his eyes." The cabbie shudders theatrically. "They were messed up, all hollow, no eyeball, no nothing, except for this faint glow."

He shakes his head. "Thinking about it now gives me the heebie jeebies, but at the time I wasn't scared; which makes *me* sound like the nutter, I know!"

He pauses and flicks the butt of the cigarillo out the window and takes a deep breath. We turn again, heading north. Traffic is moving today, but I'm not in a rush. The low summer sun turns the sky sherbet.

"Anyways, I'm looking at him and it finally clicks, what's going on. He must have caught on then too, 'cause he finally stops crying.

"So I hop back in the cab, switch off the meter, and just drive around for a while, not really sure where I'm going, only that I'm definitely supposed to get this guy somewhere.

"That's when he starts telling me things. Not about how he went. I guess I kinda assumed, but, truth be told, I got no idea how that kid landed in my cab. He was young when he went—maybe a few years outta college, if I had to guess.

"Anyway, he tells me all about his championship baseball team at some catlic school out on Staten Island, and about this big promotion he just got at work, and about how happy his folks were that he was doing alright, 'cause apparently he'd been in some trouble when he was younger. Nothing too crazy. Skipping school, missing a few curfews. Just an ordinary kid. Really, just an ordinary life. But it was his and hearing him tell it…it sounded like a movie, you know? Even though I guess I already knew how it ended."

He looks out the window for a moment before turning back to me, "But let's be honest here, all our stories get the same ending, right?"

His brow furrows then, and his smile fades. I watch him, waiting. He looks like he's trying to remember a name or a date before he gives up, shrugging, and continues.

"So, there I am, driving on autopilot, listening to this kid talk, when suddenly I see a bridge up ahead that should *not* be there. Over the East River, but by Sty Town, where there is *definitely not* a freaking bridge. Big thing, old looking, but nothing fancy…eh, you'll see it soon enough.

"Anyway, there's this on-ramp, all foggy and stuff, so you can't see to the other side, and part of me is like, 'I'm gonna get on this thing and it's gonna be another half-assed, city-run project and we're gonna plunge right into the river!'" He chuckles. "But also, I kinda knew if I was gonna get this kid where he needed to go, I had to at least give it a shot.

"So I pull onto the ramp and he gets all quiet and then—" The cabbie slaps his thigh. "Like that, I'm back on 6th where I picked up the fare. You'd think *I* had a screw or two loose! But the meter, *which I shut off*, if you remember, logged over an hour. And here's the real kicker, the odometer never changed at all. Craziest thing."

We're coming up on Sty Town now, but I don't point it out.

The cabbie sighs and adjusts his cap again. "I won't lie, I got pretty boozed up that night. Don't usually drink too much, since my pops had a real taste for it. Never hurt us or nothing, but he had a hard time holding down work. You know how it goes. Anyway, after my little bender I decided that if it's what I'm meant to do, then fu—uh, sorry, sorry, shouldn't say that in front of a lady." He pauses a moment. "Then ef it. I'm gonna be the best damn ferryman I can be. And for the last twenty or so years, that's what I've been doing…when I'm not running regular fares, of course."

The game on the radio dissolves into static as we draw closer to the bridge, but he doesn't seem to notice.

"People got other ways of getting across. They must! 'Cause I only pick up a few 'specials' a year." He grins. "I guess I get the ones who need a little help with directions, so to speak.

"I don't mind though. I don't mind. Who understands how any of this works anyway? No one. Not the scientists. Not the priests. Everyone's got a piece of it, but no one's got the whole damn puzzle. Know what I mean?"

The bridge interrupts us then, sliding into view as we come around a curve.

"There!" He points, tapping on the plexiglass. "You see it now? Ain't that something! Helluva thing, isn't it? You probably passed it a million times while you were living here. Hang on. How long have you been living here anyway? All this time I'm chewing your ear off—you shoulda shut me up!"

He reaches through the divider to give me a friendly nudge on the shoulder, just as I signal and switch lanes.

Ahead of us, fog swathes the on-ramp to the bridge.

The cabbie sits back, stunned. He opens his mouth to speak, but the words…

I meet his eyes in the rearview mirror, offer a smile.

All our stories get the same ending.

He nods, taking a deep, shaky breath; then a wry, half grin melts away some of the shock.

"You gotta laugh, right? I'm going on and on about specials and here I am…not even realizing…" The cabbie falls silent again; his eyes shift to the bridge looming ahead. His fingers drum on the armrest and his expression softens into something like wonder.

"Helluva thing."

He's not talking to me anymore, not really; still, I nod and smile as we merge onto the ramp. There's nothing else I can do.

Some of them just break your heart.

About the Authors

ALMA ALEXANDER's life so far has prepared her very well for her chosen career. She was born in a country which no longer exists on the maps, has lived and worked in seven countries on four continents (and in cyberspace!), has dived in coral reefs, flown small planes, swum with dolphins, touched 2000-year-old tiles in a gate out of Babylon. A novelist, anthologist, and short story writer, she currently shares her life between the Pacific Northwest of the USA and the wonderful fantasy worlds of her own imagination. More about Alma and her books on:
Her website: www.AlmaAlexander.org
Twitter: https://twitter.com/AlmaAlexander
Her Facebook page: https://www.facebook.com/AuthorAlmaAlexander/
Her Patreon page: .https://www.patreon.com/AlmaAlexander

A medievalist, a Type 1 diabetic, and a cyber-crime investigator, **A.J. CUNDER** graduated from Seton Hall University with a Masters in Creative Writing. Hobbies that occupy his spare time include sword fighting, playing the piano, spoiling his husky, and writing. Read more of his work in Mysterion Online, Bards & Sages Quarterly, and Bewildering Stories among other publications. He currently serves on the editorial staff of Flash Fiction Online, Cosmic Roots & Eldritch Shores, and Metaphorosis Magazine. Find him online at www.WrestlingTheDragon.com or follow him on Twitter @aj_cunder.

JENNIFER DUNNE is the author of more than a dozen romances and fantasy books, as well as the non-fiction ROAR: Overcome Obstacles in 3 Simple Steps. She also writes for multiple publications on Medium, and can be found at https://jennifer-dunne.medium.com/. Her last story for a Zombies Need Brains anthology was in Alien Artifacts. She lives in Colorado with her husband and two Siberian cats, and is working on a science fiction screenplay.

TANYA HUFF lives in rural Ontario, with her wife Fiona Patton five cats, two dogs, and an increasing number of fish. Her 32 novels and 83 short stories include horror, heroic fantasy, urban fantasy, comedy, and space opera. Her Blood series was turned into the 22 episode BLOOD TIES and writing episode nine allowed her to finally use her degree in Radio & Television Arts. Many of her short stories are available as eCollections. She's on twitter at @TanyaHuff and facebook as Tanya Huff. She has never used her Instagram account and isn't sure why she has it.

N.R. LAMBERT is a speculative fiction author from New York City. Her stories appear or are forthcoming in *Vastarien*, *99 Tiny Terrors*, *PseudoPod*, *Fireside Magazine*, and *Don't Turn Out the Lights*. She's also written for *Entertainment Weekly*, *TIME*, *LIFE*, and Tor.com. She was a 2019 U.S. National Park Service Artist-in-Residence at Fire Island National Seashore. In addition to her work as a pop culture author and freelance copywriter, she teaches creative writing workshops for young writers at The Center for Fiction, and volunteers with Read Ahead and 826NYC. Find her online at nrlambert.com.

DARYL MARCUS is a working writer living in Colorado. He's been writing horror and dark fantasy since childhood and finding creative outlets in publications such as in *Blood & Blasphemy*, by Hellbound Books Publishing, and *The Devil You Know*, edited by R. J. Carter. He and his wife travel to strange locales looking for inspiration and oddities. During the pandemic, he's been spending a lot of time on his couch watching movies. He can be found online at www.darylmarcus.com and on Facebook at https://www.facebook.com/DarylMarcusWriter.

MIKE MARCUS was raised among the tobacco fields of southern Maryland but has called Pittsburgh home for the past dozen years. An author of short horror, Mike loves a good spinetingler that makes him second guess shifting shadows and creaking doors. Mike lives in

Pittsburgh with his wife, Amy, and the world's oldest Rottweiler-mix, Millie. Mike received a bachelor's degree in Mass Communications and Political Science from Frostburg State University, in Frostburg, Md., and served 10 years in the Maryland Army National Guard. Mike is currently working on his first novel. Connect with Mike on Twitter at @ MikeMarcus77.

JULIET E. McKENNA is a British fantasy author living in the Cotswolds, UK. Loving history, myth and other worlds since she learned to read, she has written fifteen epic fantasy novels. The Thief's Gamble, began The Tales of Einarinn in 1999, followed by The Aldabreshin Compass, The Chronicles of the Lescari Revolution, and The Hadrumal Crisis trilogy. The Green Man's Heir was her first modern fantasy rooted in British folklore, followed by The Green Man's Foe and The Green Man's Silence. She writes diverse shorter stories enjoying forays into dark fantasy, steampunk and SF. Visit julietemckenna.com or @ JulietEMcKenna on Twitter.

IRENE RADFORD is a founding member of Book View Café. You can find a number of her books, both reprints and original titles at https://bookviewcafe.com/bookstore/bvc-author/phyllis-irene-radford/ Mostly she writes fantasy and historical fantasy including the best-selling *Dragon Nimbus* Series and the masterwork *Merlin's Descendants* series. Look for her new historical fantasy writing as Rachel Atwood. She also writes urban fantasy as P.R. Frost or Phyllis Ames. Lately she ventured into Steampunk as Julia Verne St. John. If you wish information on the latest releases, under any of her pen names, you can follow her on Facebook as Phyllis Irene Radford.

DANIEL ROMAN writes tales of epic fantasy from the seclusion of the Adirondacks in upstate New York, where he lives with his wife, cat, and a corgi/collie mix puppy who reminds him that the occasional break to walk outside is still a necessity. *The Teotl of Gaming* is his first published work of fiction. Daniel also pens freelance articles for the science fiction and fantasy website Winter Is Coming, where he's interviewed bestselling authors like James S.A. Corey and Evan Winter. You can find him online at daniel-roman.com, @RomanWriting on Twitter, or @ danielromanbooks on Instagram and Facebook.

CRYSTAL SARAKAS is a public radio producer, writer, editor, and cat wrangler. Her fiction has been published in the anthologies FIGHT

LIKE A GIRL and WHAT FOLLOWS, and in Lamplight Magazine. She also edited the anthology MY BATTERY IS LOW AND IT IS GETTING DARK. Originally from the oil fields of West Texas, she now lives in Upstate New York in a nearly one hundred-year-old house with her husband, three cats, four ghost cats, and a whole host of other things that go bump in the night. She's made friends with most of them. @csarakas on Twitter or at https://www.facebook.com/crystalsarakas

KARI SPERRING is the author of two novels (*Living with* Ghosts [DAW 2009] and *The Grass King's* Concubine [DAW 2012], the novella *Serpent Rose* [NewCon Press 2019] and an assortment of short stories. As Kari Maund, she has written and published five books and many articles on Celtic and Viking history and co-authored a book on the history and real people behind her favourite novel, *The Three Musketeers* (with Phil Nanson). She's British and lives in Cambridge, England, with her partner Phil and three very determined cats, who guarantee that everything she writes will have been thoroughly sat upon. Her website is http://www.karisperring .com and you can also find her on Facebook.

A.L. TOMPKINS is a writer from Ontario, Canada. She holds an honors BS in Biology, and is usually found working surrounded by animals, the bigger and more likely to eat her, the better. When not writing, A.L is usually reading anything she can get her hands on, or getting overly invested in the lives of video game characters.

JEAN MARIE WARD writes fiction, nonfiction and everything in between. Her credits include a multi-award nominated novel, two popular art books, author interview videos for BuzzyMag.com, and editing CrescentBlues.com. Her short stories have appeared everywhere from *Asimov's* to the anthologies of Zombies Need Brains. Find her on the web at JeanMarieWard.com, Facebook.com/JeanMarieWardWriter, Twitter @Jean_Marie_WardandConTinualConvention.com.

EDWARD WILLETT is an award-winning author of science fiction, fantasy, and non-fiction for all ages. His latest novel, *The Moonlit World*, is Book 3 in his *Worldshapers* series for DAW Books. He's currently writing his twelfth DAW novel, the humorous space opera *The Tangled Stars*. Ed hosts the Aurora Award-winning podcast *The Worldshapers* (theworldshapers.com), where he interviews other SF and fantasy authors, and edits the Kickstarted *Shapers of Worlds* anthologies featuring guests of the podcast, published by his own Shadowpaw Press (shadowpawpress.com). He lives in Regina, Saskatchewan with his wife and daughter. Website: edwardwillett.com; Twitter: @ewillett; Facebook: @edward.willett; Instagram: @edwardwillettauthor.

About the Editors

PATRICIA BRAY was there when Zombies Need Brains was born, and has the t-shirt to prove it. The author of a dozen novels, her storytelling skills also come in handy in her day job as a business intelligence analyst. She lives in New Hampshire, where she balances her time at a keyboard with cycling, hiking and curling. Find her on the web at www.patriciabray.com.

****

JOSHUA PALMATIER is a fantasy author with a PhD in mathematics. He currently teaches at SUNY Oneonta in upstate New York, while writing in his "spare" time, editing anthologies, and running the anthology-producing small press Zombies Need Brains LLC. His most recent fantasy novel, Reaping the Aurora, concludes the fantasy series begun in Shattering the Ley and Threading the Needle, although you can also find his "Throne of Amenkor" series and the "Well of Sorrows" series still on the shelves. He is currently hard at work writing his next novel and designing the Kickstarter for the next Zombies Need Brains anthology project. You can find out more at www.joshuapalmatier.com or at the small press' site www.zombiesneedbrains.com. Or follow him on Twitter as @bentateauthor or @ZNBLLC.

Acknowledgments

This anthology would not have been possible without the tremendous support of those who pledged during the Kickstarter. Everyone who contributed not only helped create this anthology, they also helped support the small press Zombies Need Brains LLC, which I hope will be bringing SF&F themed anthologies to the reading public for years to come. I want to thank each and every one of them for helping to bring this small dream into reality. Thank you, my zombie horde.

The Zombie Horde: Cyn Armistead, Kerry aka Trouble, Bregmann, Linda Pierce, Beth Lobdell, Beth Barany, Michael Feir, Jennifer Della'Zanna, Michele Hall, Maxim, Erin Kenny, Thomas Bätzler, AlmostHuman, Larry Strome, Chris, Jennifer Berk, Alan Smale, Lorraine J. Anderson, Pulse Publishing, Tomas Burgos-Caez, Kirsty Mackay, Kevin Lowney, Shayne Easson, P. Christie, Old Man Sparck (TyMcC), Aleis Maxim, Melissa Schultz, Richard C. White, Agnes Kormendi, ChristinecEthier, Wendy Schultz, David J. Rowe, A.J. Abrao, S.Jonda, Andy Miller, Vikki Ciaffone, jmi, Randall Brent Martin II, MJ Silversmith, John Senn, Elissa & Wolf Gray, D. A. Nulf, Lutz F. Krebs, Kammi Davis, Tina Connell, Jennifer Flora Black, George Fotopoulos, Christine Budd, Tim Jordan, William Seney, Cheryl Losinger, J. L. Brewer, Graham Robert Scott, Tommy Acuff, Kayliealien, Krystal Windsor, Erin Penn, Susan O'Fearna, Cyn Wise, Heather N. Jones., Bruce Wesley, Mandy Stein, Fiona Nowling, G.M. Persbacker, Bobbi Boyd, Kelly Wagner, Marian Goldeen, Susan Simko, Kevin Niemczyk, Lisa Kruse, Ane-Marte

Mortensen, Sure. Julie Pitzel, Dan DeVita, John T. Sapienza, Jr., OgreM, David Gillon, Gavran, Paul McErlean, Bex O, Samuel Lubell, Henry Herz, Carol Mammano, Walt Williams, Russell Ventimeglia, Levi Qışın, RM Ambrose, Lorri-Lynne Brown, Louise Dimarcello, Shaina Reisman, Leigh Ann Vaughn, Remnant, Dino Hicks, Dylan Larkin, Patrick Dugan, InarisGuardian, Vicki Greer, Sabrina M. Weiss, Ellen Kaye-Cheveldayoff, Kristine Kathryn Rusch, David Bruns, Pat Knuth, Frances Rowat, Olav Rokne, Nirven, Robyn DeRocchis, Vincent Darlage, PhD, Tracy 'Rayhne' Fretwell, E.L. Winberry, TimBlitz, Sachin K Suchak, Lace, Elizabeth Kite, Venessa Giunta, Robert V Riddell, Cory Williams, Dori-Ann Granger, Chris Brant, Greykell (werewulf!) Dutton, Kate Pennington, Tauna Sonn-LeMarbe, Marc Long, Michael Ball, James Conason, Ron Currens, Cassie A Stearns, Rebecca M, Katherine S, Sandra Bryant, T. England, eric priehs, Patrick Osbaldeston, Sheryl Ehrlich, Kristine Smith, Edward K. Beale, CDR, Fionna O'Sullivan, Duncan & Andrea Rittschof, Yankton Robins, Melissa Shumake, BUDDYH, Niall Gordon, Rae Streets, David Zurek, Samantha Sendele, CRussel, Tania Clucas, Michele 'Neverwhere' Howe, Sharan Volin, Amanda DeLand, Caryn Cameron, Jeremy Audet, Christina Roberts, Jasmine Stairs, Doug Ellis, L. E. Doggett, Gregory D. Mele, Michelle Botwinick, Michael Haynes, David Perkins, Margaret Bumby, Eric, _ALR, Michael Hanscom, Michèle Laframboise, writer & artist, Erin Subramanian, Kimberly Lucia, Tris Lawrence, Jenn Whitworth, Michael Halverson, Cindy Cripps-Prawak, Phillip Spencer, Ian Chung, Jarrod Coad, John Markley, Jeff G., Steven Halter, Jim Landis, Meyari McFarland, Chris Gerrib, Evan Ladouceur, Tanya K., Risa Wolf, Mark Carter, Sidney Whitaker, Ed Ellis, Storm Humbert, Chantelle Wilson, Cat Wyatt, Kristin Evenson Hirst, Sean P. Caballero, Camille Lofters, Brendan Burke, Rick McKnight, Jennifer Robinson, rissatoo, Kristi Chadwick, Michael Kohne, Bill and Laura Pearson, E.M. Middel, TF Newbery, Caitlin Jane Hughes, Shadowlight, Michael Abbott, Judith Mortimore, Konstanze Tants, Megan Beauchemin, Deborah A. Flores, Simon Dick, N. Engel, Susan Oke, Juliet Kemp, Colette Reap, Jim Anderson, Ivan Donati, Mustela, Petrina Hartland, M Smedley, Brenda Moon, Justin Pinner, Louise Lowenspets, Juanita J Nesbitt, James Enge, Hephaestion Christopoulos, Jaq Greenspon, Jenny Barber, Mary Alice Wuerz, Yosen Lin, Bryan Smart, Marsayus, Herbert Eder, Piet Wenings, Eva Holmquist, Jim Gotaas, Kelly J. Cooper, Mei Hua, David Lahner, Ash Morton, John Schreck, Ian Harvey, A.Chatain, F. Meilleur, Kimberly M. Lowe, Sarah Cornell, Matthew Egerton, Patricia van Ooy, Robert B Tharp, Jesse Sun, K. Kisner, Karen M, Angie Hogencamp, Blair Learn, Bill Drake, MD, Joanne Burrows, Christopher

Prew, Ruth Ann Orlansky, Scott Raun, Carl Wiseman, Camilla Avellar, Cracknot, Anita Morris, Michele Fry, Scarlett Letter, Frank M. Greco, Kortnee Bryant, Doug Porter, Beth Coll, Adam Rajski, Jerrie the filkferengi, Martin Greening, cassie and adam, Rosanne Girton, Megan Lewis, Scott Kohtz, Chad Bowden, jjmcgaffey, Richard Parker, Axisor and Firestar, Elaine Tindill-Rohr, Khinasidog, Wolf SilverOak, Beth Morris Tanner, RJ Hopkinson, John H. Bookwalter Jr., Duncan Shields, Teri J. Babcock, The Mystic Bob, Elektra, Brad L. Kicklighter, Lark Cunningham, Jason Palmatier, Christa Bowdish, Ryan Power, Krystal Bohannan, L.C., Ellie Yee, Anthony R. Cardno, Nick W, Carman C. Curton, Jonathan Adams, Anne Burner, Leane Verhulst, Eleanor Grey, Todd Stephens, Aurora Nelson, GMarkC, Patti Short, Ellen Garner Crawford, Stabby the Unicorn, Alison Sky Richards, Michael Murphy-Burton, Margaret St. John, Sam Stilwell, William Leisner, Nancy M Tice, William Rivera, Jeanne Talbourdet, Megan Miller, Ginevra Marner, Lavinia C, SwordFirey, Jeff Conner, DARIN KENNEDY, Karen Fonville, Ichabod Ebenezer, David DiCarlo, Nathan Turner, Jesse Klein, Jennifer Crow, Kathryn Smith, Robert Gilson, Gotherella Biovenom, Emily Randolph-Epstein, Millie Calistri-Yeh, LetoTheTooth, David Holden, Cathy Green, Chris Huning, EM, Sentath, Michael Axe, Taia Hartman, V Hartman DiSanto, Becky Boyer, Colleen R., Steven Peiper, Nora-Adrienne Deret, Craig "Stevo" Stephenson, Sheryl R. Hayes, Lexie Carver, Jo!, Judith Waidlich, Malcolm & Parker Curtis, Katy Manck – BooksYALove, Tom B., Nancy Holzner, Steve Arensberg, AJ Hartson, Todd Ehrenfels & The Science Fiction Society of Northern NJ, Keith E. Hartman, Timothy Pelkowski, Robin Sturgeon Abess, Aysha Rehm, Heather Fleming, Bruce Shipman, Kathleen Kennedy, Hoose Family, Fred and Mimi Bailey, Brendan Lonehawk, C. C. S. Ryan, Tony Pope, Denise Tanaka, Su Minamide, Marcel de Jong, J.P. Goodwin, Walter Bryan, Ashley McConnell, Stephen Ballentine, Richard O'Shea, Nicole Wooden, Corey T, Brooks Moses, RKBookman, David Mortman, Carolyn Mulroney, Joshuah Kusnerz, Christopher Wheeling, Tania, Jörg Tremmel, Tina M Noe Good, John Green, Jill Crowther-Peters, Richard Leis, Alex Langer, Lisa Short, Marcia Franklin, Chris Kaiser, Ronald H. Miller, Matt Celeskey, Stephanie Lucas, NewGuyDave, Janet Piele, Cliff Winnig, Robert Tienken, Annie Agostini, Steven West, Holland Dougherty, Trip Space-Parasite, Wayne Howard, Helen Ellison, Matt Taylor, Amber N. Bryant, Mark Kiraly, Phoebe Barton, Fred Herman, Brian Burgoyne, Michelle Palmer, Kate Malloy, Camille Knepper, Elise Power, R. Hunter, Gary Phillips, Nick Marone, Benjamin Hausman, Britt Hill, Julia Haynie, Carol Van Natta, Jim Willett, Robert J Andrews II,

Anna Rudholm, John Winkelman, Sonya Lawson, Katie Hallahan, Brynn, Michael Barbour, Rolf Laun, Curtis Frye, Jen1701D, Robert Balentine, Jr., James Flux, Shaun Kilgore, Mark Newman, Tibs, Caroline Westra, Robert Zoltan, Kari Kilgore, Carla B, Christine Hanolsy, Marty Poling Tool, Rowan Lambelle, Robert Claney, Kelly Lynn Colby, –Insert Name Here–, Mirranda Prowell, Juli, Kat Hodghead, Anonymous Reader, Jamieson Cobleigh, Carol J. Guess, Keith West, Future Potentate of the Solar System, Bárbara y los Víctors, Dina S, Willner, Lawrence M. Schoen, Nancy Glassman, Nancy Pimentel, Dr. Kai Herbertz, Undead Auna, Elyse M Grasso, Kiya Nicoll, Simone Pietro Spinozzi, Jessica Enfante, Michael M. Jones, Andrija Popovic, Howard J. Bampton, Connor Bliss, Debbie Matsuura, Craig Hackl, Terry Williams, David Quist, Corky Bladdernut, Olivia Montoya, Steve Salem, William R.D. Wood, Robin Hill, Michael Fedrowitz, Judy Lunsford, Céline Malgen, Katrina Knight, C.A. Rowland, Xploder, Stephanie Cranford, Dave Hermann, Holly Elliott, VeAnna Poulsen, Rhondi Salsitz, Stephannie Tallent, C.C. Finlay, James Lucas, Wilma Lingle, Charles Boyd, Sci Fi Cadre, Heidi Lambert, Greg Vose, Ryan Harron, Cat Girczyc, Danni Brigante, Leah Webber, Morva& Alan, Marco Cultrera, Paul D. Smith, Jenny and Owen Blacker, Michael Kahan, Cara Murray, Chris Matthews, Dorian Graves, Larisa LaBrant, Connor Whiteley, Carl Dershem, Andy Dibble, Tory Shade, Jen Maher, Alex Shvartman

Made in the USA
Monee, IL
31 October 2023